Maisey Yates is a *Ne...* ... of over seventy-five ... habit she has no inter... Pinterest addiction. She lives with her husband and children in the Pacific Northwest. When Maisey isn't writing she can be found singing in the grocery store, shopping for shoes online and probably not doing dishes. Check out her website maiseyyates.com.

Canadian **Dani Collins** knew in high school that she wanted to write romance for a living. Twenty-five years later, after marrying her high school sweetheart, having two kids with him, working at several generic office jobs and submitting countless manuscripts, she got The Call. Her first Mills & Boon novel won the Reviewers' Choice Award for Best First in Series from *RT Book Reviews*. She now works in her own office, writing romance.

Also by Maisey Yates

His Forbidden Pregnant Princess

Brides of Innocence miniseries

The Spaniard's Untouched Bride
The Spaniard's Stolen Bride

Once Upon a Seduction… miniseries

The Queen's Baby Scandal
Crowning His Convenient Princess

Also by Dani Collins

Cinderella's Royal Seduction

Feuding Billionaire Brothers miniseries

A Hidden Heir to Redeem Him
Beauty and Her One-Night Baby

Innocents for Billionaires miniseries

A Virgin to Redeem the Billionaire
Innocent's Nine-Month Scandal

Discover more at millsandboon.co.uk.

CROWNED FOR MY ROYAL BABY

MAISEY YATES

CONFESSIONS OF AN ITALIAN MARRIAGE

DANI COLLINS

MILLS & BOON

First Published in Great Britain 2020
by Mills & Boon, an imprint of HarperCollins*Publishers*
1 London Bridge Street, London, SE1 9GF

Crowned for My Royal Baby © 2020 Maisey Yates

Confessions of an Italian Marriage © 2020 Dani Collins

ISBN: 978-0-263-27830-9

CROWNED FOR MY ROYAL BABY

MAISEY YATES

To the librarians.
And mine especially.
At school and at the public library.
You made sure I had books. Lots of books. All the books.
If not for my love of reading, I'm sure I wouldn't be writing.
Thank you.

CHAPTER ONE

Marissa

I'LL NEVER FORGET the first time I saw Prince Hercules. A ridiculous name, and one more suited to a bronzed god than a man. The kind of god my father would have called a false one and told me to steer clear of.

If he could only have known. He would have locked me in my room for the foreseeable future if he'd had any real idea of how fallible I was.

Something in me must have known.

Because Hercules immediately became a secret. Even when I watched him from a distance.

Secrets were not allowed in my family because a secret meant that someone was concealing a truth. And if you were concealing a truth, it had to be because it was a sin.

Hercules became sin for me very, very quickly.

It was after church that first time. I had gone down to the water, as I often did on the small island of Medland, Massachusetts.

It was summer, and the elite had already descended on the tiny town as they did every year. The influx of seasonal residents as welcome as they were over-whelming.

The island ran on summer business, the money made during those months often necessarily hoarded through the rest of the year.

The collection plates at my father's church were certainly fuller during those weeks.

And while I knew, even at sixteen, that the rush of people was necessary for the economy, I still found it overwhelming.

And so I retreated, not to the most heaving parts of the beaches, but to private paths that beat through tall seagrass and down to rocky but tranquil shores that were far too rustic to attract the volume of visitors the vast stretches of sand did.

On a Saturday it was difficult to find spaces that weren't overrun, but I'd lived there all my life and barely knew anywhere else. I knew where I could find solitude if I wanted it.

And that was where I first spotted him.

He was standing in the waves, the water lapping at his knees, his pants rolled up, his shirt off.

He was surrounded by people—women specifically—laughing and chatting, splashing each other. But he stood out, his face looking like it was carved from granite.

His eyes reminded me of obsidian. The black glossy rock that both gave off light and consumed it all at once. I thought I could get lost in those eyes.

In that darkness.

I'd been taught to run from darkness, but there was a

glow in his I couldn't turn away from. I felt like I'd just discovered a creature I wasn't allowed to know existed.

He seemed lost in whatever his darkness was.

Until one of the women touched his arm, and those features shifted into a smile that seemed to eclipse the sun. And I was suddenly overcome by a strange, bitter taste in my mouth that I'd never experienced before. It made my whole body feel tight and strange.

I ran away.

But the next day, I went back after church, and he was there. This time, not out in the water, but standing on the shore.

And he saw me.

"Are you going to stare all day?" he asked.

"I wasn't staring at you," I replied. "I was simply taking in the view behind you."

"I saw you yesterday," he said. "On the shore." The way he said it made it clear he didn't believe I was looking at anything but him. "You ran away."

"I knew my father would wonder where I was. You weren't in church today?" I asked him. An inane question. I knew he wasn't there. I would have noticed. Everyone would have.

"No," he said with a laugh. "I find my worship, such as it might be, is best conducted outside four walls. And you?"

"My father is the pastor. I'll get in trouble if I don't go."

"And would you get in trouble if he found out you were here?"

He was even more beautiful up close. His chest was covered then, thank God, or I probably would have expired on the spot. It was a weakness, I knew, the way that I looked at him. The way that I hungrily took in every inch of bronze skin that was on display. Just a wedge, where the fabric of his white shirt was separated.

I knew that I was wicked.

Like a sudden answer to my restlessness had locked into place and printed the definition in my brain.

Wicked.

It was evidenced in the way I feasted on every detail of his handsome, sculpted face. But I couldn't help it, and for the first time, I didn't want to.

He looked familiar, but I couldn't place him. That square, sharp jaw and compelling mouth, those dark, intense eyes.

"Possibly," I said. "I'm supposed to be careful about talking to… Well, most people who come here during the summer are very important. And also…of a certain sort of character."

"Whoremongers and the like?" he asked, a glint of humor in his eyes.

I felt my cheeks heat. "I suppose so."

"Sadly, I'm both," he said. "You should probably run away."

"Okay," I said and instantly turned to flee, doing exactly as I was told, because I didn't know another way to be.

"Do you always do what people tell you to?" he asked me, stopping me in my tracks.

"I… Yes."

"You should stop that. Figure out what you want."

"I'll probably just get a job here. Get married." Just

mentioning that word in front of him made my insides feel jittery.

He arched a brow. "But is it what you want?"

He was looking at me so intently, and I couldn't for the life of me figure out why a man such as him would look at a girl like me the way that he was.

Of course, I didn't exactly know what the look was. I had never spoken to a man I didn't know from church. Not outside of exchanged pleasantries on a street. We didn't even know each other.

I didn't know his name, and he didn't know mine.

He was an admitted whoremonger, and someone very important. And there I was, talking to him anyway. Feeling pinned to the spot by all that intensity.

"I've never thought about it," I finally admitted.

"Do," he said. "And get back to me."

I didn't see him for the next few days, but I was consumed by schoolwork anyway. It was summer, but as I was homeschooled, my parents didn't much acknowledge breaks. It was fine, because I was on the verge of graduating at sixteen, though to what end, I didn't know. I had considered going away for a while on a mission, which was something that my parents heartily approved of.

I went back to check on Saturday again to see if I could find the mystery man.

I didn't.

But I did again, that next Sunday.

"Have you thought about what you want?" he asked.

I just stared at him blankly, because no, I hadn't. I had thought about him. And that was it.

That began a strange sort of friendship. We would

talk by the seashore when he was alone. About everything and nothing. Not about ourselves, but the world.

He'd been everywhere, and I'd been nowhere. We both found that fascinating.

We didn't exchange names. He gave me a seashell, and he told me that the way it swirled at the center reminded him of the way my hair curled. I put it in a box and hid it under my bed.

When the summer ended, I couldn't breathe.

He was gone and the world was gray. It was silly to grieve over a man who was alive, but not with me. A man whose name I didn't know.

But I grieved all the same.

Sometime in the middle of winter a photograph on the front page of a tabloid in the grocery store caught my eye—it was him. It was him with a beautiful woman on his arm and his name plastered right there on the newsprint, and I had to ask myself how I could be so stupid.

I wasn't one to pay attention to popular culture—in fact, my father expressly forbade it—and often I averted my eyes even when waiting in the checkout line, so there was a certain sort of sense in the fact that I hadn't realized immediately who my seaside friend was.

Not just someone important.

A *prince*.

Prince Hercules Xenakis of Pelion, one of the most renowned playboys in the entire world.

That night I took the box out from under my bed and stared at the seashell, and I told myself I should get rid of it.

He wouldn't be coming back to the island—I was certain of it.

I would never see him again. Our meeting—our friendship—had been a fluke, and what was more, I was sure that I meant nothing to him. I was a schoolgirl, a common one at that, and he was one of the most wealthy, desirable men on the planet.

I couldn't bring myself to throw it away.

Summer rolled around, marking my birthday and marking the return of the seasonal residents.

And there he was.

Sunday afternoon.

I told myself not to smile like a giddy fool when I saw him, but I did. And he smiled at me.

"You're still here," he said, shoving his hands in his pockets.

"I live here. So it's not truly that surprising. You came back," I said. I looked away from him. "You're a prince."

"Ah," he said. "So you've discovered my secret." He sounded regretful.

I peered at him while still trying to keep my head tilted down. "I'm not sure how it can be a secret, given you are frequently on the cover of newspapers."

He touched me then. His fingertips brushed my chin, and I lifted my head, my eyes meeting his. The impact left me breathless. "Does that change things?"

I was stunned. "Doesn't it have to?"

"I don't think so," he said. "I knew I was a prince this whole time. And anyway, that you didn't is part of why I liked spending time with you."

I held that close for the rest of the week.

He liked me. He liked me because I didn't know he was a prince, and he didn't think I was a fool.

That next week I told him my name. "Marissa," I said. "Since I know yours."

"Yes, it's quite a difficult name to use in conversation, don't you think?"

"I assume that's helped by the fact that most people probably call you by an honorific."

"Indeed. But I would rather you did not."

"Hercules?" His name tasted strange on my lips, and not just because it was foreign.

"Yes," he said, smiling at me.

"Then I will."

I knew he was older than me, richer than me, more experienced than me, impossible in every way. But in that moment, as his smile lit his face, I fell in love with him.

He gave me another seashell, and I thought maybe he might feel something for me.

When he went away that summer, I couldn't help but follow the headlines about him. I made myself sick with them.

Because there he was, with beautiful women on his arm, and if he felt for me even a fraction of what I did for him, there was no way that he would be with them. I bought an entertainment magazine with his picture on it, and I knew that if my father found it, I would be in trouble. I put it in the box with the seashells. I felt guilty, because now I had secrets.

Now I didn't do what I was told.

I seemed to do things because of Hercules instead, and that was something entirely different.

I finished school, but I didn't want to go away on a mission trip, because he would be coming back. So I made an excuse about wanting a job, got one at a local coffeehouse called the Snowy Owl.

And mostly, I lived for Sundays.

Of course, nobody scheduled me to work on a Sunday, because my father would forbid that I do anything on the Sabbath.

I didn't care about that. I cared about him.

"You're back," I said to him. First thing, just as I had done the year before.

I was eighteen, and I burned with a strange kind of conviction in my chest, because I didn't feel quite so helpless. Quite like there was such a barrier between us.

Oh sure, there was the Prince thing. The fact that he spent the year dating supermodels and traveling around on private jets. But I was a woman now. And I felt like that had to mean something.

"Of course."

"I'm glad," I said.

"So am I."

Then he reached out his hand and took hold of mine. "Shall we go for a walk?"

"Yes," I said.

And for the first time, I held a man's hand. His fingers were so warm, and it made my stomach turn over, made my heart feel like it was going to race right out of my chest. I looked at him, and he looked completely unaffected, but he still held on to me, and so I held on to that.

He kissed me on one of those Sunday afternoons.

My whole body felt like it would burst into flame.

His lips were firm and sure on mine, and he was so impossibly beautiful.

Every feeling he called up in me I had been taught to identify as a sin, but it was so beautiful, and part of him, and I couldn't bring myself to turn away from it.

So instead, I wrapped my arms around him and kissed him back. Parted my lips for him and allowed him to brush his tongue against mine.

I allowed all kinds of things on those Sunday afternoons. For his touch to become more familiar. For the feeling of his body against mine to become the dearest and most precious thing in the world. All that hard, powerful muscle, gentled as he held me.

I wanted to tell him he didn't have to leash that strength. But I didn't have the words for it. I didn't have the vocabulary for what I wanted at all.

"Can you meet me tonight?"

It was near the end of summer when he asked me that, and I wanted to. Desperately. But I knew that I would get in so much trouble if I were caught.

Do you always do what you're told?

That earlier question came back to haunt me. And no, I didn't do what I was told. Not anymore. Not now.

I lived for Hercules.

It wasn't about whether I might marry him and become a princess. I never thought about the future. I only thought about us, as we were, there on the beach. His life outside of that didn't matter, and neither did mine.

And so I made the decision to expand it. To push outside those isolated Sunday afternoons and see something more.

"Yes."

I climbed out my window that night and met him there at our spot, in the darkness. He had a blanket and a bottle of wine, and I had never tried alcohol before. I declined the wine, but I got drunk on his mouth, on his touch. And before I knew it, things had gone much further than I had intended.

It went on like that over the weeks, until I didn't care anymore what was supposed to be right. The only thing that felt right was being in his arms. And when I gave him my virginity, I gave it easily, joyously. And he showed me what pleasure meant, and why people jumped into ruin with careless abandon and joy in their hearts.

It was the night he left that it happened.

He had to go. He couldn't stay away from home any longer.

He didn't ask me to go with him.

I told myself he couldn't.

He and I forgot everything. We made love on a blanket in the sand until neither of us could breathe, and it wasn't until later that I realized he'd forgotten protection of any kind.

He was gone the next day.

And three weeks later I knew my life had changed forever.

I had no idea how to begin contacting the palace.

But that wasn't even what worried me, not right at first. It was telling my parents. But I knew that I had to call Hercules first.

I knew you couldn't just call up a palace. Still, I had to try.

I called the palace directory. I left a message. I heard nothing.

I called again. Again and again.

Finally, in my desperation I told the person on the other end of the line that I had to get in touch with Prince Hercules, since I was having his baby.

The next day, men in suits came to the coffeehouse.

They whisked me into the manager's office, and they told me that I was never to reach out to Hercules again. And that if I agreed to sign stacks of thick legal documents and never reveal the paternity of my child, I would be given enough money to live more than comfortably forever.

My heart shattered into pieces. Desperate, enraged, I threw the papers and ran. I ran all the way back home.

My secret burst out of me. Flowing like the tears that were pouring down my face. I admitted to my parents that I was pregnant.

My father's face turned to stone. He asked if I intended to marry the father of my child, and quickly. I told him I could not, because he had abandoned me.

He didn't have to say anything. His face said it all. He had warned me. He had told me. And I had failed. I was wicked, just like the rest of them. And that was when he told me he would have to wash his hands of me. Because there was no way that he could have his daughter wandering into Sunday service visibly fallen as I was.

I stumbled out of the house on numb feet, trembling.

And the men in suits were there.

They opened the door to the limousine and bade me to get inside. I obeyed, because I had reverted to being obedient again, there at the center of my grand demolition.

"What does the paperwork demand of me?" I asked.

The men looked at me, hard, neither of them sympathetic at all. "You must stay away from here for a period of five years at least. You must never attempt to contact Prince Hercules. You must never come to the country. If you do that, the sum of money will be yours."

He pointed to a figure outlined on the contract, and my vision blurred. I would never have to work again. My child would want for nothing. And given that I was currently homeless, that was important.

But I could only think of one thing.

"How many times have you had to do this for him?"

"All these things are a matter of private palace business. Will you sign or not?"

And I knew that I'd been had. My virginity taken by a careless seducer of women. He hadn't waited for me because he cared; he had simply waited until it was legal. And then he had sent strangers to do this to me. To dehumanize me, to take what had been a beautiful gift on my part and turn it into something tawdry and worse than common.

"I'll sign."

And so I had. Because what other choice did I have?

Yes, I remembered the first time I saw Hercules Xenakis.

It had been the beginning of the utter destruction of my life as I knew it.

But I rebuilt it into something beautiful. Something that centered around our daughter. *My* daughter.

And I did not violate that agreement. Not in that whole time. Except…

Except I had come back to Medland for the first time, at the end of my five-year exile. And there had been rumors he would be here in the lead-up to his wedding.

I'd told myself I was going for a walk.

But that walk ended at a place I knew I was likely to find him.

There he was on a balcony at the country club, overlooking the ocean below. With a woman standing next to him, a giant ring glittering on her fourth finger. I knew who she was—I wasn't a fool. I didn't avoid headlines about him. I didn't seek them out either. I refused to let him become a sickness for me, ever again.

But I knew he was getting married.

A part of me had to wonder if I was here out of a true desire to reconcile with my mother, now that my father was gone, or if I had really come in the hope of this.

Because of course he still came here. This site of my ruin. The site of his betrayal.

And he was with her.

There had been many *hers* over the years.

I'd forced myself to look at them all and imagine what lies he told them.

But seeing them in person…

It made my whole body ache. I suddenly wished that I had Lily with me. Because at least then I could've turned to her, used her as some sort of distraction.

No.

I would never, ever allow Lily to be exposed to him.

He didn't want her. He didn't want her, and he didn't deserve to see her. Did not deserve to set eyes on the miracle that we had created. The only good and beautiful thing that I had in my life. He had rejected her, and he never, ever deserved to have even a moment of that pure love that she possessed.

But then he turned, as if an invisible force had tapped him on the shoulder. And his eyes caught mine.

And the expression I saw there was one of pure hatred.

CHAPTER TWO

Hercules

MARISSA. HER NAME echoed inside me, as it always had. And for one moment I was stopped utterly and completely. For one moment I was transported back in time. To the strangest, most unaccountable three years of my life.

Three summers spent obsessed with a dowdy brunette who hadn't even known who I was upon our first meeting.

That was what had intrigued me at first. Women tried all kinds of things to get close to me. To get into my sphere and seize whatever power they thought they might have. But not her.

Oh, I hadn't believed her doe-eyed innocence at first. I had been waiting for her to show her hand at some point, the whole summer that first time we met. But there was never a hand to show.

We never exchanged names, and if she knew that I was Hercules Xenakis, Prince of Pelion, she did not let on.

I talked to her. And I could not remember a time

when I had ever talked to another person the way that I did her. And even now, years later, I could not quite account for why.

At first, it had felt like a game. I was one of the most recognizable men in the world and had been from the day of my birth, so the novelty of being anonymous was one that amused me greatly.

But there came a point where I began avoiding any and all others on Sunday afternoons so that I could go and meet the pastor's daughter, who had somehow captured my attention.

She became a sickness.

I was obsessed with her smile. Her eyes. The way the sunlight caught her hair and created a halo of gold around her. Like she was an angel. The kind who shouldn't associate with a devil like me.

It has never been my habit to question my motivations. An entire staff of hundreds exists, and always has, to see to my every whim. I've never had to put much thought into why I do anything. If I want something, it appears.

And so I didn't put any thought into why my little fascination had a hold of me the way that she did. It was innocent, that first summer.

But things changed.

The way that she looked at me, with that hunger in her eyes. And I knew that she didn't understand what was burning between us, which should have been my first warning to stay away.

But as the Prince of Pelion, I did not have to heed warnings. The world rearranged itself around my desires, so denying myself the diversion never crossed my mind.

My first mistake, and one that I would come to understand as a weakness.

The kind of weakness that my father worked to train out of me from the time I was a boy.

A man, in my father's opinion, had to be able to withstand anything. Any pain, any betrayal, without a hint of emotion. If his child was to be tortured in order for an enemy to gain secrets, the man must not bend then.

He had done his best to ensure that I could withstand any physical torture.

Even if he'd had to be the one to test me.

And he had.

But in my father's view of the world, that same man could not put shackles on his excess. It was balance, he had told me, that a man be the hardest, cruelest of weapons when the time came, and that he indulged his baser urges when it was not a time of war.

Well-fed appetites for drink and women contributed to strength in lean times, or so he'd said.

Weakness in himself was the only thing that a ruler need fear. My father ruled Pelion with an iron fist, and he ruled his life the same way.

He ruled his children in that manner as well. Making sure that from infancy I was fit to take the throne when he passed on. If he could have taken on the Roman practice of leaving his issue out in the dirt overnight to see if it was strong enough to survive, I knew he would have done so.

Being the son of King Xerxes was not for the faint of heart. Or mind or body.

But one petite brunette that I met on the shores of a deserted ocean could hardly be a threat. That was what I told myself.

My heart had been forged in fire, covered in iron from the time I was a child. I excelled at playing a part. The international playboy who cared for nothing.

But in truth, behind the scenes, I was always ensuring that my father did no damage to the country. Did no damage to my mother.

For her part, she removed herself from the palace whenever she could.

I had been hurt by that, as a boy. Left to my father's particular brand of care, which included torture and time spent in solitary confinement.

I'd ached for my mother then.

But there was no point in regretting anything.

My father had made me a weapon. One intent on being turned around on him.

And I would have engaged in a more open rebellion in the beginning if I had not known it would come back tenfold on my much younger sister and the Queen.

There was no place in my life for softness, nor any place for a commoner who would endanger the plans that I had carefully put in place.

The Council of Pelion and I worked together to find an existing precedent for change of leadership. Once the current ruler surpassed his seventieth birthday, if the successor had produced an heir, he could take control.

It was a complicated process, and as I did not want to create a Civil War, I knew I had to play my cards right.

My father was nothing if not a self-preservationist. And I knew that I would have to do everything in my power to have the full favor of the people. And that meant, of course, marrying a woman from Pelion, one who came from the high echelons of society and who was well loved by many.

And I had done my part. I had managed to gain an agreement from my father that he would allow this, once his birthday passed and I had fulfilled my obligations.

One of which was marrying a woman he found suitable.

But in my foolishness, I had begun to negotiate in my own mind, as one summer with Marissa turned to two. And then it became three, and the heat of passion had burned between us, so hot and bright it obliterated the memory of any woman who had come before her.

I had to leave, had to return to Pelion to make a case for why this woman was worth upending the existing agreement that I had with the daughter of a politician.

But when I returned to Medland she was gone. Nowhere to be found at all. Her father simply opened the door with a stony face and said she had gone.

And I wondered if she had gone off on the mission trip she had spoken of all that time ago, but it had seemed to me that her devotion had rather turned to the worship of me and my body rather than a deity.

I was not content with that. I sent my security detail out on a search for her, engaged the resources of the palace, and still, it turned up nothing.

She had abandoned me.

The woman that I had been willing to risk an agreement over was gone.

No one had ever dared to defy me before.

That she would felt like a near unendurable blow, one that had left a great crack inside my chest.

But I had repaired that. Let it go.

Still, as I stood there, looking at her and her shocked face, I knew that it wasn't fully repaired. No. But it had changed.

It had been pain at first—a shock to me, as I had no idea I was capable of such fine feelings. But then it had changed, shifted into a deep, raging fury that had propelled me on. Had cemented my motives.

I had allowed myself to become distracted, and that was unacceptable.

I had gone back to Pelion, reaffirmed my commitment to my future marriage.

And now, five years on, it was set to take place. It had all been put on hold until my fiancée, Vanessa, was ready, and I had been happy enough to wait, as I knew that I could not rush something like this, so poised on the knife's edge.

Once, once I had been impatient. Once I had nearly ruined everything. It would not happen again.

Except, I forgot why in the moment that I stared at Marissa.

But there came a point where I began avoiding any and all others. And then she did what she had done that first day, the very first time I saw her.

She turned and she ran away.

I spared a glance at the woman by my side. "I have business to attend to."

"What is it?" she asked, only half-interested.

She was more interested in taking in the surroundings at the country club's deck. And the people who were there. Not so she could see them so much as she could know who had seen her. Vanessa was accustomed to status and luxury. It was one thing I valued in her.

Vanessa and I had an arrangement that centered squarely on politics and personal gain. She was not interested in my comings and goings, not any more than I was interested in hers.

She tucked her blond hair behind her ear, and her ring glittered in the light. "If I don't return soon, have security detail escort you back to the house."

"Very thoughtful of you," she responded, smiling at me, ever conscious of the fact that we might be photographed at a given moment.

A good thing she remembered, because I could not spare a thought for it. I charged away from the deck, going back the way that Marissa had gone. And I saw just enough to see which direction she fled, rounding a corner down one of the quaint streets.

I wondered if she was going to her parents' house, though I had checked periodically for months with palace security, and they swore she had not gone to her parents' home.

But she was here, so clearly something had changed.

It occurred to me suddenly that I should perhaps feel like a fool, chasing down the footsteps of a ghost from my past wearing a custom-made suit on the night of my engagement party. But I was a man who was accustomed to his word being law, and the matter felt as if it bore more importance than it did.

So I felt it. So it was.

And I ignored the slight kick in my gut that told

me it was a shade too close to something my father might think.

I didn't know why I was going after her. I'd had countless lovers before her, and countless sins stained my soul.

I didn't know why she mattered.

Because she got beneath the armor. That was why. Because she had done something to me that no one else had ever done. Not before, not since. Because she had made me question my primary goal in life. Had made me question the very foundation that it had been built upon.

Because of her, I nearly put the plan to rescue my nation in jeopardy.

I would have chanced marrying a commoner, a woman unapproved, who could add nothing to the throne, ensuring that my father stayed seated for years longer than he might have otherwise.

My father was too mean to die. Far too cruel to do anything quite so prosaic as give up the ghost.

And she had walked away from me. It was not I who had come to my good senses, no.

It both incensed and fascinated me even still, and that was why—I told myself—I was now chasing after her through the streets of Medland.

Her family home was small, a classic saltbox house with shingled siding like every other house on the street. I crossed the lawn, prepared to walk in without knocking, because princes did not knock, when I realized that it was probably for the best if I attempted to open with a small modicum of courtesy, as I had no idea if her parents still lived there, or if it was the home she had in fact gone into.

I rapped on the door and waited.

It opened wide, to reveal an older woman with the same color eyes as Marissa. She swung the door just wide enough that I caught sight of Marissa standing behind her. Marissa quickly retreated into the kitchen. The older woman looked behind her. "Can I help you?"

"I think we both know why I'm here."

"I don't, I'm afraid. I'm the only one here."

I admired how brazen she was. But that didn't mean that I was going to allow her to get away with it.

"I'm here for your daughter."

"She is not here for you," the woman said. "How dare you show your face?"

No one save my father had ever spoken to me with that tone of voice. This woman, who only came to the middle of my chest, spoke as if she would cheerfully remove my head from my shoulders. "Go off and have your wedding. Leave us in peace."

"I have questions for Marissa."

"And she has none for you. If she did, she would be out here. My daughter is strong. Made stronger because of you. We don't need you here."

"I am very sorry," I said, feeling nothing of the kind. "But I can't take no for an answer."

I stepped inside, and she moved back, allowing the entry. My footsteps fell heavy on the wood floor, and I knew that was what signaled Marissa, who came charging in from the next room.

Damn, she was beautiful.

Even more than the last time I'd seen her. She'd been

a woman then, but she… She had blossomed in the years since.

Her curves were more exaggerated, hollows in her cheekbones, rather than the pleasant roundness that had been there before. Her dark hair was long, curling at the ends, and there was a wildness to it now. I had thought, the first time I'd seen her, that she did look every inch the church secretary.

She did not now.

There was an edge of sophistication to the way she was dressed, even though it was simple and not designed to draw attention to her. She was wearing makeup, which I had never known her to do before.

I resented it. I wanted to wipe it away, just like I wanted to wipe away the years. Wanted to go back to a time when things had made sense to me in a way that they never had before.

When my world had been contained in an empty stretch of shore and this woman.

But I had been wrong then. Wrong about what mattered. Wrong about everything. So there was no point going back.

And there was no point mourning the passing of the years.

"How dare you?" she asked. "My mother told you to leave."

"And I said no." I took a step forward. "Have you forgotten who I am, Marissa?"

"In the five years since I've seen you? Almost. Your name has not crossed my lips once, Hercules. This is the first time in all that time. I swear it."

Her expression was guarded, the words hard, and

she was nothing like the girl I had once known. And I believed her.

"I want to know where you went."

"You want to know where I went?" Confusion and anger contorted her beautiful features.

And it hit me then that however much Marissa had changed, it was strange that she was angry at me.

She was the one who had left. And I had racked my brain over the years to try to think of reasons why. But I had been faithful to her. And yes, I had gone back to Pelion and left her in Medland, but I had assumed she would understand I would be back. And I had been.

She was the one who had abandoned us. A good thing, I could see now. But that made me question why rage still burned in my chest.

I heard the clatter of footsteps on the stairs, but they did not sound heavy or even enough to be an adult's. I looked and saw a little girl leaping down the steep staircase, her dark curls bouncing with the motion. And everything in me went still. I'm not a man who believes in premonitions. I believe in what can be seen, felt and touched, but in that moment, I felt something supernatural steal over me.

And when that child looked up at me, her chocolate eyes connecting with mine, I felt a stirring of recognition down in my soul.

I knew this girl. I, who had never had exposure to any child and who had never had a strong feeling about one, was suddenly overcome, immobilized by the strength of the connection that I felt to this one.

Because looking in her eyes was like looking into a mirror. I recognized her face, because it was mine, but smaller, rounder, cherubic in a way I was certain I had never been. I looked up at Marissa and saw she had gone pale.

"What the hell game are you playing?"

CHAPTER THREE

Marissa

IT WAS THE shock on his face that confused me. I don't know what I had been prepared for. But I had always rejected the idea that he might lay eyes on Lily, because he didn't deserve to. Because he had rejected her. I had thought in terms of protecting my daughter, because what mother wouldn't? He didn't deserve to see what a wonderful child we created, because he had rejected her. Because he had sold her when he bought my silence.

But the look on his face was not that of a man who saw this child as being inconsequential. No. The look that he had on his face was that of a man who was... shocked. As though he had been struck by lightning. Of all the things I had expected, I had not expected this. I had done my best never to think about it, of course. But...

No, something was wrong about the way he was looking at her, and I knew it. Deep down I knew. I had seen his face when he thought no one was looking. That sort of blank hardness that I'd witnessed on his features the first day I'd seen him all those years ago.

I'd seen him smile. Laugh.

I'd watched as his guard dropped completely and he'd given himself over to pleasure.

But I had never seen him look like this.

It was not rage; it was something beyond that. His skin had taken on a waxen pallor, and for the first time he seemed…

Well, human, and not so like a god.

"Explain this," he said, his voice hard.

My mother looked at him and then at me, her expression helpless.

My mother had worked hard to repair the relationship that had been severed by my father. She had secretly traveled to visit me and Lily a few times over the years. And I hated that my father's death had brought me a sense of relief, but it had. Because it had returned my childhood home to me, and my mother and I no longer had to stoop to subterfuge to see one another.

She felt nothing but sympathy for me, and I wondered if sometimes she felt a bit of envy.

Because I'd found a sort of passion that had made me behave the way that I had.

Because I had then gone out and raised a child on my own, which she'd not had the courage to do.

In spite of how unhappy she had been.

And now I could see that she was prepared to fight for Lily and me if need be.

"What do you mean what is this?" I asked. "You know perfectly well."

"I don't know anything," he said, his eyes never leaving Lily.

"We cannot have this conversation in front of her," I said.

Lily, being four and full of inquisitiveness without an ounce of perception, tilted her head back and stared up at the man I knew to be her father.

"Who are you?" she asked him.

"I was going to ask you the same thing," he responded, his voice far too hard to speak to a child.

"I'm Lily Rivero," she said. "It's nice to meet you."

Lily was precocious and polite, and I was happy that I had been able to stay home and take care of her. That we'd been able to afford to buy a wonderful house in a beautiful neighborhood. I had made the absolute most of all that I had been given, if for no other reason than to throw it in the face of Hercules, whether he could see it or not.

When he looked at me, the fury in his eyes was terrifying. It wasn't fire. It was like ice. And I sensed that it had the power to utterly destroy me.

But then, he always had. He was my weakness. My undoing.

My brightest and most beautiful sin.

My father had repeated the quote that the wages of sin was death.

Looking at Hercules now, I was beginning to wonder.

The words were quite literal and not spiritual as I had originally taken them to mean.

"Perhaps there is a place where we can talk," he said.

And I feared slightly for my own safety and health. It was like staring at a stranger. A large, incredibly muscular stranger, who bore no small amount of anger inside him.

But then…

The light hit him, just so, a shaft of sun coming through the window. And I knew him.

It was like being cast back to those sunny days on the beach.

When I had trusted him. When I had given myself to him.

When I had known him, better than I had ever known anyone.

It was still true.

That this man would always have a piece of me that no one else would. What we had shared, my father had called a *sin*. The result of which he had called the *consequence*.

But it had been *intimacy*.

And it had been real.

Whatever had happened after, it had been real for me.

And that was why I found myself unable to deny him. That was why, in spite of the years of pain, anger and anguish, I could not deny this man now when he asked for an audience with me.

Or maybe I was weak.

I would have to allow for that, I knew. I had always been weak for Hercules.

But strong for Lily.

Strong for Lily from the very beginning.

I would be strong for her now.

I followed him into the kitchen, and then I gestured to the back door. It was his turn to follow me, out to the backyard with a scant covering of crabgrass, peppered down a rolling slope.

You could just barely see the ocean through the trees,

the most beautiful views on the island not afforded to a family like mine.

I had always found that unfair when I was a child. That the bright, brilliant ocean views were granted to those who only lived here a few months out of the year.

As an adult, of course, I understood. The cost of such beauty.

I looked back at Hercules, and my previous thought echoed in my head.

The cost of such beauty.

I knew the cost of touching beauty like his.

Or so I'd thought.

I had not realized a further payment might be required.

"Is she mine?" The question was a growl.

It took me a full minute to process those words. Because it was not the question I had expected him to ask.

There had been papers. Demands. He had never wanted her. He didn't want me.

"How can you ask me that?" I sputtered.

"What else could I ask? Is that child mine?"

"You know she is," I said. "You know. You sent men. You made me sign papers. I was never supposed to come and see you, and here you are at my parents' house…"

"What men? What papers?"

"They were your men," I said. "Men from the palace. I called, Hercules. So many times. I was pregnant, and I was terrified. And do you have any idea what my father…? I needed you. I needed you, and you sent a nondisclosure agreement."

"I did no such thing," he said.

The light in his eyes had gone obsidian, and for the first time I was staring full in the face of the blackness I had witnessed in that unguarded moment when he thought no one had been looking at him that first day I'd seen him.

There was something beneath that careless playboy facade that the paper saw, something beneath the caring lover that I had spent time with years ago.

It was something I had not touched. Had not tasted.

Until now.

"I don't know what to tell you," I said. "I called the palace and left messages, and no one returned them. Finally, I said… I told them that I was pregnant with your baby."

"You told someone at the palace?"

"Yes. There was nothing else I could do."

"You told someone at the palace and then men arrived." It wasn't a question, more grim statement.

"Yes. Men came, and they offered me a sum of money if I never spoke to you again. If I never contacted you again."

"You took a payoff in order to avoid telling me about my child?"

"I thought you were the one offering the payoff," I said, my heart fluttering in my chest like a trapped bird. I was beginning to feel sick, because the implications of the words being spoken between us were starting to turn over inside of me, revealing facets that I had not immediately understood or seen. "I didn't choose money over you. I thought you were demanding that I never see you…"

"This child is my heir," he said.

"She's a girl," I said, defensively.

"That doesn't matter. A law as old as time in my country, which my father would have changed if he could have, believe me. But he could not, alas for him. And so it remains. Any child of mine—as long as she is legitimate—can take the throne."

"Well," I said, drawing myself up as tall as I possibly could. I still fell laughably short of the top of his shoulder. "She's not legitimate. She won't be. She can't be. Surely you know that already."

"That isn't how it works. If I choose to recognize her by marrying you, then she will be legitimate."

"I don't… I don't understand any of this," I said, panic rising up inside of me.

How was I supposed to make sense of it? I had thought all these years that he never wanted to see her. That he would rather pay exorbitant sums to keep Lily and myself as his dirty secret. Making sense of the fact that he seemed to want Lily was almost impossible.

It was untangling a web that had been stretched across my life five years ago. One that I had built myself with the remnants I'd had left.

I'd lost him.

I'd lost my parents.

And now here he was, larger than life and every inch as heartbreakingly beautiful as he'd been at the first, and he was telling me that he wanted Lily.

"This is my father's doing," he said, reiterating what he'd said before. "He and I have an agreement. I don't know if you know much about the history of my country."

"I steer clear of everything concerning you to the best of my ability."

His lip lifted into a curl. "Except for my money."

Anger sizzled through my veins. "I'm sorry. Should I have sat in poverty and virtue with your child after being rejected by you and by my parents? Would that have made a more beautiful and sympathetic picture of maternal suffering for you? When I had an offer of comfort and riches on the table, should I have opted to take something else? There is no shame in poverty, not when life has given you no choice. But I was given a choice. A choice to make sure that no matter what happened, my child would have food. Would have shelter. That I would be able to be home to take care of her. I have been all she's had. Her only parent. It is my job, and mine alone, to care for her. There has been no one else. If you would have preferred to come back to a life in ruin so that you could rebuild it again, I am sorry to disappoint you. When you left, my life *was* ruin. My father looked at me and called me a whore. I had nowhere and nothing, and I rebuilt it with what I was given. I will not feel shame for that."

"Do you know what I think?"

I crossed my arms and took a step toward him, and I could see shock flickered behind his dark eyes. If he thought that I was still the young girl in love that he had met back then, then he was to be reeducated, and quickly.

Five years I had been without him. Five years I had been on my own in the world. Learning what it meant to live beneath the judgment of others, sleepless nights spent caring for my daughter, without any help when I found myself in a state of utter exhaustion.

And I had become strong.

Arguments in doctors' offices when I knew my child had pneumonia and they simply wanted to send me home. Standing up for Lily when she had pushed someone to the ground in her preschool class because they had said her mother was bad since Lily didn't have a father.

Standing up for myself when people sometimes didn't let their children associate with mine for those same reasons.

Years alone and motherhood had sharpened me, and sometimes I resented it.

Because I had been soft once, and I had believed in love.

The only kind of love left that I believed in was the kind between a mother and daughter, strengthened when my own had attempted to mend the bridge that had been broken between us by my father.

Fathers I could do without, thank you.

Mothers I had found strength in.

But like a stone battered about, my smooth edges had been cracked against the hardships of life, creating hard, sharp edges.

And he was about to understand just how much I'd changed.

"I'm sure you're going to tell me what you think," I said, "because you think the world stops and starts on your word. Because once you were able to make my world stop and start at your word. But I made a life without you in it. And I will tell you gladly that there is nothing for you here. So whatever you say, it better be compelling, and not predictable as I suspect it will be."

"I think that you didn't want to hassle with me, and when you were offered a payoff, you took it rather than making sure you did the right thing."

I scoffed. "The right thing? The right thing. To ensure that a man who goes about the world spreading his seed whenever he feels the urge knows about a child he didn't even want? How many other women are like me, do you think?"

He drew back. "None."

"You don't know that."

"I have always used condoms," he said ferociously. "With every other woman."

"Oh," I said. "So I'm special. The woman who had never even touched a man's hand before you is the one that you couldn't be bothered to protect? I'm glad that our dalliance meant so much to you."

"Say what you want, Marissa, but I came back for you. I came back for you, and you were not here. And a damn good thing, I have told myself over the years, because I had a responsibility to my country and to my people, and you did not fit anywhere into that responsibility. But now there is her. Lily. And I cannot ignore the implications of her existence. My father has ruled Pelion with an iron fist for generations. And the only reason that I have not overthrown him in some kind of civil war is that the casualties would be too great, and there is a law that states the current leader is to step aside at seventy if the successor has married and produces an heir. I found that suitable woman some time ago."

"Yes. I know. I've seen photos of you with her."

"But Lily is my heir. And my father has had a significant birthday. That ushers in a new order in my country immediately. And that must be fulfilled. Because over the years my father's tyrannical tendencies have gotten worse. He is beginning to crack down on even the most basic of freedoms people in my country used to experience. And while there is breath in my body and power to do so, I cannot allow it. But the consideration of the cost to civilian life and the danger to my mother and sister has weighed heavily on me. But this... We have a binding document."

"Your father is a tyrant—do you think he would honor it?"

"It is not him that I need to honor it. It is the military. They serve the King. Not only that, it's whether or not I am King in the eyes of allies."

"It all seems trivial to me."

"It is the nature of being royal. Tradition is what it is."

"But will I be deemed acceptable?"

"That is for the Council to decide, but I suspect that the existence of an heir and the law as it is written will trump any concerns about your suitability."

"I have a life. I have built a life for Lily and myself in Boston. I am terribly sorry about your country. Not for your sake, but for the sake of your people.But I fail to see how it's my problem."

"It is your problem because you had my child."

I stepped forward, rage simmering in my blood, boiling over. "She is my child. Your contribution to her genetics does not make you a father. It does not make her yours. I gave birth alone. The pain and fear that I felt in that moment was horrible, and if not for a nurse who felt sorry for me and sat there and held my hand the entire time, there would've been no one there for me. I took an infant back to my home by myself, and I'm the one who didn't sleep for months. I'm the one who paced the halls rocking a crying baby."

I took a jagged breath and continued, all my anger—at him, my parents, the world—spilling out now. "And you… You were at parties. You had a new lover that same week that I gave birth, and she was on the cover of magazines with you, all slim and beautiful and perfectly made up, and my hair was in one giant mat, my pajama pants were too tight and I wanted to weep from lack of sleep. Lily is *mine*. She is mine by rights. You have parties. And endless photos to document the way that you enjoy spending your time, and all the glittering, sparkling objects you can lay claim to. But I am not one of them, and neither is she. Your father might be a bastard, but it's his money that kept us off the streets, if I'm understanding this correctly."

His face went grim, the light behind his eyes unreadable, opaque.

"I don't have room for emotion in this," he said. "There is a means here to liberate my country, and it will be done. Lily is coming with me whether or not you like it."

"What are you going to do?"

"Take her from you forcibly if I must, and deal with whatever fallout results. But I would rather that you came with me, as it would make things easier for the child."

Horror stole through me, and I could see that he

wasn't kidding. I could see the hardness in him. And I wondered how in the world I had ever thought this man to be a creature of pleasure and lightness, when I could see now that he was all rock and cold.

"You can't do this."

"I can. Even legally. I have diplomatic immunity, first of all. Second of all, Lily is a citizen of Pelion. And I am her father."

"Your name isn't on the birth certificate."

"It doesn't matter. Or have you not been listening? I am a prince in line to be a king and my word is law, even here."

I felt some of the fight begin to drain out of me, but then I steeled myself, took a breath and did my best to renew it. "I will not go easily. I will not uproot my child from everything that she knows, everything that she is, because you have decided that it's time to take responsibility."

"I didn't know. And if you want to make it about Lily, then you have to ask yourself what the ramifications of your decision are. She could be Queen."

The words shocked me, because it had honestly never occurred to me. That Lily was royal. That she was a princess. One that was in line for the throne of Pelion, but only if Hercules and I married.

"Would you rob your child of her rightful place in this world?"

I didn't want my child to be a queen. That was my very first thought. Because the very idea of her being a world leader, of her having such scrutiny placed on her, such a broad target painted on her back… It filled me with dread. I couldn't stand it when children made fun

of her parentage. The very idea of her being a leader—
a woman leader in this world—and the kinds of things
that would be said about her… It scared me to my bones.

But on the other hand, there was a truth to what he
said that I found difficult to deny.

But the idea of being married to this man that I had
hated for so long, who had hurt me so much…

A little bubble welled up inside my chest, and I despised it. Because I recognized it for what it was.

Joy.

That I could feel joy in some part of myself that
Hercules was back, that he was proposing marriage…

Well, it made me feel like the foolish idiot my father thought I was. The immoral fool who would throw
over all scruples and morality for the touch of a good-
looking man.

This wasn't about me. And if I was to claim truth for
all the things that I'd said to him in the past few minutes, I had to take myself out of the equation.

I had to think of Lily. Only of Lily.

"It's not my permission you need," I said. "But you
will ask my daughter's."

"I'm sorry," he responded, arching a black brow.
"You expect me to go to a child and explain all of this."

"She has friends," I said. "She's just now reconnect-
ing with her grandmother. It is her future you're talking
about, and yes, I know she's four. And I know that…" I
blinked back tears, because I knew that what my daughter would see was this tall, beautiful man telling her that
he was her father. And that she was a princess. And I
already knew what Lily would say.

But it was that vision in my mind that made me so resolute.

That Lily would be a princess. That she would have a father.

Whatever my feelings about him were…

He hadn't known.

He hadn't rejected me. He hadn't rejected her. And I couldn't shrug off the layers of armor that I had put on over the years with the ease of that revelation, but it was what made me give him time to speak, rather than simply attempting to run him through with a kebab skewer that I might have found in my mother's kitchen drawer.

"It's her life," I said. "And so, yes. I expect you to speak to her." I sighed heavily. "If she says no…you'll have to kidnap us both, I guess."

CHAPTER FOUR

Hercules

UTTER DISBELIEF FIRED through me as I stared down at
Marissa. I hardly recognized the woman who stood before me, and I had known her intimately five years ago.
But she was not the scared creature who had fled, no
matter that I had thought she might be, given the way
she had run from me back at the restaurant.

She had not been running to protect herself, but to
protect Lily.

Lily.

Who was undeniably mine.

But I could not afford to falter, could not afford to
allow emotion to have any purchase on this moment,
because I had a responsibility.

First and foremost, Lily was the heir to the throne
of Pelion. Lily was the key to ousting my father from
power, and she would have to be treated as such.

But somehow I had been thrust into a position where
I was going to have to make political negotiations with
a child.

Marissa was staring me down, her dark eyes never

wavering from mine, and I had no doubt that every-thing she said was true.

I would have to bundle them up and carry them out of the house, forcing them onto a plane, if I did not do this.

Now, whatever Marissa thought, I was not ashamed at the thought that I might take that action. I would do what I had to do.

But I was also happy to avoid it, given it was an ac-tion that was guaranteed to draw press.

It was a tangled mess. I was set to marry Vanessa in just two weeks' time, and now there was no question of that happening.

I didn't need allegations of me being a kidnapper to come out on top of it.

I was not a man who dealt in uncertainty—a man in my position could not afford to be. But as I followed Marissa up the stairs, I felt a shadow of it. And I real-ized that the only reason I even knew what I could be feeling was because of her. Because Marissa had, all those years ago, taken that bedrock certainty of who I was—and my confidence that I could make whatever life I chose to arrange for myself—and dashed it against the rocks, as if she were the siren to my wayward sailor.

She pushed the door open at the top of the stairs, and I followed her in. "Lily," she said, "Hercules would like to speak to you." There was a tremor in her voice for the first time. And if I had been a different man, I might have felt some uncertainty along with it.

But I could not afford to waver. Not ever. And I could not afford sympathy in any measure.

Lily looked confused. Curious. Her dark eyes swept over me, and even amid the confusion, even in her youth, I could see an imperiousness there. Inherited, I knew.

Lily.

What would her name have been if I had been there? Her name would have been a family name. Aphrodite or Apollonia, perhaps.

Lily was so simple.

It sounded like something that could be easily crushed, and everything inside of me rebelled at that. But when I looked back down at the child and her steady expression as she looked me full in the face with an ease that men found next to impossible at times, I knew the name suited her well.

Because her enemies would never know that she was made of steel at her core. They would be distracted and confused by her apparent softness, and they would never see her hit coming.

I would teach her to hone that. I would teach her all she needed in order to ascend the throne of Pelion. She was young enough that it was not too late, and I might have missed her earliest years, but I would not miss anymore. I kept my gaze on Lily, because this discussion was between us, and only us.

"I have something I wish to speak to you about," I said, trying to decide if I should loom over the child or crouch down and meet her eyes.

I was a prince. I did not crouch. It was near to a bow, and I wasn't entirely sure my body could form such a submissive posture.

But speaking over her as I was didn't seem right either.

And so for the first time I could remember, I bent a knee.

"Your mother and I were…" How the hell did you explain such a thing to a child? I had no idea. Did she even know a man and woman had to *know* each other in order to reproduce? And I could not say something that would cast her mother in a negative light. That was just diplomacy. She was on her mother's side. Clearly, she would not take kindly to an interloper telling her that her mother was anything less than perfect. So I would have to select my wording carefully. Not out of deference to Marissa, but out of care for my particular political mission.

With a four-year-old.

My child. My *daughter*.

It was something I could not fathom still. It settled on my skin like a crackle of electricity, rather than sinking in.

"We knew each other for a time," I continued. "And we were…separated. I had to go back to my country, and you moved away from here."

She scrunched up her face. "You talk funny. Is it because you're from another country?"

It was not a question I expected, and one that came in slightly from left field, given the direction my line of speaking was headed.

"Yes," I said. "I imagine so." Though, I did not think I had a very marked accent. I've been told my English was nothing short of excellent.

"Okay," she said, apparently satisfied by my admission.

"I am from a country far away," I continued. "Across

the ocean. An island in the middle of the Mediterranean Sea. It's beautiful. You see, I had to return there to see to business because I am a prince."

"A prince?" Her eyes got round.

"Yes," I said, satisfied that that statement had landed anyway. "And I have just discovered something, Lily. You are my Princess. You're my daughter. I… I'm your father."

And then she did something I couldn't have anticipated.

I didn't realize that children felt emotion in that way, but she demonstrated to me that I knew nothing. Her face crumpled, almost immediately, and the sound that came out of her tiny body was almost inhuman. A high-pitched wail that pierced my heart, pierced any defense I thought I might have had. And then she wrapped her arms around my neck and held me, as if I weren't a stranger. As if I weren't a man who had stormed into her grandmother's house and made all manner of threats to her mother.

I went stiff, completely uncertain of what to do. And for the first time, I looked to Marissa. Her expression was neutral, but there were tears in her eyes. I tried to straighten, but Lily would not let me go. So I wrapped an arm around her and stood, holding her against me as she wept. "Your mother told me that I had to ask you," I continued, "if you want to come with your mother and live with me in my castle."

I realized how truly unfair a line of questioning that was, and also realized that by asking me to go and speak to Lily, Marissa had not set me up for failure. Her motive had not been selfish, not at all. Because anyone would know that a four-year-old would not have the willpower to turn down such an offer.

She lifted her head, wiping at her eyes with closed fists. "What about my nana?"

"Your nana can come too," I said. "It's a very big castle."

I didn't know how I'd come into the position of negotiating details of something so delicate with a preschooler, but there I was.

"Mommy," Lily said, her voice plaintive. She reached for Marissa.

Marissa stepped forward, and I transferred the warm weight of the child to her.

It was a strange thing, one that I imagined normal parents did.

Mine certainly never had. There had been no affection spared for me in my youth. I imagine my mother had felt inclined to give it to me, but my father had not allowed it.

And I...

I had spent so much time planning for what it would be like politically when I had an heir that I had never once spared a thought to what kind of father I would be.

Only what kind of king I might be.

But Lily was not a hypothetical—she was very real, and seemed to need something from me that I could not quite fathom, but knew I had to find it in myself to give.

"It's true," Marissa said, brushing Lily's hair back from her face. "Everything he said is true. You're a princess. If you want to be a princess, it means moving away from here. Away from our home in Boston. Away from what we know. But I'll be with you. And...

you were born a princess, Lily." Her voice broke. "You were born a princess, and whether you go to Pelion or not, you're still a princess. But everything that your father has belongs to you too. And it wouldn't be right for me to ask you not to have it."

It was clear to me that Lily didn't understand Marissa's impassioned speech. But I did. I appreciated how difficult this was for her, even though it couldn't affect my ultimate action.

Lily's expression was serious, and she looked at me with luminous eyes. "Daddy?"

The word hit like a bullet. I felt as though it had ripped its way through my chest and torn my heart utterly into pieces.

The heart that I didn't realize had been quite so vulnerable, or quite so…

Quite so able to feel.

This child was innocent. Of everything.

Of what had happened between her mother and me, whether it was subterfuge on the part of Marissa or not. Of the royal lineage she had been born into.

She had no control over any of it, and I knew exactly what that felt like.

Except when my father had taken me in hand, they had been the hands of a monster, and there had never been any question that I call him something so affectionate as Daddy.

But this child was handing me trust. A moniker of affection that I had done nothing to earn, and I feared might never.

I felt utterly and wildly adrift in that moment, in a way that I had only ever done two other times in my life.

The first time I had seen Marissa—when it hadn't even been sexual in nature—and when I had come back to discover she was gone.

"Yes," I said, my voice less than steady, which was unacceptable.

And yet we were not in the throne room. Not before the press.

It was just me and this child. My child.

And Marissa.

"I want to go with you," the little girl said, while simultaneously tightening her hold on her mother.

"Then we will go together," Marissa said, holding even more tightly to Lily. "We will go together."

"And you will be my wife," I returned. "My Princess. Both of you."

I was resolved. And it was done.

"My mother?"

"Is welcome to come."

Marissa nodded slowly. "Okay. I'll... I'll talk to her."

"We must leave tonight," I said, decisively. "I will send men to handle my things, and to handle Vanessa as well."

"Oh..." Marissa looked crestfallen. "Vanessa. What are you going to do about Vanessa? You're engaged to her. You're supposed to get married in two weeks. How are you going to...?"

"I just told you," I replied. "I will send men to handle her. And to help mitigate any disappointment that she might feel. I'm not a monster. Whatever you might think."

"You're breaking up with your fiancée via your goon squad. Who, by the way, are likely the very same men who told me that you wanted—"

She cut herself off, and I saw her flick a glance at Lily.

"You and I will have to discuss this at another time."

"We will."

I picked up my phone. "Have my private jet ready to go in one hour. Please arrange alternative transport for Ms. Carlson."

And with that I hung up, not cowed by Marissa's disapproving gaze. She could disapprove all she wanted. We were in a mess that I suspected had been made by my father, and I refused to let him win. Absolutely and utterly refused. Marissa may not have liked my methods, but I knew that in the end my way would be the best way.

"An hour? That's not enough time to pack. What about all our things? Lily and I don't live here. We have a house in Boston. All of her toys…"

"Someone will be sent to retrieve them," I replied. "But I will not delay taking the two of you back to your rightful place."

"My mother…"

"I suggest you speak to her quickly."

"So all of this will be your way?" Marissa asked.

"I did this part your way," I said, nodding toward Lily, indicating the fact that I had asked her permission. "Yes. The rest will be done mine. I regret to tell you that there is no other option."

"Somehow, I very much doubt that you're filled with regret of any kind."

But she was wrong. Because what I felt swirling in my chest right now as I looked at my child, as I looked at the way she fitted in Marissa's arms, was a tangle of regret that I had not felt before in my entire life.

I did not like it. And so I did what I must do. I took action.

"We are going. Now. Don't tempt me to change the deadline."

Marissa turned away from me and bumped against a box on the edge of the dresser. She cursed—which surprised me—as the box hit the ground. The lid fell open and out spilled two shells. A larger one and a smaller one.

She looked at me, and my eyes went to her hair. The way it curled.

And then I looked back at the shells.

I'd given those to her. Because in my madness I'd seen her in everything, even in nature.

And she'd kept them. Even while claiming to hate me.

She bent down and picked up the box, put the shells back in and cradled the box to her chest. She stared me down for a moment, as if daring me to say something.

I didn't.

Then, without a word, Marissa nodded and swept from the room, leaving me standing there.

Something no one would typically dare to do.

But Marissa had never been typical. She hated me, and yet she had my shells. And I was fascinated all over again in spite of myself.

But Marissa had nothing to do with the decision that I had made.

This was about Lily. This was about the throne.

This was about making sure my father knew he would never win against me.

Of that I would be certain.

CHAPTER FIVE

Marissa

I HAD KNOWN that he was a prince. I had followed news stories about him over the years and seen the lavish way he lived his life in stunning photographs splashed across search engines and tabloid newspapers.

But it hadn't really taken hold of me just what that meant until we boarded his private plane.

Luxury on that scale was something so theoretical to me that I could only imagine it, and even then, I could only imagine it at a reduced scale.

My brain hadn't had the textural vocabulary for leather as soft as what was found on the plush couch in the seating area of the plane. It didn't have the concept of the scale that something like a prince's private plane might have. I had imagined something like I had seen in movies, where one still had to duck down when they stood, and there were a few seats with ample legroom, and glasses of champagne.

No.

This plane was mammoth. One that could easily fit the same number of people as commercial planes that did domestic flights. And there were rooms. Multiple rooms, though I didn't know what they all were.

The stewardess quickly ushered Lily to a beautifully appointed bedroom and did the same for my mother. Then she made herself vanish, and I knew that everyone had been carefully dealt with so that Hercules and I could talk.

My mother had of course decided to come with us. There was nothing left for her in Medland, except the beautiful house that she had once shared unhappily with my father.

I could tell that my mother was hesitant to leave me, but it was also clear to an extent that pushing back against Hercules was futile. Far better to try to negotiate with him and get a handle on what this new reality was. And what it would be in the future.

"This is…nice," I said, taking a seat on the couch and sinking into the buttery softness. But I refused to show him that I took pleasure in it.

"Champagne?" he asked.

"A toast to our upcoming union?" I asked. And I immediately regretted making the dry comment, because I was in no place where I could joke about such things.

I couldn't take it lightly.

It made my insides twist into a knot.

And that hope bubble in my chest became more pronounced.

I wanted to pop it.

I felt so foolish, revealing to him that I'd kept those shells. And even more foolish that I hadn't dumped them straight in the trash but had packed them instead.

"If you like."

"I don't drink," I said.

"Do you still not drink? I thought that you also didn't have premarital sex. And yet..."

I didn't tell him that I hadn't had sex since. That he was the only person I'd ever made the exception for.

I didn't tell him that I didn't drink because holdovers from my childhood were still hard to shake, and sometimes I worried a little bit about hellfire being in every breath I took wrong.

"Well, when do you suggest I might have started? During my pregnancy? After? When I was single parenting a young child? There never seemed a good time. And at the moments when I thought I might need a drink most, it occurred to me that perhaps it wasn't healthy to be thinking of it as a crutch."

"Fair enough."

He put the bottle of champagne back and then to my surprise opened a cooler and took out a bottle of sparkling cider.

"You can have champagne," I said.

"I don't need it," he said. "And, as you pointed out, perhaps if one is using it as a crutch, it's not a very good thing."

"I wouldn't think that Your Royal Highness needed crutches."

"In this current situation, I'm finding that I might need more than I think."

I didn't know what to say to that. The admission of weakness was so unexpected that it momentarily silenced me.

"Well, I find that I'm in want of some as well. But... but again, it seems an inadvisable reason to start."

"I don't disagree with you," he said. "And so, in the interest of fending off addictions, we can have this together."

"I did try to contact you," I said. "Whatever you think of me… I could have had much more if you would have known. Surely you must see that. If you can't believe in who I am as a person, if you can't believe that maybe what we had for a while was real, then believe that, even if I'm grasping, I'm not stupid. Believe that if I really wanted to take you for your money, I would have done so in a spectacular fashion. I would have shamed you publicly, but I had no interest in that. All I wanted was what was best for Lily. When those men came… Hercules, I thought I was nothing to you. Nothing more than one of the many women that you seduce and leave behind. I had no reason to believe that I was anything else. And I had no reason to believe those men were not sent by you."

He began to pour a glass of cider, and then he paused. Suddenly, the look on his face became one of stone. "It's why they couldn't find you," he said. "They didn't look. They were working for him, not for me. They had orders not to find you."

"What?"

"I searched for you," he said. "Your father said you were gone, and I didn't accept it. I had my men go after you. I had them search. I have resources that stretch far beyond that of a normal man. I should have been able to find you. They should have been able to find you. The fact that they did not…" He shook his head. "Why did I not realize it before now?"

"He wanted to keep you from her," I said.

"He did. Because he knew that when his birthday passed, I would succeed him. As is the law in Pelion. He wanted to delay my heir, wanted to set up hoops for me to jump through. Vanessa was a hoop. A suitable bride that was not ready to marry and reproduce immediately when my father passed his deadline."

"We don't need to punish each other," I said softly.

For the first time, I honestly felt some sympathy for him. He didn't know.

But I couldn't just turn my whole sense of the last five years on its head.

"I… I felt so utterly abandoned, Hercules. I betrayed who I thought I was for you."

He shook his head. "No. Don't tell me that. You are a strong woman, Marissa. If you did not want to have sex you wouldn't have."

The truth in those words set me back on my heels. He was right. I hadn't been seduced. Not in the way that I often let myself think of it. Yes, he was new and exciting, a window into sensations that I hadn't even known I wanted. But I had wanted him. I had wanted him deep in my soul. Wanted him with a desperation that defied sanity.

It reminded me of when he had asked me if I always did as I was told.

I had, because it had never occurred to me to do things a different way.

And when I stopped doing as I was told, it wasn't because I had simply replaced one set of commands with another.

It was because I had realized what I was. Who I was. And that I wanted it to be something different than I had been fashioned into.

It had nothing to do with faith, for mine had remained intact all these years. But it had become something deeper in many ways, something more personal, because I wasn't following commandments and dictates because my father said so, but because of what rang true in my own soul.

And perhaps I didn't have a life that looked perfect to everyone from the outside, but something in my heart felt healed.

No, it had never been about rebellion. It had never been about burning down what I believed in and starting from scratch.

It had been about finding me.

In the midst of everything that I had been taught to be, I found the person I was born to be.

I didn't have to hide. Not now. Not behind excuses, and not behind the idea that I had somehow succumbed to the temptation only because of his wickedness. Or even my own.

"It doesn't matter. Not now. I've changed. I assume you have too."

"No," he said, his expression opaque. "I have not changed. I am as I ever was. I'm a man who has the responsibility and the weight of an entire nation on his shoulders. And I never forget it. It doesn't matter what you see in the media. If you see photos of me looking carefree. All that time we spent together on the beach. I am never carefree."

I looked him right in the eyes. "I know that."

He appeared shocked by that. "What is it you think you know?"

"The first time that I saw you, standing there on the

shore. None of your friends had caught up to you yet, and you were standing there with your hands shoved into your pockets and a grim look on your face. You were clearly a man with a great weight on you. I could see it. A man who carried darkness around inside of him and understood that there might be a cost to that. I knew it. I did. I knew it then, and I know it now. All of what you show the world is… It's an oversimplification. And even what you showed me, back when we were together."

"Well, isn't that a neat trick that you managed to speak of it now, and yet you didn't say anything then."

"I always felt like there was a timer ticking down on what we had. I didn't want to clutter it up with unpleasant topics. And I never wanted to betray how much I cared. But I'm not a girl now. And while you may carry the weight of the fate of your nation on your shoulders, I carry the responsibility of taking care of our daughter. She is my primary concern, and she always will be. Lily is the most important thing in my universe. You must worry for millions. I worry for only one. And that means my focus is not split. I will defend her and her interest with all of me. Forever."

"And what about your own?"

"I am second. And I chose to be second when I committed to being her mother. When I knew that I wouldn't give her up. My father threw me out. He said I was an embarrassment. But it didn't matter. Because at that moment it ceased to be about me. It was about Lily, and me doing the best that I could for her. It was a free and wonderful realization, and it has been a free and wonderful way to live. And maybe…maybe this isn't what I want. I didn't sign on for this. For the life of public scrutiny, or to be…at the center of your engagement falling apart, which I can only imagine is going to make headlines everywhere."

"Yes. We are about to create something of an incident. I won't lie to you."

"I'm doing it for her."

Suddenly, he closed the distance between us, reaching out, his large hand cupping my cheek. He was like fire. His touch was a flame. And I had not expected that. I had thought that all those years would have given me a sort of immunity to the man, and yet there was none. "Is it?"

The words were husky, and his breath was warm and I could feel it across my lips.

It made me ache. Everywhere.

"Is it just for her?" he pressed. "You do not think that even a small part of yourself is going to find some enjoyment in this?"

My heart was thundering hard, so hard that I was convinced he could hear it. I swallowed.

I would not give him the satisfaction of seeing that he had shaken me. I would not let him come in and simply think that he could assume control of not only everything outside, but all the things inside me too. I had raised my daughter on my own for years. And yes, I was affected by him, but I would not simply give him the satisfaction of knowing that.

"Are you sure that this is entirely for your country?" I shot back. "And not you satisfying your thwarted hunter's instinct? You've caught me. And wasn't that what you wanted all those years ago?"

He growled and closed the distance almost entirely between us. And I faced the black fire, so close that I thought it might reduce me to ash. "No one leaves me," he gritted out. "No one abandons me."

"Don't they?"

I didn't know why I asked the question, or if it would have a particular sort of significance to him, but he released his hold on me, dropping his hand and turning away.

He raked his fingers through his black hair and then moved to face me again.

"Rearranging a wedding should not be too difficult. We have the venue. Guess all we need to do is change out the bride."

I gritted my teeth. "Just as I dreamed. From the time I was a little girl. That I might be a replacement bride for the Prince."

"She was your replacement."

The words were stunning. Rough, and for a moment I was certain that he had actually been speaking in a foreign language and my brain had translated them incorrectly. It took me a moment to realize that I hadn't been insulted in some way. Quite the contrary. He had admitted something to me that I didn't think he was happy to have spoken into existence.

"Well, then isn't it good that we put things to rights," I said. The words were barely above a whisper.

The problem was nothing felt put to rights at all. It all felt wrong and strange, deeply disconcerting.

And yet…

When he touched me, there was still heat. When he was near me, I still felt a kick of desire.

And if I was perfectly honest with myself, I would have been unhappy to go back home now.

No. That could not be. He could not have that kind of power over me. Never again.

I was not so weak that my attraction to Hercules could cause me to abandon reason.

"Perhaps we should toast," he said, lifting his glass. "To our union."

I raised my glass, my eyes never leaving his. It was a challenge, and I was not going to back down. Because I had changed. I had become someone different, forged in steel, in the fires of the conflagration that had occurred between us.

I had been a fool then. A girl easily wounded.

"This is for Lily," I said, more for myself than for him. "And our marriage is for Lily. It is not for us."

"Is that so?" he asked, his voice rough.

"Yes," I responded, pleased that I managed to keep my voice steady then.

It was the fire that terrified me. But more than that… it was the hope.

Because I could not seem to banish it no matter how much I tried.

"I don't care who you sleep with," I continued, the words catching in my throat. "But it won't be me."

"Excuse me?" The cold, dark ice in his tone sent a chill through me.

"We must be good parents to our daughter," I said. "Unless you're willing to drop down on your knees now and profess undying love, it won't work. We must be able to parent together, to exist together. To attend functions together and present a united front."

"My parents managed to do it for years. And trust me when I tell you they do not care much for each other."

"I am not your mother," I said. "And you are not your father. I'm confident of that, without ever having met either of them."

He stiffened. "Have it your way, Marissa. But I have to tell you I think your goals might be unrealistic here."

"Why?"

He smiled at me, and he didn't have to say a word, because electricity passed between us in that space, a switch flipped by the crook of his lips. And he knew it.

"We are not animals. We managed to go five years without touching one another, after all."

"True," he said, leaning in. "But that was when we were nowhere near each other. With an ocean between us it's quite easy to resist, is it not?" He reached out, the rough edge of his thumb resting against my upper lip. "But is it so easy to resist now? When I am here. And you still want me, so very much." My heart was tripping over itself, like the fool that I was, giddy and excited over the touch of this man.

"There is unfinished business between us," he continued.

"No," I whispered, calling on all of my strength and taking a step away from him. A step toward sanity.

"The business between us is Lily. And when she is finished, when she is grown, we will be too."

"Divorce then?" he asked. "How dull."

"It doesn't have to be divorce. We can simply separate. Whatever you need for your perfect royal image."

"You will not shame me by going out with other men," he said, the words shot through with iron.

I might have taken pleasure in the thought that he was jealous if I wasn't so desperate to release my hold on any sort of feelings for him. "I have no problem with that. I've managed just fine on my own this whole time."

"Have it your way, then." He downed the rest of the contents of his glass and took a step away from me, and I felt unaccountably cold when he did.

Then he removed his presence entirely from beside me.

"You might want to get some sleep. When we land, it will be morning in Pelion. And there will be much to attend to."

CHAPTER SIX

Hercules

OF THE MANY rebellions I had expected of Marissa, this refusal to be my wife in anything beyond name had thrown me off entirely.

It was one thing that I knew we could count on between us. Our passion.

Yes, we'd had an innocent relationship at first, but when passion had ignited between us it had been undeniable, unstoppable. We had traded in words for sighs of pleasure, and I had never regretted it. But this... This could not be endured.

I gritted my teeth. What man was this inside of me who could not handle being absent the touch of a particular woman? Since when had it ever mattered to me? I had more pressing matters to deal with than Marissa and her reluctance to be my bride in any real sense.

I had my father to deal with.

There was no question of having Marissa and Lily or Marissa's mother come to the palace.

Instead, I had them driven to my home that was nestled in the mountains of Pelion, on the opposite side of our major city from the palace.

My home was not a castle, but in many ways my father's home and mine had been set up like two warring palaces on opposing hills, facing each other down.

But now I was ready.

Ready to cross the gulf, ready to go to war.

I had steadied my hand; I had played at diplomacy. And I had done so in order to keep my father's wrath away from my mother and sister.

Though I knew at the moment neither of them were in residence in Pelion. They were in the French Riviera, as both of them preferred.

Even if not…

My father had already done the unforgivable.

He had kept me from my child.

I would not be civil.

I was given admittance into the palace immediately, and I walked directly through the glimmering obsidian halls down to the throne room.

It was Gothic, this palace. It always had been. As if the black heart of the Xenakis family resided at the center of this gilded mausoleum.

But then, I supposed it was true.

Whoever sat on the throne was the heart.

And my father had been up there spreading poison for far too long.

I would be better than the heart of this palace, than the heart of this nation.

I would be the brain.

That at least had a basis for reason. That at least had a code.

There were so many people who thought that the heart deserved to be followed. That the heart was the core of our humanity, but I knew the truth.

The heart could produce both humanity and unspeakable horror.

The heart was wicked. And it was deceptive. If you could find justification for your behavior deep in your heart, then a man could do anything.

However, reason would win out. I was confident in that. Reason I trusted in.

Reason I had violated only once.

With Marissa.

But it was funny how in the end she was the key to Pelion salvation. She had caused a shift in what was possible, and therefore a shift in my reasoning.

Something fascinating to be explored later, perhaps, but not when I was about to cross swords with my father.

I pushed the double doors of the throne room open without signaling my arrival.

The two Secret Service agents standing next to my father reached for their weapons, and I held up my hand. "Prince Hercules," I said.

"Prince Hercules," the other men repeated, nodding once.

"To what do I owe the pleasure?"

I had not been home in some time, and I was surprised by how diminished my father looked.

It was not just aging, for the Xenakis family tended to remain strong like oxen until the end. He looked weathered, and he looked weak, and my father was many things, but he had never been that.

"Have you climbed off of your latest whore long enough to see to issues of state?"

His voice was not frail, and apparently the meanness that coursed through his veins was well intact.

"I have been on a fact-finding mission," I said. "And I am not certain you will like what I uncovered."

"Is that so?"

The gleam in his eye seemed to swallow the light rather than give it off. Like the obsidian walls all around us.

That darkness was my legacy. And I would wield it against him happily now.

"Yes. Perhaps there is a secret that you forgot to tell me."

He did not look cowed by this; instead, he looked smug. "Oh, there are many, Hercules. Did you imagine all this time that you were sitting back pulling my strings and I never pulled yours? A common error of the youth. You think you know more. You think you know better. And because of that, you never take a moment to consider that I might be an opponent that is equal to you."

My lip curled. "I am not you," I said.

"That may be. But whether or not we are the same, we are an equal match."

"You're a monster."

"There are reasons that monsters live in caves for hundreds of years terrorizing the townspeople, and it isn't because they are stupid. You don't have to be good to win, Hercules. Perhaps you should remember that. If you're looking at your victory as an opportunity to measure the purity of your morality, I feel that might come to a disappointing end."

"Moral absolutism is not exactly at the core of what I've come to talk to you about. I found my child."

That I could see impacted him. "Have you?"

"Yes."

"Her mother was happy enough to sign away your rights for a payout."

"Because you made her think it was what I wanted. Marissa is a proud woman and she would no more beg me for anything, for my attention, than she would submit her child to a life on the streets."

Marissa's own words filled me, and I found I believed them with a great conviction in that moment.

"She is a woman of absolute strength and dignity, and she has done what we all should have done for the past years. She has raised Lily. Lily is the heir to the throne of Pelion. We owe her the same that we have owed every ruler that has come before her."

"A girl," my father sneered. "Of course you would produce a girl."

"She will be Queen. She will be Queen after me, and I daresay that whatever I don't manage to blot out that you brought on this country, she will erase entirely."

"Do you imagine I will step aside for you? For her?"

"You have to. Your birthday has passed. And I can see that age has begun to eat away at you."

He chuckled. "It is not age. But illness. It has long been said that I am too mean to die. I suspect soon we will see whether or not that is true."

"Step aside now."

"Have you not even a flicker of emotion for your father?"

"No," I said, "and you are not shocked. You concealed my child from me, and I have told you that I brought your granddaughter back to the country and you have no emotion to spare for that except disdain over her gender. No, I have no emotion to spare for you. None at all. You had none to spare for me. You had none to spare for her. I will stage a coup. We can end this in blood if you like."

"What if you didn't like the blood that was spilled?"

"If that is a threat against my family, I will end you now with my own hand."

"Do not speak of threats, Hercules, for we are more civilized than that, are we not? Political warfare is best waged with words and bureaucracy, don't you think?"

"The war is won. Engaging in a battle with you is a pointless waste of time. I marry Marissa in less than two weeks' time. The original wedding date stands. And upon that wedding you will abdicate."

"Will I?"

"Yes. Because if you don't, trust that I will make public what has occurred with Lily. Trust that I will destroy whatever fragment of a reputation you have left in this world. What do you want in the history books, Father? That in your current state is your primary concern anyway."

"I will require medical staff," he said. "I will require a residence."

"All to be provided," I said. "I will send you off with the most lavish of severance packages. You will want for nothing, and to all the world it will look as if the

Xenakis line has continued as it should. No one need know that I had to wrest it from you."

"If I resisted, what would you do?"

"I would have the military on my side, Father, and I think we both know it. No matter your threats, the blood that spilled would be yours."

My father was dying, and I knew that he was not fighting me because he wanted to extend his time as ruler, not when the tasks were clearly going to be too much for him and soon.

No, my father was fighting to avoid losing to me.

And that was why, whatever he said, I always would find victory.

Because I was not fighting a war of pettiness, but one for the people of my country.

"You have until the wedding to vacate this place. We will notify the Council that power is changing hands, and we will notify the press that my bride has changed. And we will come up with a suitable story for how I have only just now discovered my heir. And if you do anything that I do not care for in the meantime, that story will become more fact than fiction, and you will not like the results."

I considered how much I was counting on my father's ego to remain predictable as I made my way back to my home across the city.

He was a dying man, and many could argue he had nothing to lose. It was true enough. But for my father, legacy would always count in the end.

I wondered if it occurred to him that I had control of that legacy. Because whatever I told him while he drew breath I could change once he was gone.

The ultimate tragedy for a man who sought to control everything in his life, I supposed. A man who did not think he had to give deference to a son who was beneath him.

Not even my father could manipulate death. And once he was gone, he would have power over nothing.

The house on the hill was not my home.

I had never given much thought to homes.

The castle had always felt very much like my father's domain, and like it was sadly tainted by the sins of the previous generations.

One thing my father would get to live to see, and it gave me an extreme amount of pleasure, was the joy that our people would feel when he was finally removed from the throne.

My wedding would be a cause for celebration in a way no one had anticipated.

And—something I had not thought of—Marissa would be a welcome bride, even though she was not from Pelion, by sheer virtue of the fact that she was the method by which my father was uninstalled.

In contrast to the darkness of the palace, my home was made of light. Windows and stark walls, and white marble on the floors.

Not because I was a creature of virtue so much as even devils got tired of hell.

I was so used to my staff being invisible and everything being in a certain order that the disruption in the white—Marissa's figure and Lily's small one—gave me pause.

"You're back," she said.

"Yes," I said, battling against the warring responses

to the sight of both of them that were occurring in my body. There was an ache when I looked at Lily and I did not know what to call it.

I *knew* what I felt for Marissa.

And I disliked very much the sensation that she was holding the most vulnerable part of me in her hand and guiding me around by it.

If she wanted to do that, she had to give me pleasure, rather than just attempts to manipulate.

"Have you not found everything to your liking?"

"Lily wanted to see more of the house," Marissa said.

"It's the biggest house I've ever seen. Is it the castle?" Lily asked.

"No," I said, working to gentle my tone. "We will move into the castle after the…after the wedding."

Lily's eyes were shining. "You're going to marry my mom."

"Yes," I said. "And she will be a princess too."

Lily was enraptured, clearly captured by what to her felt like a real-life fairy tale. She wrapped her arms around her mother's leg. "We'll be princesses together," she said.

Marissa, for her part, tried to force a smile and patted Lily on the back. "Yes. We will."

"Can I go and get Nana?"

"Sure," Marissa responded.

Lily bounded up the stairs, her dark curls bouncing behind her.

"What were you doing?" Marissa asked.

"You don't care what I was doing," I said. "Remember, I have permission to be with anyone I choose at any time I choose. Your edict, Marissa, not mine."

"It was not a question of where your private parts were, Hercules, but your person."

"I was speaking to my father," I said. "And somehow I managed not to kill him." I made my way over to the bar that sat in the corner of the living area and I poured myself some scotch. Crutches be damned, some things were better done with alcohol.

"I see."

"It has never been a secret to me that he was a monster. But he kept my child from me, Marissa, and I cannot forgive that. I will not."

"Why should you? If you had come back into my life simply telling me you had changed your mind... If you had known about Lily all this time, I would not have forgiven you. There are some things that are simply unforgivable."

I thought of her, as she had been. Young and pregnant and alone. And for the first time, I could see clearly enough through my rage to truly think of her as a victim.

I had cast her in the role of defector for so many years. And then the shock of discovering that I had a child had...

It had undone my world.

And then it had put it back together with strange and new possibilities, and I had not been able to ignore the political implications.

"I'm going to need you," I said.

Because it did no good for me to dwell on the past. On what might have been, and who she was to me. On how terrified she must have been. Alone and...heartbroken.

It didn't sit well with me.

When I had touched her, I had known that I had crossed a boundary I normally would not.

Virgins were not something I had ever cared to trifle with before. There were too many unintended consequences.

But I had decided on some level that I would make Marissa mine, and so I had justified it.

And then, when she abandoned me, I had recast her in my mind in the role of scarlet woman somehow, even though I knew full well that she had never known the touch of a man before me.

Marissa.

No, there was no point in thinking of her that way. It was better to focus on now.

"Need me for what?"

"We have to speak to the press."

"Why do you need me for that?"

"Because. Because I need to put a face to my new bride, for all the world to see. Because there is going to be an interest."

"I'm exhausted," she said.

"And we are getting married in two weeks' time. Sleep now if you can. Try to catch up. Tomorrow, they will be here."

"In the house? I don't want Lily on camera."

"You understand that is impractical. Lily will be on camera from now on to the rest of her life. She is going to be a public figure. An object of interest and curiosity. It is far better that we have Lily on camera when we decide. Far better that we have official photographers taking her photos. It will be better, trust me."

"I… But she's very little. And this is all very new."

"Tomorrow I will only need you. But you will have to look the part. And whatever your personal feelings on me or the subject…you will have to look as if you can bear my touch."

The air went thick between us, and she captured her lower lip between her teeth. Worrying it.

I reached out and then dropped my hand quickly. I had been about to touch her. But I refused.

I would not allow her that kind of power. I would not allow her that kind of control.

Everything had been put in motion. By my hand.

I had the power here, not her.

We would both do well to remember it.

CHAPTER SEVEN

Marissa

I SLEPT TERRIBLY. I kept waiting for Lily to crawl into my bed, because I was certain that the new environment would be uncomfortable for her, but she didn't come.

And when I woke up early in the morning, unable to stand staying in bed any longer, I tiptoed down the hall to her room and found her sleeping like the little princess she was in the middle of a giant king-size bed. She barely made a dent in the feather mattress; her dark hair spilled over the pillow.

She felt happy here. She felt safe. I was the one with the issue.

But then, I was the one who had a history with Hercules.

I sighed heavily and padded down the stairs, searching for coffee. I kept waiting to see Hercules. But he didn't materialize.

And when the sun finally came up, I could see the breathtaking view out the window. The craggy, glorious mountains all around limned with gold. And below…

The sea. The glorious Mediterranean burning like a jewel in the early morning.

This place was beautiful.

It would be my home.

I could see the ocean.

The wave of relief I felt at that realization surprised me.

Lily and I were near enough to the water in Boston. We didn't have a view, but we could easily walk down to the harbor.

Even so, sometimes I ached for the beautiful simplicity of the shorelines in Medland. The bristling seagrass that grew from the soft sand hills and the rich blue water.

This was different. But it was so close. The sea as if it was illuminated from its center.

My heart felt inexplicably tied to the ocean.

And it made sense suddenly that it was by the ocean I had first seen Hercules.

I stood out on the balcony, looking down over the water for an untold amount of time, until I heard the sound of footsteps behind me.

It still wasn't Hercules.

It was a woman, immaculately dressed, her hair and makeup flawless.

"You must be Marissa?" She spoke with faintly accented English, her voice gloriously cultured. "I am Isabella. I'm here to help you get dressed for the press conference."

It turned out that Isabella's statement was an understatement. She was not there simply to help me get dressed, but to acquaint me with an entirely new wardrobe that she had selected sometime between the moment I had been whisked away from Medland and when we landed in Pelion.

We set aside multiple items to be altered and chose one formfitting red dress that fell past my knees and was cut classically, that needed only a bare minimum of sewing sorcery. Isabella accomplished it in moments. Then she did some expert styling on my hair, promising that I needed a bit of salon time and would get it later on.

She also did makeup, miraculous things with it—things that I hadn't known were possible.

With a bit of shading, she made my face look narrower, more sharply defined, and with some glue and fake lashes made my eyes look stunningly wide.

"Camera ready," she said.

I turned and looked in the mirror, feeling shocked by what I saw. "That doesn't look like me."

"It doesn't have to. It has to look like a princess."

I recognized the truth of that. It wasn't meant to be insulting, not in any way. It was simply the truth.

Hercules needed to present a woman to the country—to the world—who was believable. Who could be likable enough to smooth over the narrative that was going to have to be spun about the existence of Lily.

Come to think of it, I didn't even know what that narrative was going to be. And I still hadn't seen Hercules. So we had not had a chance to talk about it.

As soon as Isabella was finished, she whisked me out of my bedroom and down the stairs. And then suddenly she was gone, and Hercules was there.

"We will be meeting the members of the press out in the courtyard."

His eyes flicked over me, and I saw heat there that made my skin feel like it was prickling.

"She's done a good job."

"Yes," I responded.

"We will tell them you did not know my identity, and I didn't know about Lily, and it was only recently when headlines of my engagement hit the news that you realized who I was. You came to me, not to destroy my wedding, but to make sure that I knew about my daughter. And that was when we decided it would be best if we were together."

It was so close to the truth, and it made my heart twist. I should be happy with that. That it wasn't an outright lie. But…

"It's not exactly a story that will sweep people away."

"What do you want?"

"It's not about what I want," I said. "But…people want to know. They'll want to dig in deep. And I… It all sounds so practical, and there's nothing beautiful to weave from it. People want to weave a story."

"We are marrying for practical reasons."

"Yes," I said softly. "But don't you think it would be more impacting if you said that when I came to find you, you realized that… I was what you had been missing all along?"

The words tasted so strange on my lips, almost like honey, and a surge of longing welled up inside of me, and worse, hope.

Hope was a beast inside me I could not seem to banish.

"I like that," he said. "I'll use it. You're right. It is

much more compelling. Unfortunately, not much can be done for Vanessa's feelings."

"Did she love you?"

He shook his head. "No. I don't believe so. She will be angry that she isn't going to be Queen. On that you can trust me. It has been a goal of hers most of her life. She has always known that she was the most suitable woman in all the land for the heir apparent."

"Bloodlines."

"Bloodlines," he said. "They are all important when you are royal."

"For all that my father was difficult, and there were things that he…that he did and said that I feel were wrong… I was taught that people were more than blood. That we are spiritual. That our souls are what truly matter. This idea of blood overshadowing everything is so foreign to me."

"It's a lovely concept," he said. "That a human being's spiritual self might matter more than, say, who his father was. But in my experience that is simply not the case. Man is a physical being. He wants power. Above all else. And the best way to consolidate that is with money. And then you can make rules. Any rules you like. About how the power can only be passed down through blood. When a man is hungry, he eats. When he desires a woman, he finds physical release with her. When he is tired, he sleeps."

"And what does he do when he is sad? What does he do when he's lonely? When he has a fear, or a hope or a dream, who does he confide in? And when he finds satisfaction for those things, what does it feed? His body? Or his soul?"

"I don't believe in what I can't see. What I cannot touch."

"That's very sad."

"Everything else is simply the way man builds justification for things. All manner of things. We dress our selfish desires up as matters of the heart, as dreams and callings… Morality can be lost much easier than when we view the world through black-and-white terms."

"Well, for the purposes of the press conference, perhaps we should borrow from my philosophy more than yours."

"I believe it likely we should."

I didn't know why the conversation with him made me sad and happy all at the same time. It reminded me a bit of the kinds of talks we used to have down by the shore. All kinds of things.

Ideas that challenged my view on the world and on myself.

But there hadn't been an edge to him then, not like this. It was as if he'd let his guard down with me then, rather than wrapping his every word in hardened cynicism.

I studied his face. There were new lines there. Grooves that had settled in by his mouth, by his eyes, just in the years since I had seen him.

I wanted to will them away. To will him back in time.

But I couldn't. And I knew it.

But we were in the here and now, and he was propelling me out the door and toward the courtyard. It was beautiful, flagstone and vivid green grass, surrounded by glorious flowering bushes.

The security detail was there, and a limited number of press members had arrived as well.

"We will stand in the front. You will stand beside me. You do not need to speak. I will do the talking."

And then I was following him, right into the public eye. I stood beside him, my hands clasped in front of me as I had seen any number of political wives do at press conferences over the years. I did my best to mimic that pose. That smile, and those rigid, resolute shoulders that they seemed required to possess, whatever their husband might be confessing to.

"I thank you for coming today for this announcement. I appreciate that it is a bit unorthodox. But it seemed the best way to proceed. After I am done speaking, I will give the opportunity for three members of the press to ask a question. And only one question. Then we will be done, and you will be escorted from the premises."

I could feel the need to ask questions radiating from the people in the audience, but they all seemed too afraid to do anything out of turn.

"To begin with, my marriage will still proceed on the appointed date. But I have an important announcement regarding the bride. Vanessa and I will no longer be getting married. Instead, I am marrying Ms. Marissa Rivero of Medland, Massachusetts."

To those who didn't know, that might make it sound as if I had a pedigree. Medland was known for being the preferred second, third or fourth home location of the rich, connected and political. But anyone who truly understood would know that if I was from Medland, I was not one of those people.

If you were well-off, you spent summers there. You didn't live there.

You certainly weren't from there.

"I knew Marissa years ago, and we had a romance," he continued, yet again being very careful with his wording. "Due to the delicate nature of my position, I did not reveal to her who I was, and she was not aware. When our relationship was cut short during a time when I had to return to Pelion, she could not locate me, and when I returned to find her, I could not locate her. Over the course of years, she discovered who I was, and was only recently able to establish contact. When she did, I discovered that she'd had my child."

The members of the press couldn't help it—a wave of shock went through them, and chatter rose up in the serene garden.

Hercules held his hand up. And as if he'd roared, they silenced. "I'm not finished. When she found me, not only was I overjoyed to discover that I was a father, but I also found I was overjoyed to be reconnected with her. It was a relationship that I…was never ready to let go of. And I knew that I could not let her get away from me again. It is with great regret that I broke my engagement to Vanessa off, but she understands the extraordinary circumstances that were at play."

The crowd shifted, and scattered observers began to stand, lurching forward, questions competing with each other to exit their mouths first.

"I'm not finished," he said again, and again, the crowd stilled. "Further, on the date of our marriage, I will be crowned King of Pelion. Marissa will be my consort, and that is the final word on it."

They all stood frozen, like dogs on the hunt waiting to be given the command. They didn't want to incur a scolding from him yet again, Marissa assumed. The disapproval of Hercules Xenakis was a powerful thing.

He inclined his head. "Now you may speak."

They all jostled for position, raising their hands and hurling out queries. But Hercules pointed to one.

"This question is for Ms. Rivero," the first man said.

I didn't know that I would be asked questions, and I wasn't certain if it was allowed, but Hercules did not deny them, so I turned my focus to the reporter. "Did you track him down finally solely because he was getting married?"

My tongue felt thick and my heart was pounding hard. I didn't have experience speaking in front of people. I'd even avoided it in church, during prayer or when we'd been asked to share good news in our lives.

But this was for Lily.

I would be a reflection on her, and I had to deal with my nerves, I had to deal with my reservations, my issues, because they would rebound onto her. It couldn't be helped.

"Yes and no," I said. Which was true enough. "I had no other way of getting in contact with him. But his location for his celebration before the wedding was revealed. And so I was able to approach him. And I was able to tell him…to tell him about our daughter. The timing is unfortunate, I know, but believe me, if I had been able to tell him sooner, I would have done."

Hercules looked at me, the expression in his dark eyes unreadable. Unknowable. I would have given much to be able to see into his mind. "There is a duty that a man in my position must assume for his country. A responsibility. Making Lily legitimate is part of that responsibility. She is my heir, and the future ruler of this country. Therefore, whatever speculation you might want to apply to Marissa's motives, you should know that the right thing was done here. What sort of man would I be, what sort of King would I be, if I ignored my child? If I refused to recognize her, to grant her the legitimacy that she requires. What sort of man would I be if I replaced my heir with another simply to avoid making waves? What would that mean for her? Indeed, for the fate of a nation. But quite beyond that… A man might have responsibilities, but a man has a heart as well. And when I saw Marissa again, I knew that I could not ignore mine."

I was shocked by the words that had come out of his mouth, for they were in direct opposition to the sort of thing that he had said to me just before we came out here. He wrapped his arm around my waist and then he was pulling me to him. And I couldn't breathe. I couldn't think. All I could do was feel. All I could do was breathe him in. Him. Hercules.

My greatest triumph and my greatest sin.

The man who had made me a woman. In so many different ways. More ways than just the simple euphemism that was often used for that phrase. No. It was his attention that had given me strength. His touch that had made me wild, and his betrayal that had made me fearless.

And now it was his hand on my chin making my heart beat so fast that I thought I might fall over.

When he claimed my mouth with his, it was like the

world exploded. Brilliant bursts of light behind my eyes that left me trembling, shaking.

His mouth was like I remembered it. Warm and firm, but so much better now for all the years of separation.

Like going home.

I had just returned home after a five-year absence, and it had not been like this.

It was as if I'd been struggling with a door for years, and he'd handed me the key to the lock, only to have it click in place and turn easily.

I felt walls collapse inside of me. Walls that had been protecting me. That had been closing off so much in the way of feeling.

Of being a woman.

I had become Lily's mother. And when I had taken that role on, I had assumed it entirely. I had made myself forget. I had made myself forget the rude insanity of what had caused my change in identity in the first place.

I had done it deliberately. And I had done it well.

But it had only been sleeping. It had not been banished.

That mouth.

He parted my lips with his, sliding his tongue against mine, and that was not for the press, I knew. Because a kiss to the mouth would've been just fine without increasing the intimacy.

He had done that for me.

To show me. To show me that no matter what I said I still wanted him.

Of course, I had known that already. I didn't need his games as a reminder.

It was why I had told him that we would not be having a physical relationship in the first place.

Because I understood that in that equation I was the one who was vulnerable. I was the one who would be wounded.

But right now, I was just the one on fire.

And I was gladly allowing myself to burn.

His hands were large and warm, pressed in the space between my shoulder blades, holding me firmly. He was such a breathless temptation. And I wanted to give in. I remembered all too well how it felt. To leap off the edge of reason and into his beautiful obsidian abyss.

It took me minutes—at least it seemed so to me—to realize that I was making a fool of myself on a public stage. I was melting in the arms of this man for all the world to see.

But I couldn't pull away, because we were being watched. Because this was the moment he'd warned me about.

It was for show.

It was for show.

That doused some of that fire in me.

It wasn't that Hercules wanted me so. He wanted to drive the point home to the press that what he'd done he did out of duty and love, to instill in his people a sense of confidence that he was a ruler who would do things in a much more measured way than his father.

When we parted, he still held me, his arm around my waist.

And he took a breath. Just one, but it was ragged at the edges, and it gave me the hope that he had not been unaffected by what had passed between us.

I shouldn't care.

I truly shouldn't care.

"So you see," he said, his voice slightly lower. Slightly rougher. "There is duty, and then there is something that goes beyond it. It would've been a grave misstep for me to carry on with my engagement to Vanessa, even though it would have been the path of least resistance. But I'm not a man who takes the path of least resistance. I'm a man who acts for the best interests of all those involved. And I am a man who will do more than simply lead clinically, as has been done before me.

"And I will make change where change must be made. To ensure that the citizens of Pelion are living with freedom and are not being shut out of the comforts which the royal family has enjoyed without them for far too long. I hope, if you can, that you will see these actions I've taken now as an indicator of who I am, and that you will find it to be positive."

Another reporter stood up.

"No further questions," Hercules said.

"You said we got three," the man said.

"I did," Hercules confirmed. "I have changed my mind. And as I told you, I reserve the right to do so."

And then he whisked me away from the reporters, and from the clamor behind us, ushering me back into the house.

I had to lean against the wall for strength, my energy suddenly draining out of me as if those questions had punctured a hole in me. And I told myself it was because all of this was overwhelming. Not because Hercules himself was overwhelming.

"You did well," he said, his dark eyes appraising me,

but I saw it there. That he wasn't unaffected. And my own heart tripped over in response.

"The wedding is in two weeks' time," he said. "I have no doubt you'll be prepared for it."

"I'm glad you don't have any doubt, because I… We don't really know each other, Hercules. We had stolen time together away from both of our real lives. I'm a pastor's daughter who never left the island the whole time I was growing up. I wasn't thrust into the real world until after I had Lily… And I had to become so…so hard to protect myself. To protect her. To stop myself from missing what I'd left behind so much that I ached. All the time. And you… All of this is yours. It's your legacy. But it isn't mine."

"But it is Lily's," he said, his voice firm. "And that you are bringing yourself into it so she can have it is a great thing you've done."

I was floored by the compliment. "That might be the first nice thing you've said about my parenting."

"I've had time to accept that what you did… You had no other choice. That it was my father who did this to us. Not you."

"It's forced you to have empathy."

"I wouldn't call it that. I would simply say that there is no logical way to look at it that casts you as a villain, Marissa, and I am a man of logic, always willing to be corrected if a more reasonable scenario presents itself."

"Well, I'm happy that my villain status seemed unreasonable to you."

"There is much to be done in the lead-up to the wedding. Much diplomacy to be handled, seeing as I am assuming the throne the day of the wedding, and there will be policy ready to be enacted upon the exact hour. I will not see much of you over this time."

It was a relief, though I didn't tell him that. "Okay. I think I can handle that. Since I haven't seen much of you over the past five years."

"Lily will be the flower girl for the wedding."

My heart squeezed tight. Because somewhere in all this was a mixed-up fantasy of what I had dreamed would happen all this time, even if it hadn't been a conscious dream. That my Prince had come, even if he was late. That our daughter would share in our special day.

Except, it was not our special day. It was Lily's, perhaps. It was the kingdom of Pelion's. And those were good things. But the last thing it was about was myself and Hercules. And, no matter how incendiary a kiss between us might be, I had to remember that.

If I didn't, I was in danger of breaking all over again.

And I wasn't sure that I had it in me to emerge stronger the second time. I didn't know if I would be able to emerge at all.

"In two weeks," I said, nodding my head purposefully and turning away from him.

Because I had to turn away. Because I had to be strong.

Because none of this was for me.

And it never would be.

CHAPTER EIGHT

Hercules

THE DAY OF the wedding, of the coronation, dawned bright and clear. My father was nowhere to be seen, and I was not unhappy with that. I was told by members of staff that he had gone up to his new home—a lavish keep nestled in the mountains—and would likely not be coming down.

It was fine by me, and I would be making an announcement regarding the King's health for the benefit of the media.

I was ready.

Ready for all of this to be cemented. Ready for it to be over.

We had settled into a pattern at my home, the four of us. Lily chattered and filled the awkward spaces that existed between the adults, and Marissa's mother had assumed an easy and content position nannying the child. Marissa had been undergoing a crash course in the customs and laws of the country, and what duties were required of a royal spouse.

Meanwhile I had made sure that every piece was in

place for an easy transition of power and that I could swiftly repudiate the prohibitive laws my father had placed that kept the people in poverty.

Change what happened. And I knew that change would not be instantaneous, but it would be as close to it as possible under my watch.

And Lily would bear witness to it. To the changes that a good ruler would make, and I had confidence that she would make changes of her own. Her sweet nature—which seemed natural to her—surprised me at every turn.

And it made me wonder if she would have turned out half so well at this point in time if she had been raised with me.

There was something in that child—a lightness—that was not in me. And I knew that it could have only come from Marissa.

I wouldn't see Marissa until she actually began to walk down the aisle, but I did see Lily, dressed all in white, with ribbons woven through her dark hair and a basket of flowers in her hand. She lit up, and she ran to me, opening her arms.

And the sight was enough to bring me to my knees.

I did not understand how this worked. I had never cared for children much at all. I didn't dislike them, but they weren't often in my presence. My sister had been born when I was fifteen, but my father had never allowed me much interaction with her.

But every fiber of my being responded to this child, and I knew beyond a shadow of a doubt that I would wage war for her.

Essentially, I had. And it had nothing to do really

with fairness to her. Everything to do with the fact that I wanted her. She was my child, and I wanted her as mine. I could not go on in a world where I knew she existed and pretended that she did not. An emotional revelation for a man like me, especially one who had a father such as mine.

Every so often that terrified me.

Because wanting just for the sake of it was a dangerous sort of drug. The beginning of all those outrageous justifications that my father himself engaged in.

A man had to act from a more morally superior place than his own soul. And I knew that well.

My father acted from a place of using his own desires as guidance, and he had not been a good father.

I might not know how to be one either, but one thing I knew for sure: I did not want to be like him.

"Daddy," Lily said, "do you like my dress?"

I was frozen. I didn't know quite what to do or say. "Yes," I said, the word sticking in my throat.

"It's good for twirling." She spun in a circle happily, and the freedom and simplicity with which she did things struck me. Because while I was contemplating the future of the country, of my humanity, just before my wedding to Marissa, Lily was spinning circles.

I had never been a carefree child. I had not been allowed. I wondered how different I might have been…

But then, there was no point mourning the loss of childlike joy.

What I had become was what was needed for Pelion, for my people, my country. And I would honor my responsibilities.

Right now, that responsibility included seeing to Lily's happiness.

That was a logical choice.

I liked what Marissa had built in her. And I could see how she was the future of Pelion.

I could see that I would have to work at being a softer parent than my own had been.

That satisfied me because it was a logical conclusion that would put me in a position where I would not crush my daughter's spirit. The very thought of crushing my Lily made my chest feel like it was so tight I couldn't breathe.

I moved to my position at the front of the church, and I looked around. It was amazing, the number of people that had come for this. Who were looking to the future of Pelion. We were all done with business as it had been conducted under my father's reign. So many of the people in my country didn't even know life out from under his thumb. But it would change.

It was all changing today.

And I kept my thoughts on the state of the country as music began to play. As my daughter came down the aisle with her flower petals and a grin on her face to light up the entire church.

And then the music changed, and the spectators stood. And I knew beyond a shadow of a doubt that if it had been Vanessa I was waiting for, if it had been Vanessa concealed by those double doors, my chest would not be locked up like there was a rock directly in the center of it. I knew. I knew. I knew.

But as it was, I found that I could not breathe.

That kiss…

Two weeks ago, my lips had touched Marissa's for the first time in years. And I remembered.

Remembered why that particular spark was an insanity that transcended all else. I remembered why I had been willing to overturn cars, my life, anything in order to get another taste of the passion that was between us. A passion that was unlike anything else I had ever experienced. Marissa. An intoxicating flavor unlike any other. I needed it like none I had ever known before.

And then those doors parted, and it was like the sun had been let into that old stone building.

She was an angel. An angel of light come down into hell with me.

I was going to take her back to that glittering obsidian palace, full of darkness and soaked in centuries of despair.

And I did not even regret it. How could I? How could I win this vision of beauty that was mine to capture? Mine to hold an ethereality just short of heaven that had fallen down to earth so that I might pick her up and conceal her in all that darkness.

The dress was a cloud, falling effortlessly over her body, swirling around her legs with each step she took. The neck was square and low, revealing a tantalizing amount of her beautiful curves.

Her dark hair was pulled back, wisps of curls cascading around her face.

I was thankful that the makeup for the wedding day was more natural than what she'd had the day of the press conference. She had been beautiful—she was always beautiful—but I had missed that familiar beauty.

As she drew closer, she filled my vision, made the edges of the view before me go fuzzy, until it was only her I saw.

For three years I had seen only Marissa.

So this was a familiar state for me.

But not a comfortable one.

And she thought that we would not consummate this marriage.

I reached out, and she took my hand.

It was trembling.

I was cast back to that first time we'd been together on the beach in Medland.

She'd been a virgin, and I had ached with a strange sense of humility.

That she had given her body to me. That she had done so with joy, in spite of her nerves.

I had never known such a feeling. I had never been given such a gift.

I was struck with the parallels between that moment and this. This vision in white walking toward me like a virgin sacrifice.

But she was not a virgin.

And she was not giving herself as a gift.

I had to remember that.

I had not told her about what was to happen after the wedding. She would not be happy.

But the decision had been made, and I had not consulted her. She would have to get used to such things.

The vows felt like they had an especially heavy weight to them. Perhaps because I was promising myself to her for the sake of a nation and promising myself to the nation as well. And to Lily. Because the vows were a tangle of vines around the both of us, and so many other things.

But then, nothing else mattered. Because then it was time for me to kiss her again. And it consumed me.

When the minister gave the command, I was more than ready. And it didn't matter to me that we were in a church, or that we had onlookers. All that mattered was her.

I cupped her face with my hands, and the silk of her skin made me shudder. I leaned in, inhaling the scent of her. Her beauty. Her perfection.

Her.

And then I tasted her.

Slowly at first, encouraging her to part her lips for me that I might taste her even deeper.

And she obeyed.

I would feast on her, except that I knew I would not be able to gorge myself entirely on her beauty because there were limits to what could be expressed here and now. So I ended the kiss, with much more regret than I care to admit.

We were then pronounced man and wife, and immediately after I took bonding vows to become the King, as she vowed to be consort and, like myself, put the kingdom of Pelion before all else.

It was a funny thing, but as she took the vows, I knew that they were a lie. She would not put the kingdom above all else, because she would always place Lily above anything else in the world. And I found a measure of satisfaction in that. Because whatever my feelings, they would not be hers. She would be the one who compensated for all my shortcomings. And I would rule. As I should. As I must.

When it was done, I bent down and picked Lily up from the ground, holding her, and she clung to me as if it were the most natural thing in the world.

It was not. Not for me, still not. But that it was for her was one of the more revelatory things I had ever experienced.

We would do official portraits later, but for now, these would be the first photographs together of us as the royal family.

Family.

It was one of those words that was thrown around often enough, though in my family, it was more likely that you would hear about blood. Blood, that most important of connectors, that essential component that made a person, and/or Royal, worthy or not in the eyes of my father.

It meant something different to me in that moment, and I could not credit why, which was added to the list of unsettling things I'd been grappling with for the past two weeks.

There were postwedding celebrations planned, but we would not attend them. It was not customary for a royal couple to do so. They would either retire to small, private parties, or they would do as we were about to do.

I set Lily down, taking hold of her hand, and we walked down the aisle together.

Marissa's mother, who had been seated in the front row, joined us, and when we were in a private room at the back of the church, I knelt down in front of my daughter. "Will you be all right staying with Nana for the next week?"

Lily frowned. "What?"

"We are going to move from the big house into the palace," I said. "But it will take some time." Some of that to do with the fact that I was having every piece of my father's legacy removed from the place.

"And your mother and I are going on a honeymoon."

Marissa sputtered, "You didn't say anything about a honeymoon."

"I know I didn't, because I suspected you would fight me. But this is not something worth having a fight over, my Queen. It is a tradition among royal families that we retreat to the private island for this period of time away from the spotlight, away from all others. It has been prepared for our arrival, and there is no question of whether or not we will go."

"You would have gone with Vanessa?" she asked, and I was surprised at how quickly she reversed the immediate spark of rage in her eye.

"Yes," I responded. "I would have. As tradition dictates."

"Our agreement stands."

I cast a glance at my new mother-in-law. "Our agreement stands," I said, and I wonder if her mother had any idea what that agreement was.

I gritted my teeth, because of course I could not help but imagine demolishing that resolve of hers.

"You might have asked me," she said.

"Did you have other plans?" I asked.

Perhaps not the best tone to take immediately with one's mother-in-law looking on, but I was King, after all.

"You know I didn't," she said.

"You and Lily will have free run of the house while the palace is being prepared," I said to her mother. "When Marissa and I return, we will all go together."

"Are you all right?" her mother asked.

"I'm fine," Marissa responded. "If not blissfully happy."

It was all quite a bit much in the way of family connection for me. Given that I had been raised by wolves essentially. Blue blood notwithstanding.

"We must go," I said.

"Now?"

Marissa suddenly looked terrified.

"Is that a problem?"

"I've never left Lily."

Lily patted her mother's arm pragmatically. "You'll be back," she said.

Marissa looked stunned.

"Yes," she responded, looking down at her daughter with wide eyes.

"And I'll be with Nana," Lily said.

"Yes again," came Marissa's reply.

"Then it's settled," I said.

"Do I have to go in this dress?"

"No, don't be silly. I've had your going-away outfit selected for you."

"What is it?"

"Something befitting a honeymoon on a private island."

CHAPTER NINE

Marissa

I WAS MARRIED, and I was a queen.

And still, my predominant concern was the fact that I was going to a private island dressed in a very brief gold dress that left little to the imagination with a man who I was going to have a very hard time resisting if he put his mind to doing any sort of seducing.

I felt the strangest things in that moment, and I had no idea what to do with them. I was…sad and terrified and filled with guilt at leaving Lily, but there was also a strange sense of exhilaration inside of me.

I hadn't spent even one night apart from Lily since I'd given birth four years earlier. I didn't know what it meant to be away from her. And now I was going to a private island for a week with only this man for company. No responsibilities. Nothing.

It was an invitation to the kind of sin that I had only gotten a taste of all that time ago. If only things weren't so complicated.

Being pampered the last couple of weeks had reminded me…that I was a woman.

Kissing Hercules twice in the last couple of weeks had reminded me that I was a woman.

Not just a mother. Not just a caregiver. But a woman. One who was sensual, and who had…needs, whether or not I had tried to suppress them. And I had tried.

Lily was well cared for, and the island was certain to be beautiful, and if it wasn't for the fact that I didn't trust myself, everything would be fine.

But Hercules was so big, so hot and hard and beautiful, and I had been reminded yet again today when he had kissed me at the wedding. But at least then I'd had layers of wedding gown in between our bodies, and now I had been reduced to the flimsy article made of netting and gems, and it felt like his heat, his body, was that much closer to mine.

"How come you stayed in a tux?" I asked as our plane touched the ground.

"Because you didn't choose anything for me."

The grin that he treated me to was wicked, almost light, and it made my heart lift, because I had not seen him look like that in…

A long time.

"Can you really leave for a week after being crowned King?"

"Yes. Everything necessary to create a smooth transition was put into place some time ago. And I knew that I would be away. Everything is set in motion. And we are a twenty-minute plane ride away. It's not as if we can't return home quickly if need be."

Considering that Lily was on another island, it was a comforting thought. "There was no one else here," he said, as the door to the plane opened.

"Well," I said, "the pilot is here for now."

"He will be leaving with the plane."

He stepped out of the door and held his hand out toward me, his right foot on the second stair. "Come with me."

I had taken his hand once before, and I had followed him wherever it led. I would be foolish to do it again, and yet I found myself grasping on to him, allowing him to usher me down the steps.

The surroundings were beautiful. Breathlessly so. This island was a rough-cut gem in the middle of the Mediterranean, without another soul or another building in sight. I hadn't realized that a place like this might exist. Or that it would be part of Hercules's legacy. He was so urbane, so very smooth, that I had imagined him out of place on the small island of Medland. Even though it was a sophisticated old-world form of rural living, he had seemed like a fish out of water there. But now I wondered.

There was a car parked partway across the runway, and he led us toward it.

"We will take this," he said. "The house is across the island."

"On a mountain?"

"Naturally," he responded.

"Do rich people live on mountains just for the views?"

"Well, yes, and to remind others of their place in the world. How will people get the full sense of how above them we are if we don't place our houses up off the ground?"

"Good point," I said. "But there are other ways to

lord superiority over people. To make them feel small. My father was an expert at doing it through religion."

"Your father threw you out," he said.

"Yes. When he found out about Lily."

We got into the car and he began to drive.

The scenery outside the window was stunning, lush trees and bright pink flowers with the clear breathtaking sea beyond.

"Your father died," he said, clearly intent on pushing this line of personal conversation.

"Yes," I responded.

"And that's why you were able to reconnect with your mother."

"Yes. She sneaked away to see us sometimes. She lied to him. He controlled her, but...not in the way he thought he did. He...he was terrible. He was a man who liked power more than he loved God. Believe me when I tell you that. And people trusted him... They... I did too. I trusted what he had to say because I didn't know any better. I believed that I had no other choice but to feel guilty all of my life because there was something wrong with me. You don't need money to make people feel small. But in the end... In the end, when you live a life like my father did, I don't know that you leave a lot of people behind to mourn you. More than anything, I mourn what could have been."

"Do you?"

"I mean, I try not to. But sometimes I wonder what it might have been like if we had a different relationship. But then I realize he would've had to be a different man altogether. And that's impossible. I had the relationship with my father he was capable of having. It's sad, but it's true. And there's ultimately nothing that can be done."

"As long as my father is in the history books in the way that he wants to be, he will be happy." He laughed. "I'm not sure how he'll know, but…maybe the view from hell is clear."

I rubbed my chest, but didn't say anything more. After that I didn't need to anyway, because the house came into view. I had thought I was quite past having my breath taken away, but apparently I wasn't.

Apparently, there were still levels of luxury that could shock me.

This house seemed to be made entirely of glass, set into the mountain, facing the sea. If his home in Pelion was beautiful, then this was otherworldly.

The inside was even more amazing, the pale coastal light bathing everything in a glow. Everything was white, as it was in his home.

"You know, this really is an impractical color scheme for children."

"Children?" He arched a dark brow and looked at me.

And for the first time, I saw the future. A possible future, anyway, one that wounded me and lifted me in ways that I could not begin to describe.

Children. Plural. I had not meant to say that, but it was all too easy to imagine.

The two of us having more children, together. Having him with me while I felt sick, while I grew round and while the baby stayed up all night. Seeing him hold a tiny new life that we had created together.

My heart stuttered. "I misspoke. Or rather, I meant children in general."

"Of course," he said.

"Lily could easily turn this room into a Pollock painting in ten minutes."

"I have no doubt. Although, I must tell you, this hideaway was not designed for children."

"I don't doubt it."

"It has always been the place where the Royals could escape to engage in fun. Obviously the house has been updated."

"Your parents came here together?"

"No. My father took lovers here. But I have had the house that he used razed to the ground. It has been under refurbishment for the past five years. This is the first time I have been here since."

"I find that all comforting."

"I thought you might. There is something quite distasteful about bringing your new bride into your father's former den of sin." His lip curled upward. "I find something distasteful about being in it myself. But as I said, none of that original structure remains."

His words seemed oddly symbolic, and I let them settle there for a while, but he didn't continue. Didn't elaborate on it all.

"So here we are, on our honeymoon," he said.

I shifted. "Yes. Here we are."

"You are welcome to change your mind about your rules."

Suddenly, my throat was dry. I felt parched, down to my soul, and he looked... Well, he looked like water. Like the only thing that might make me feel right.

"No," I said, stumbling backward. The moment brought to mind the story of Joseph in the Bible. When his master's wife had tried to seduce him, and he had run away, leaving his jacket behind.

I could imagine doing such a thing now. Running away and, if he grabbed hold of me, slipping out of my dress if I needed to.

But that only put me in mind of being naked with him, and that destroyed the point of the image in the first place. Which was to remind myself that sometimes the better part of valor was absolutely fleeing temptation.

"Then you will find your room at the end of the hall. Upstairs. You will not be bothered. It is perfectly fine for us to spend a week in solitude, I suppose."

"We don't have to be in solitude," I said.

He looked at me, and the expression in his eyes left the soles of my feet scorched. "Believe me," he said. "We do."

Isolation was easy in theory, but not so much in practice. My room was beautiful, my view of the beach, the white sand stretching out empty and pristine as far as my eye could see. And the ocean beyond might have kept me mesmerized for days on end, but I itched to be out in it.

The fact was, we were the only two people on the island, and even given all the space, we couldn't seem to stay away from each other.

Not quite.

We would pass each other on the stairs, down in the kitchen. The kitchen was the worst. Because there was something so unaccountably domestic about those familiar, everyday movements in a kitchen.

The opening and shutting of drawers, the clanging of

silverware, and there was no way that familiarity and domesticity should be attached to a king, especially not a king like Hercules, and yet it was even more impacting than those moments when I had stood in awe of him and his power.

He was a human. He drank coffee.

He walked around in bare feet.

And I was fascinated by him even more than when he had been a man of my fantasies. Something immortal and untouchable. A god from Mount Olympus.

I was fascinated by the way he ate fruit in the morning, by the way he took his coffee.

But I was also afraid to let him know that.

I would look at him out of the corner of my eye and then I would scurry back to safety, to isolation.

I would call Lily and then take a walk on the beach.

On the third day, he found me down there, by the water.

"You do love the beach, don't you?"

"I didn't know anything else for years. And it was always where I would go to be by myself."

"Until you met me."

I took a breath to say something to set him back, but…it left me. Because he was right. Until him. Solitude had been my escape, and then I had met him down by the water, and he had become my escape instead.

"All right. Until you."

"Tell me about Medland. Living on it."

"Why?"

He looked at me as though he was helpless to come up with the answer. "You're the mother of my child, and while we talked about a great many things, we avoided personal details. Someday it might come up in an interview."

But I didn't believe the answer.

"So quiet when no one was around. The people on the islands year-round don't have stacks of money. Or status. It's almost like a place set forty years back in time. Until the seasonal people come. And you know Medland is a high-end escape, for royalty such as yourself. Politicians. Actors. It moves from being the sleepiest, most down-to-earth little community you could possibly imagine into a strange collection of the world's elite, if only for a couple of months at a time. It was a wonderful and strange place to grow up. And being my father's daughter was… Well, I was homeschooled. I didn't attend school with any of the other kids. And no one would have wanted to be my friend anyway, because… Well, no one wanted my father getting wind of anyone's sins."

"I did whatever I wanted," he said. "Always. My father didn't care about debauchery, but he did care that I was strong. He wanted to turn me into a weapon. Strong for him and…callous, I think. And he wanted me to be like him. To care about the quest for power more than anything else, to consolidate our bloodline. To make us richer while the people continued to get poorer. But that is not me. I knew at a young age that I had to defeat him. Not join him."

"I don't know very many boys who would have come to that conclusion on their own."

"Surely it can't be that uncommon."

"I had to meet you to know that I could make another choice. That you discovered that on your own is… Well, it's truly wonderful."

I wanted to close the distance between us, because it felt right, out here on the sand with the ocean bearing witness, because it was something we'd done any number of times before. But not now. Not in this part of the lifetime.

"How did he try to make you tough?" I almost didn't want to know, but I felt that I had to ask. I was so curious about this man. This man that I'd only gotten a piece of all those years ago. But it had felt like everything to me. Only now was I realizing that physical nudity just scratched the surface of intimacy.

And did I really want to court intimacy with him? After all my talk of keeping things simple between us...

It wasn't sex. It was just talking.

"It doesn't matter," he said.

"Yes," I said. "It does."

"No," he said, his tone decisive. "It doesn't matter. Leave it alone."

And then he turned and left me alone, which was what I had said that I wanted.

And now I found I bitterly regretted it.

CHAPTER TEN

Hercules

SHE WAS TEMPTATION. Temptation in a way I was not inured to. In truth, I had never much tested myself when it came to resisting what I might want.

My childhood had been a harsh landscape. My father had taught me to withstand torture. Starvation. Isolation.

And then he had told me that as a man I was free to indulge my appetites as long as I knew how to go without them.

It was a strange life. A firm, iron hand, combined with no discipline at all.

I knew how to go without certain things. Affection, food, water.

Apparently, I did not know how to go without Marissa when she was near.

She fascinated me. And I could tell that I fascinated her. When she approached me, it was often with the trepidation of a small mouse approaching a predator. Her hands were often clasped, just below her chest, her eyes bright as she would speak to me about something she liked—the food, the view, the way that the sun painted the sea with gold before it sank behind the horizon—and then she would scamper off as if she was afraid I might pounce on her at any moment.

She was not entirely wrong to be afraid.

I could not understand the point of resisting the thing between us, and yet she seemed to find it a moral necessity.

Except... I did understand. Why would she take a chance on a man like me?

I was not in the habit of talking to myself, but that had been happening more and more lately. As I questioned her, only to end up questioning myself.

All was running smoothly back in Pelion, at least as it had been reported to me. I received calls every day letting me know of the state of the nation. And I would take any necessary action that was required before going out of my office and into the rest of the house.

Going to Marissa.

To torture.

In many ways, Marissa was the perfect realization of what my father had raised me to endure. Indulgence and torture all rolled into one.

For I looked at her, and I was filled with desire, filled with lust, and I wanted her more than I had ever wanted anyone or anything.

And I constantly made sure that I was in her orbit, just to test my resolve. To test my strength. I wanted her.

I could not figure out why. I had never been able to.

It always came back to the way she had looked at me.

To the fact she wanted to talk to me. Didn't assume she knew what I thought about anything, but rather asked with an openness and innocence that shocked me.

I was distracted, thinking about Marissa when I should be thinking of the tasks ahead of me for the day, when the phone rang.

I answered, and the revelation on the other line turned the blood in my veins to ice as surely as Marissa turned it molten.

"Your father is dead." The palace official went on to tell me that my father had been found dead of an apparent suicide.

I could not fathom it. My father, the most self-interested man in the entire world, had ended his own life. He had never been anything but a master of his own self-preservation.

But then it suddenly made sense to me as I sat there in my office, my head reeling in darkness even as the sun rose high over the ocean.

He had chosen how it ended.

He had chosen it in a way that would make things the hardest for me. Because he knew that it would leave me with guilt, and if he left me with guilt, then how could I go on to sabotage his entire reputation? It was his final manipulation.

His final bit of torture. Rage tore me up inside as I tried to put the thoughts in my head in order.

Should I feel grief? Because he was dead, and there was no coming back from it. His revenge was hollow whether or not that was his intent.

Anger?

I did not want to bargain. Unless…

If I could only have had a few more words with him. He would never know now. He thought he had won.

He would never see that he was the one in the wrong.

Because I could not believe that he had taken his own life in a moment of despair. No. My father didn't have it in him to feel despair.

He would never see. Now he never would.

There was something so desperately hollow in that. Something appalling and vastly terrible in its scope.

Suddenly, I couldn't breathe. It reminded me of when I had been a boy and he had put me inside of a box. The kind of training that the military went through, he had told me. And the leader of Pelion could not afford to be any less stalwart than the military that protected it, because they would go for the King first. My father had told me that.

Isolation for hours, trapped inside of a box where I couldn't even stand up.

That was how I felt now. Unable to breathe. Unable to move. And I had to get out, because the walls of my office were closing in around me in spite of the fact that there were windows on all sides.

I did not know this feeling. I did not know helplessness. I did not know weakness.

Those things had been banished from me when I was a boy. Banished at the hand of the man who put me in that state now, and I hated him. Never had I hated him more in life than I did now in death.

I stormed downstairs, the blackness inside of me an entity that was beginning to escape. It had always been there. It was not new. I knew that. I had always known it was there. But I had always kept it locked behind a wall. Only allowing glimpses out. Reminded when I walked through the obsidian halls of the palace and had it reflected back at me.

But I did not let it out.

But now it was as a torrent of living water. Destroying all that might come into its path.

But I was on an island where there were so few other souls.

But there was one.

And I knew… I knew that if she came near me now I would only destroy her.

I stumbled out of the house, down the path that led to the beach. And she was there. I had gone to find her. I had gone to find her because I no longer had it in me to fight. Not myself, not the beast inside of me and not the desire that I felt for her. Why had I resisted? All this time, why had I resisted?

Why had I allowed her these proclamations?

I was the King.

I was her husband.

She looked up at me, the wind whipping her dark hair around, those eyes bright as that little creature I had only just imagined her to be.

"We are through playing games." I stopped with just a foot between us. "I want you. Do not deny me."

"What has happened to you?"

But any words she might have intended to say next I cut off. I pulled her up against my body, and a muffled squeak rose from her mouth.

"You're mine," I said. "You have been mine for eight years. Since that first moment that I saw you on the beach. Do you not understand that every woman I took into my bed after you was a paltry imitation? Do you not understand that you took me and you turned me into a creature of longing, when I have never had to want for anything in my entire life? If I demanded it, it was mine. But not you. You ran from me. No one runs from me."

And I remembered her questioning that proclamation I had made when we had first reunited. I remembered her asking me if that was true.

And I pushed away the disquiet in my soul. I pushed away the answer.

And I held on to the lie.

And I held on to her.

"There you are," she whispered. And she did not look at me like she was terrified. Those bright eyes examined me, and she lifted her hand, brushing her fingertips against my mouth. "I've seen you like this before."

"You have not," I said. "You don't know who I am. No one does."

"I do," she said. "I saw it. That first day. It might not have been this close to the surface, but I saw it. You hide it from the world. You hide from yourself, but it's there, Hercules. I know it is."

"Is it why you ran away from me?"

"No. I ran away from you that first time because of how badly I wanted to run to you. And I was taught. I knew better. To want something the way that I want you… To feel that sickness inside of me… It could only be wickedness on my part, and so I ran from temptation. And I have run from temptation. Every moment since you have been back in my company, but it was not to please my father, and it was not to save my soul. It was just to save... I am in your world. There must be something of mine that remains."

"I need you," I said. And it galled me to say it. It was why I did not press the issue before, because I had been unwilling to show her how much I needed her. Unwilling to show her what her denial of her body to me cost me.

But I had no pride left.

My father was dead, and for the first time in my life, I had no idea what to do.

And I had run to her.

I was not a man who ran, and yet I had.

But not away from anything.

Just to her.

And I wondered if she would deny me, or if she would demand conversation first.

But instead, she stretched up on her toes and pressed her mouth to mine.

Marissa

He was falling apart inside, and I could see it. And I knew that there was every chance that touching him would pull me into the darkness right along with him. That I would not be able to protect myself once I'd allowed myself to be stripped bare with him. Especially when he was like this.

But this—as little as it made sense—was the part of him that I had always craved. And it was the part of him I had always been denied.

He had been the smooth playboy around me. He had

found something a little bit deeper, and a little bit more authentic, conversations with me that weren't about trading innuendo, but were about the things that we believed in our hearts.

But he had not shown me this.

I had witnessed it, like a voyeur staring through a window, that first time I had seen him when he had thought that no one was watching.

And that was what had ensnared me. I realized the truth of it now.

The whole truth.

For I had not known who he was.

It was not his wealth, his title, his reputation that had fascinated.

It was not the way he teased me. Not the way he laughed. Not the way he touched me or made me call his name.

It was knowing that there was more to him. That he had shown me something just a little more than he had shown anyone else. And that there was yet another secret I might reach.

And he was giving it to me now.

I didn't know why. And in the moment, I didn't want to ask. I didn't feel that I should.

Because he didn't want me to know. And if I asked him now it would break the spell. He might be able to gain his composure. And I did not want that. I wanted him like this.

And later, much later, perhaps I would ask myself where my sense of preservation had gone.

But I already knew the answer.

It went where it always had when it came to Hercules.

And here on this island, we were man and wife. King and Queen of each other and nothing more.

Lily wasn't here.

Here on this island, we were not parents who had been thrown together by our compatible fertility. We were not essential strangers who'd had to marry for a bloodline, for the throne.

We were not those who had taken vows in front of the church only days ago, to each other, to a nation.

We were just Hercules and Marissa.

Even our names seemed at odds, mine so typical.

His, that of a god.

But in this moment my god had fallen, and he needed me to hold him. He needed me to be there for him. To bear witness to this brokenness.

I would ask later why.

Later, we would talk.

But now…

Now I wanted only this. Only him.

I was not a saint, and I had given up the idea that I might be long ago.

In his arms, I was just a woman. And I needed him to satisfy me as only a man could. "If you want me, then take me," I said.

"Give yourself," he said, his voice rough. "Give yourself to me because you have to be in this. All of you. Because if you are not I might hurt you. I might do something you don't like. I need to know that this is not me taking with my darkness but you giving in to it. Step into it, Marissa, but do so of your own free will, because I do not trust myself. Not now."

Perhaps that should scare me.

But nothing about him had ever scared me. Not really. It had been my own self that I was always the most afraid of. The feelings that he called up inside of me, and the way that he made me act in a way that I thought was out of character. A way that I had discovered was my character, at least with him.

He had put me in touch with places and pieces and feelings inside of myself that I had not known existed. And he had made me like them.

Then he had taken himself away from me, and I had been left sitting in charred ruin. Not knowing what to do with this new version of myself, unable to go back to who I had been, unwilling to.

And cut off from the joy that I had found in being new at the same time.

He had taken my journey of discovery and made it a hard climb.

And yes, there was joy in being at the summit, joy in holding my daughter in my arms. Joy in who I had become after that long, hard slog.

But I wanted to return to that spark of joy.

I wanted to go back in time to the first moment I'd seen him and be woman enough to handle the bleakness that I had seen there.

But the good news was I could handle it now.

I had been given a gift. A gift of time. A gift of being able to be with him in the way that we both needed.

Desperately.

And so I did as he asked. So I stepped in with both feet.

I pressed my hands to his face and stretched up on my toes, and I claimed his mouth.

Doing that was exhilarating. Being the one to lean in. To take responsibility for all that we were, rather than being the helpless, innocent virgin. The seducer rather than the seduced.

Oh, I knew enough to know that we were both, he and I, wrapped up in this thing that we could not control. That we didn't want to—not anymore.

A bubble of laughter rose up in my throat, even as I kissed him.

"Something is funny?" he asked, his voice rough, and I knew that I was on dangerous ground.

"It's not really funny," I said. I pressed my hand to his chest. "I always imagined parents as some other *thing*. Off in the distance, remote and mature, and in possession of every answer to the universe. In my father's case, I imagined that he was basically omniscient. And here we are. Parents. And yet the same as we ever were. Still…with this. Between us."

"Because children make the mistake of believing that parents are something different entirely," he said, something dangerous and sharp on the edge of his voice. "That they are not human. When, in fact, that is all they are. And as fallible as any other."

"Yes," I agreed. "Yes." But I didn't say anything more. I simply kissed him again, my lips on his, moving, desperate for access so that I could go deeper. So that we could be consumed in this.

And he gave in, growling and wrapping his arms around me, folding me into the strength of his embrace. I had never felt so safe, so protected and yet so perilously close to danger as I did in that moment.

This was not the sweet touch of a man having deference for his much younger, less experienced lover.

This was a desperation between equals.

And nothing had ever made me more certain of the fact that this had to happen than realizing that.

That this King was standing with me, not above me.

I stripped his T-shirt from his body, marveling at all that golden skin. At the way the years had only improved him. Made his chest deeper, his waist slimmer and more defined. He had more hair on his body, and I found that I liked it. The touch of it. The way that it reminded me he was a man, and so very different from me.

He pulled my dress away, leaving me standing there in nothing but the brief bathing suit that had been provided for me on the island. But I wasn't embarrassed. Then he stood and began to examine me, and suddenly each and every difference in my body felt large and highlighted to me.

My curves were fuller, my stomach softer. White lines marred the place beneath my belly button and my thighs.

I'd had his child, and I bore the evidence of that.

And I wondered what he would say. What he would think.

There was nothing but that endless black fire in his eyes, and he said nothing. Then he reached behind me and untied the top on my bikini, sending it to the sand. He knelt before me and undid the ties on the bottoms. He looked up at me and I was engulfed in the black fire. But I didn't burn away. No, if anything, I only became stronger.

He leaned in, and he pressed his mouth to my stomach. Right to the spot where my skin had stretched, where it was looser now and nothing like how it had been the first time he'd been with me.

I closed my eyes tight, fighting back against tears. I didn't want to cry. I wanted to seize this moment with both hands, to dive into the debauchery of it. To be consumed in the intensity. I wanted to have this. With no thought for the future. No thought for consequences.

For the first time in my life, that was what I wanted.

But I couldn't banish the feeling. The deep, heavy emotion that wound itself around my heart, around my soul.

Because this wasn't just sex, and he wasn't just a man.

And we might not primarily be parents here on this island, but we made a life together.

And there was a heaviness to what we were.

Marissa and Hercules.

We couldn't erase the history between us. And in that moment I didn't even want to. Because it made it all that much more.

The weight was a blessing. The weight was a curse.

The tears spoke of the beauty as much as the sadness, and I wanted to embrace both.

And he was embracing me. The changes in my body. He took a tour of the map that spoke of the years we'd been apart. Of those nine months when I'd carried his daughter inside me.

He kissed every single one of those marks. His big hands explored my thighs, around to my bottom. And he ignited me.

More than just my skin, more than just desire, it was a feeling that was almost too big to be contained inside of my body.

An ache welled up between my legs, my breasts heavy, my nipples aching for his touch.

But if it had been only that, I could have walked away.

He had captured me somewhere deeper. Had made me want in a way that only he could satisfy.

And when I opened my eyes, when I looked at him again, the bleakness there terrified and compelled me.

Hercules.

My only lover. My only love.

My husband.

The list of all the things he was to me was long, and I wondered if it could ever be true for him.

Oh yes, I was his wife. The mother of his daughter.

But did that mean something to him? Did it mean anything beyond the legality?

It didn't matter. Not now.

Because now there were no barriers between us. Now he was taking his jeans off for me. Showing me that body that haunted my dreams.

His powerful thighs, his very powerful... The rest of him.

And when he came back to me, his naked body pressed against mine, he kissed me.

And every hot, hard inch of him was against every pliant, willing inch of me. It was right that it was here on the beach. Because it had always been the beach for us. Always the ocean.

As if we were ready to sail away at any moment, he and I.

But it had always been an illusion. There had always been a duty for him to return to, and there had always been reality to return to for me.

But not now.

Not now.

We were enfolded in his darkness, and I welcomed it. His hands were rough on my body, his whiskers a hard scrape against the tender skin of my breasts as he took my nipple into his mouth and sucked it deep.

The sharp sensation it created between my legs a glorious and honeyed pleasure that I craved. More.

More.

That was what my father had said about the road to ruin.

One step.

One step on the wide path.

The easy path.

You would keep going that way.

But nothing about this felt easy. It was hard in the most beautiful way. Too much and not enough all at the same time.

Heaven and hell converging on a beach.

As we had always been.

He slid his hands down my back, gripped my hips and pulled me up against him, urged me to stand on my toes, and then he lifted me up off of the sand by my thighs, wrapping my legs around his back as he took advantage of the fact that he now opened me to him. He braced me with one arm and put his hand between my legs, stroking me, stroking me until I cried out.

Until I thought I might cry.

He was brilliant. And we were brilliant together.

I had missed this.

As if a part of myself had been revived and I was now whole.

Then he laid me down on the sand, his hardness pressed against my center, and I arched against him, seeking to find the thing that I knew only he could give.

He had ruined even that for me.

Because the pursuit of my own pleasure, when I ached in the middle of the night and couldn't sleep, always took the shape of him.

He was a fantasy I could not banish.

I could want nothing and no one else.

So I had forgone even the pleasure of release on my own, because I couldn't bear to fantasize about the man who had abandoned me and my daughter.

But he hadn't.

And he was here. And he was mine.

And I was his.

"Give it to me," I whispered. "Give me your darkness."

And I did not have to ask him twice.

He wrapped his hand around my head, burying his fingers in my hair, lifting my head from the sand and kissing me with a punishing strength that took my breath away.

He shifted between my legs and surged inside of me, his strength, thickness and power causing me to gasp.

I was unused to this kind of penetration, and it hurt just a little bit.

And somehow that felt all right.

Somehow it felt fitting.

That this was like the first time.

He was in me. All around me.

We were one again, and that was the most right thing in the world even if I couldn't explain it. Even if I couldn't understand it.

His touch left trails of heat across my skin, and as he surged inside of me, over and over again, I was close to completion.

Not just in the sense of pleasure, but in the sense of a wholeness, a fullness and realness that I hadn't known had been absent from me.

The sun was behind his head, and each time he moved, a flash of light would blind my eyes and then it was him. Hercules.

And even when I closed my eyes, he filled my vision, the light from the sun painting ghosts behind my lids.

Hercules.

It had always been him.

He had always been my sanity and insanity. My joy and my sadness. My ruin and my triumph.

He had always been.

He always would be.

And I realized in that moment, as I opened my eyes again and stared at that dear, beautiful face carved from rock, at those eyes that were capable of making me feel desired and making me feel destroyed. That mouth that I knew could deliver the most beautiful of compliments and the most cutting of cruelties, that this was what I had avoided.

Because I knew that once he touched me, it would be undeniable.

And I had thought that perhaps we could parent side by side and have some sort of sweet, amicable relationship. A marriage that was in a marriage. A life together that wasn't together. Hercules and Marissa with a space between them rather than wrapped around each other, but that had never been possible. And it never would be.

Because he was my other piece, whether or not I was ever his.

He had been the path to myself, and I had spent years living away from him, and I had not lost that.

My strength. The fortitude to stand on my own feet.

Even when I thought he had caused my diminishment, I had known that he had also created in me the strength to endure it.

The strength to go against my father, the confidence that what I felt and what I wanted was right.

A whole woman. Not a girl who was under the oppressive thumb of her father, who knew nothing of the real world or what she could be.

Hercules's woman. And that was when I shattered. Not slowly as he was doing, but one moment I was whole, come together completely, and then I was shattered, tossed into the wind like a billion stars in the sky.

And being broken with him was better than being whole had ever been.

Because he was the one who had made me.

And he was the one who had broken me.

I cried out his name as reality shattered through me, digging my fingernails into his shoulders. I had never done that before. I had never left a mark on him. But I would now. The joy that I took in our union would stay on his skin.

And I was proud of that.

With a growl, he froze, finding his own release that left him panting and spent just as I was, his forehead pressed against mine.

We shared the same air. Shared the same breath.

And for a moment we even seemed to share the same heartbeat.

But then that moment was over, and I remembered.

I remembered that he was bleeding something black and ugly from his soul, and I had managed to put a tourniquet on the wound, but I had not healed it.

I looked up at him, and I pressed my hand against his chest. "Tell me."

And on a ragged curse, still buried deep inside of me, he pressed his head against my neck and groaned. "My father is dead."

CHAPTER ELEVEN

Hercules

I DID NOT know what had possessed me to make that confession, still inside of her, still in reach of heaven.

I should not have done what I did. I should not have gone to her as I was. More beast than man, jagged and sharp and unable to control the rage that was coursing through me.

And Marissa did not deserve that.

Whatever I might have thought about her, she did not deserve that.

But she had said yes, and more than yes, she had taken the step toward me as I had demanded.

As if that had somehow taken the blame away from me. To put that squarely on her shoulders as I had done.

Take me.

She had commanded that I take her.

But she had taken me, and thoroughly at that.

In the sand, yet again.

Would I ever have this woman in a bed?

It was a question that I wanted an answer to.

But she had asked me a question, and it had nothing to do with when we might come together again.

I had answered.

And now there was a deathly, still silence between us.

She shifted beneath me. "I'm sorry," she said.

Two words. So quiet. Infused with sympathy.

Empathy.

She knew. She understood. That a horrible father could still be mourned, that the grief for someone such as him could be complicated and double-edged.

I barely understood it myself, but she did. Because she had been through it before. "It means it's over," she said softly. "And that is a terrible blessing."

Terrible blessing. A strange pairing of words, but she was right. It was a wholly terrible sort of blessing. To never have to deal with my father again, but also to never be able to experience the satisfaction of him being forced to change.

"For all I know," she said softly, "my father died believing that he did what's right where I was concerned."

I shifted, moving to lie beside her on the sand.

"Believing that ostracizing me, disowning his granddaughter… That it was the height of his piety. We never got to reconcile. Our final words were… Well, I didn't even speak. It was just him, telling me that I had to leave. Telling me it was the punishment for my sin. That Lily was a punishment. Perhaps it was something too large to repair. I don't know. But I would have very much liked for him to say he was sorry. To know that he knew he was wrong. Even if we could never have a relationship again, I would've wanted that."

"My father was a man beyond redemption," I said. "But I think I was waiting for that as well. For him to understand that he was the villain. But I believe that he died under the illusion that he was going to defeat me in his way. That he was the center of the story. And that he was the one who deserved triumph in the end. And that is…"

"It's not a good story," she said. "It's a terrible story. No one would want to read it, unless they were looking to feel sort of self-important. Unless they were looking to marinate in the gray areas of life, in which case I can only assume they don't have much experience with them. It's only a good story if it's not your reality. And for us…"

"It's uninteresting to watch them continue to be the heroes in their own worlds," I said.

"Very," she agreed.

"He was not a good man." I repeated it, mostly to myself.

She sat up, sand covering her bare body.

She looked so beautiful. She was different now, fuller breasts, fuller curves. She had a dusting of sand over her breasts, and I wanted to brush them off. And then put them in my hands. I was fascinated by her stretch marks. It made her pregnancy with Lily more real to me.

I wanted to focus on that, and not on the situation with my father. Not on the truth of him. Of my childhood.

But that darkness… I could not control it.

And everything was about to come spilling out.

"Do you know how elite military soldiers are trained?"

"No," Marissa said. "I can't say that I do."

She was clearly confused by the direction the conversation was going.

"In almost every country, a variant of these methods is used. But it is not just physical strength they must learn to withstand. They must learn to withstand physical torture. Because they are at risk for being tortured in order for the enemy to gain information. Torture is not simply shoving bamboo under people's fingernails. It is psychological as well. And the military in Pelion is well trained to withstand many forms of torture." I gritted my teeth. "My father believed that the ruler of Pelion must be trained to withstand it as well. He believed that I must be no less trained than our military. He started my training when I was a boy."

"When you were a boy?" She looked so horrified and I had regret that I was bringing my ugliness into her world. But we were the only people here. And she was the only one who had ever listened.

And for the first time in my life, I wanted to talk. Really talk. About what had created me. And what I really was.

"Yes. It was his belief that you created strength in a man early, or he would be compromised at the foundation. He approached me that way. As if I was something he was building. And I… I knew no different."

"Your mother…"

My heart felt like it was being squeezed. "Much like your mother, she did not have a say in most of her life."

She didn't try.

I clenched my jaw tight. There was no opposing the King. I'd had to go to great lengths in order to maneuver into a position where I might oppose my father. What hope would she have had?

Marissa looked away. "I think she would have put a stop to physically harming me."

"But you don't know. When powerful men with dangerous ideals ensnare those around them, when they feel powerless, what are they to do?"

I had repeated the same mantra to myself countless times over the years.

I ignored the hollow ache in my chest.

Like always.

"There were beatings, to be sure. Administered by some of his most elite soldiers. They knew how to make it hurt, but to avoid killing me. Very important, as killing me would defeat the purpose. But the beatings were easier to withstand than the other things. Being locked in a box with sound playing on a loop. Babies crying. Endlessly. I couldn't escape the noise. Sometimes they would strip me bare and hose me off with water as I lay on the cold ground. Shouting at me… Things I couldn't even understand.

"And they would demand that I denounce my father, and I would refuse. And that was how I won. Every time. That was how I proved my loyalty to the throne."

"Hercules…"

"No one has ever pitied me before," I said, marveling at her. "It is something of a novelty."

"Because everyone sees one piece of you. Everyone sees the money. Everyone sees the power, the money, the prestige. They don't know this."

"My upbringing was strict. Isolated. And then I was turned loose when I was fifteen. My father was confident that I had been trained, and he sent me out into the world and told me it was my buffet. I had the foundation I required."

"Why do you suppose he did that?"

"Truthfully? I think because he wanted to have it confirmed that his own debaucher nature was somehow ingrained in his blood. He wanted to watch me go out and do the very same. Have any woman that I pleased, buy expensive yachts and jets and go to the most exclusive parties and indulge myself in drinks and mood-altering substances. He wanted to believe that was the best a man could be, even when he was the very best man. He used me in a variety of ways, and that was just one of them. He created with me a perfect soldier—so he thought—and he created a mirror that showed him what he wanted. But inside I have always been different. I have always known that he was wrong. And when those men told me to denounce my father, I did it a thousand times inside. I didn't speak, not because I was afraid, but because I knew that my father could not see into my mind. Because I knew that I had to stage my coup in the neatest way possible. I feared, always, that any bad behavior would blow back on my mother, and later my sister."

"You feared for your mother's safety?" Marissa asked.

"Yes, of course."

"But she did not fear for yours. Or she was too afraid to act out and protect you. How can you worry for her?"

I shifted, and so did something in my chest. "She was not created to be strong. I was. I was not going to allow what he did to me to break me, Marissa. You must understand that. I had no control over it. No control over what happened to me. But I could allow it to forge me into the blade that would eventually kill my father. I didn't know that it would be quite so literal. I had imagined that it would be political in nature, and it very nearly was. I suspect… I suspect in essence he wanted me to feel that it was me who made that fatal blow."

"Because he knew that it would hurt you."

"Perhaps. Though, I think *hurt* is too strong a word. I'm not sure that he believes I possess the ability to be hurt. I'm not sure if I do either."

"You are hurt. I saw you when you came down from the house. This hurts you terribly."

I shook my head. "Animals feel pain. It's not the same."

"You think you're more like an animal?"

"Elemental. As I was trained to be. I do not feel far beyond what the basest creatures do. I do not have the ability."

"I think you do. I've watched you with Lily."

"It is beneficial for me to be kind to Lily."

I felt nothing when I spoke her name, and I was glad of it. I suddenly felt hollow, and I was glad of that as well.

"That's not the only reason," she said.

"Don't make the mistake of thinking that you know me," I said to her. But I was saying it to my own self as well. For it was easy to lie here with her in the sand, a moment out of time. Which was what we had always had. But when we returned, we would be returning to the palace, and I would be King. I could not afford to take that lightly, nor could I afford to assume that I knew everything about myself or what I was capable of.

I had been created by the hand of a monster, after all.

And the real danger was assuming that I could control the matching creature that lived inside myself.

That darkness.

She said nothing, but the way she looked at me clearly spoke the words for her.

She was intent on seeing the best in me. And I wondered if it was because she had consented to be mine again.

If she had to tell herself that on some level I was a good man or feel sullied by what had happened between us.

Marissa was a good woman.

Of that I was confident.

If anything had changed over the course of the week at the island, it was my certainty of that.

I had spent five years thinking of her as a defector. As one who had betrayed me in a way that no other woman had—because no other woman abandoning me would have felt like a betrayal.

But I had relearned her.

And perhaps the best thing was having confirmed that I had been right about one thing at least.

She was exceptional. She was like no one else. And that meant that I would have to be careful.

She was the one who would have to take the largest part in raising Lily. Because she was the one who would shape the best ruler, one who had not been touched by my father at all. I would make a conscious decision to correct what I could, but Lily would be unspoiled.

Of that, I was certain. Of that, I was resolved.

"Let us go back to the house," I said.

"Will we need to return for your father's funeral?"

I leaned in, and I kissed her, fiercely. "That man has stolen enough from me. He will not steal this too."

That seemed to soothe her, and she leaned against me. Trust. She should trust in me, as did Lily.

I would do my utmost not to disappoint them.

But that would mean keeping my distance.

But we had until the end of this week.

And I would take that with both hands, and her as well.

For when we returned to Pelion, things would have to change.

CHAPTER TWELVE

Marissa

THE TIME ON the island slipped away too quickly. I was angry at myself for spending a week avoiding him, when we could have been together. I was blissfully happy, but I missed Lily.

Of course, when we left here, I would miss being with him as we were now. I knew that. I somehow sensed that things were going to change.

Of course they would.

We would be back in a world that was completely foreign to me. I didn't know how to be a queen.

I didn't know how to live in this country; I didn't know the customs; I didn't know the way of it. Much less how to be royalty within it.

And so, I decided to ask him.

I felt raw, wounded by our coming together down at the beach, but more than that, the conversation we had after.

Thinking of what his father had done to him...

It tore me to pieces inside.

To think that a parent could do such a thing to their child… It was beyond imagining.

And he seemed to think…that he was fine. But I could see that he was not.

Or if not fine, he seemed to think that whatever remained in him was for the best, something that made him the sort of opponent that his father had required.

When I looked at him, I saw a wounded boy. And I knew he would not like that. Not at all.

So I didn't say that to him. Instead, I would touch him whenever I could, not just to solidify the sexual connection, but to find closeness. To offer comfort. I found myself wondering if anyone had ever touched him kindly when he was a child.

Or if all he had known was abuse and negligence. In some ways, he was right. And my mother could easily be accused of actions similar to his own. She had certainly been unable to act against my father in a meaningful way in those years when I had been banished from the home.

But I had read about his mother. About all the traveling she did, the way that she flitted off to tropical islands at her leisure. The rumors that the young Princess was not the daughter of the King.

And I did not doubt that Hercules had believed he needed to protect them. I could see it in the way that he spoke. In every line of his body. He was protective of them.

And from what I had heard about his father, possibly rightly so.

But I had a suspicion that his father more or less

ignored his wife and daughter, and did as he pleased with other women, and did as he saw fit to Hercules.

I wondered how much of the threat directed at Hercules's mother and sister was simply a smoke screen set up by his father. A way to take advantage of the good nature that his son had. Because of course the King possessed none of his own.

I knew that Hercules mourned him in a strange way. But I would not mourn King Xerxes. Not for a moment. Not after the way I had learned he had harmed Hercules.

The physical scars might have long healed, but his emotional scars were deep.

I thought about Lily and the way he seemed afraid to connect with her. Though, he seemed to try at that more than he did anything else. He was a good man, of that I was convinced.

It wasn't that he was incapable of connecting with Lily, or that he didn't want to. To me it seemed as if he was truly frightened.

Of her, of something in himself, I didn't know.

I wanted to fix it.

But I knew that I couldn't.

So instead, I decided to give him a chance to fix me, because that might give him something to tether him to the earth.

"I don't know how to be a queen," I said to him over coffee the morning before our last here on the island.

"Come to think of it," he said, his tone dry, "I'm not sure there is a very decent precedent set for a queen in Pelion."

It was the first time I had ever heard him come remotely close to insulting his mother.

"In what way?"

"You may have noticed that my mother is absent from the country most of the time."

"Yes. Will she return for your father's funeral?"

"Oh, I suppose. They were still married, whether or not they had a relationship."

"And you are not concerned about the rumors that will come from you not going?"

"There will be rumors, of course. But I stand ready to repudiate nearly everything about my father's rule. I will lead with this. And I will make a statement."

I was struck by his strength. By the way his face seemed almost carved from granite.

He was truly an incredible man.

"You're not afraid of scandal, then," I said.

"The only reason that I cared about marrying a suitable woman was that was part of the rules set for my father's early abdication. Once I found out about Lily, I was able to institute a bit of blackmail to ask him to step aside. But then he did the most convenient thing I could imagine and died."

"Well," I said, laughing reluctantly at his dark comment. "I suppose."

"I have never cared anything for convention. For in my eyes, the conventions established in my country were little more than a joke. Ways to keep pompous men like my father in power."

"Has there ever been a queen? I mean…a queen like Lily."

"No," he said. "In fact, that makes me suspicious that they might have…" He grimaced. "I don't even want to think about it. Hopefully no one made a practice of eliminating heirs to the throne based on their gender. Though, they might have just made them go away, the way that he did with Lily."

"He didn't know her gender when he did that."

"No, indeed. But that had everything to do with keeping me from taking power any sooner than I might have." He shook his head. "No. I don't care one bit for the pomp and circumstance of the Xenakis family. We are making a new country. And so you will be the Queen that you decide to be."

"I'm just a girl from an island who happened to meet a prince."

"A prince with very poor self-control," he said.

"That's not true. I think you have amazing self-control, and any indication to the contrary is a little bit of a put-on."

"I didn't have self-control with you."

I took that and held it close to my chest. "Well, I suppose that makes me special."

"There is no *suppose* about it. You are unlike anyone else I have ever known."

The admission seemed uncomfortable for him. Seemed torn from him.

"Then I suppose I will keep aiming for that as Queen."

"Do you have any special interests?"

"The care of single mothers," I said instantly. "Believe me when I tell you we face an inordinate amount of judgment while the men often responsible walk around without any."

"Perfect," he said.

"Perfect?" I repeated.

"Not perfect that they face judgment. But perfect that

you have such a strong and clear interest. That will be your vocation, if you would like."

"I would," I said. "You know, I was so focused on taking care of Lily that I never truly thought about having work. Or…a calling, I suppose. I was given so much money by…well, your father…that I was able to buy a house, and we were able to live quite comfortably. When she was older, I would have had to find something to do, but that wasn't encouraged in my home either. Women working. Having aspirations. So I just didn't. But I like the idea of this."

"Being Queen can be a vocation. A calling. No one else has taken it that way for my country in the past, but you could be the first."

"I imagine I'd also be the first to marry the King after our child is born?"

"Likely. Unless, again, there has been some revision in the history books."

"Well, we can always assume there might be. I don't mind being the first. Just another way that we are an oddity. Just another way that we will help change the country. I mean, not to co-opt your revolution."

He laughed. "No, it's perfectly fine if you want to join the revolution with me. You're free to pick up a sword."

"I hadn't realized that swords would be part of the job description."

"I can get you one."

"I don't think that's necessary." Our eyes caught and held, and heat spiked between us.

What a strange and wonderful thing to have both, this ability to laugh with him and want him all at the same time.

"I have some things to see to," he said. "I will... I'll find you."

There was something deep in that. Enduring. A promise that echoed in my soul. At least, I chose to let it.

"Okay," I said.

I chose not to dwell on the end of our time here.

I had to start thinking of it as a beginning. No matter how difficult it was. When we returned to the palace, we settled into a pattern. But it was one I didn't expect. It was reminiscent of our first days on the island. Hercules avoided me. At least, that was what it felt like. Perhaps that wasn't what was happening.

He was wrapped up in affairs of state. I discovered quickly that life as royalty did not simply mean a life doing whatever you wanted.

Not that I didn't have a sense of that before—I had seen news stories about royals all my life, but it wasn't as if I had paid close attention to them, and I definitely hadn't considered it some kind of guide for my potential later life.

I had never imagined that I might become a queen.

But here I was.

I spent a few hours a day working on ideas for outreach to single mothers in the community. I looked at budgets and talked to palace officials about things like free day-care centers and maternity leave.

It was fulfilling work. And when I wasn't doing that, I was taking care of Lily. Lily made me happy too, as she always had.

It was nice, also, spending time with my mother. We had years spent apart, and we hadn't talked like we did in the palace in... Ever.

But I was still lonely. I missed Hercules. I missed wasting hours talking to him about everything and nothing. I missed sleeping with him at night.

We kept separate bedrooms here.

I didn't like it.

"What's wrong?" my mother asked one day as we sat in the garden of the palace, where a massive play structure had been erected for Lily. She was running around, her dark hair flying behind her as she ran, her laughter filling the staid silence of the royal grounds.

I loved that.

Especially knowing what I did about Hercules's childhood.

"Nothing," I said.

"That's a lie," my mother said. "I know you well enough to know that, even if I haven't known you as well as I should have for the past few years."

"You couldn't help any of that. There's no point in regret."

"I don't say this because I am experiencing regret. At least, not so much. But I can tell that you're not happy. When you came back from your honeymoon you seemed…different."

"Well, it's nice to be on a private island without any responsibilities."

"And now you have responsibilities."

"Good ones," I said. "But it is a lot."

"I don't think hard work has ever scared you, Marissa. Somehow, I don't think that's what's bothering you."

"It's… Hercules has been very busy."

"I've never known as much about the two of you as I should. I was forbidden from speaking about you when your father was still alive. And we never got a chance to…"

"I fell in love with him," I said. "The first time I ever saw him. I was sixteen. He didn't touch me then," I said hurriedly. "But we got to know each other. Every summer. More and more. And I… I didn't have the willpower to resist him."

My mother looked thoughtful. I didn't know what to expect from her. If she would judge me for that weakness or not.

"I was envious of you in some ways," my mother said. "I was never carried away by passion of any kind. I married sensibly. I married a man that my parents approved of. There was no joy in our marriage. And we couldn't speak. I could never tell your father what I wanted from life. I let him send my daughter away because I didn't have the fortitude to stand on my own two feet and speak for myself. I let you be badly treated because I didn't stand up for you. And I have regretted it every day since."

"There is room for regret between us," I said. "Mom, I know how Dad was. I don't blame you."

"Perhaps you should. I look at the way you protect Lily, how you've given everything to her, and I should have done the same for you."

"You weren't able to. I know that. I understand it."

"I wish… I wish I would have had a different life. I wish I would have stood up and said what I wanted."

"Do you really think that he would have given it to you?"

"He might have given me a divorce, and in the end, perhaps that would have been better."

"Maybe," I said.

But I didn't really think so. I don't know what my mother would have done. I was glad that she was coming into her own strength now, but she couldn't regret who she had been all those years. She couldn't change it.

And I didn't want her to make herself sick over it.

"I guess my point in bringing any of this up is that if you want something different with Hercules, then you should speak up. Otherwise you end up with a lifetime of regret and sadness. You look back and you wonder how you spent so many great years just enduring. Brittle silence and the full absence of a loving touch. I don't know how or why I subjected myself to that. And maybe I couldn't have had a different marriage with your father, but perhaps I could have had a different life. Perhaps you could have had a different life. But you still can. Don't build castles made of regret, because they're what you'll live in in the future. Believe me."

"What if he doesn't want different?"

Because that was the thing that really scared me.

"Then you'll be angry. And hurt. But you won't have to wonder. You won't have to wonder if there was something you could have done but were too afraid. Your relationship with Hercules…it's for Lily too. If you need that, then remember that as well. But if you could do it just for yourself… Marissa, that would be a very brave thing to do." She sighed. "To do more than just endure is a brave thing." My mother's words stayed with me for the rest of the day.

I did know how to endure. I had gotten very good at it. I had accepted a life where I wouldn't have love.

Where I wouldn't have Hercules. In many ways, I had accepted my fate as a martyr to the cause of my daughter, and that was what had made it so easy to go back with Hercules and use Lily as the sole excuse.

But that hope…

That hope inside of me meant something.

It was for me. It was for him. For us and for our love. For what could be.

I had seen the possibility of all that five years ago, and I could still see it now. I wanted it. I craved it.

But I was denying myself because I had looked into my father's icy stare and been sent away before. Because my mother hadn't stood up and told me to stay. Or that she would go with me.

Because I had felt abandoned, by my parents, by Hercules.

It had been so much easier to let go, to accept the fact that I walked through life alone, except for Lily. That I lived for her, that I breathed for her.

And there was nothing wrong with that. I did. She was my daughter, and it was my great joy to sacrifice for her.

But there was more. I wanted more.

And wanting more for myself meant wanting more for Lily.

I wanted her to have a happy home. And no, it would never be conventional, because we lived in a castle. There would always be staff around; there would always be matters of state to see to. But we would never want for anything. There were incredibly wonderful, privileged things we could have as well, but why couldn't we have love on top of that?

The house that I had grown up in had been stale.

My mother had been right. It had been gray.

And I had gone to escape the gray down at the shores of the ocean, where I had found Hercules.

He had been my escape. He had been my salvation, not my ruin.

But only if I was willing to reach out a hand and ask.

Ask to be saved. For both of our sakes.

Because we could have one of two lives. The gray and the bleak, or we could have it all.

We could have paradise. A walk through the fog, or a life staring out at the bright, brilliant sea.

And I knew which one I felt we were meant to have. I knew what I wanted. But one of us was going to have to be brave enough to take it.

I knew all that Hercules had been through, and I could understand why the inside of him felt a little bit too broken for things like love.

But I also knew that he could make a decision to put it behind him.

I also knew that we could have more, that bravery might have a cost, and love might take work, but it was worth it in the end.

For what Hercules and I could have was a jewel beyond price, and I had to be willing to sell everything I owned to possess it. All of it.

I had to be willing to do more than exist in the possibility of a relationship and throw down a definitive gauntlet.

Do you always do as you're told?

He had asked me that once, so long ago. And that was when I had realized that I did, and that I didn't want to, not anymore.

It was the same now.

I didn't want to simply do as was expected. I didn't want to do as I was told.

I wanted to live bright and brilliant, with him, with our hearts twined around each other as I knew they could be.

Not two separate people living two separate lives in a massive palace, but two souls that had become one.

He might not believe in that, but I did.

And that meant that I had to be the one to fight for it.

He wanted reason, and I didn't have reason.

But I had love.

Hercules had told me once that he believed in the physical. Well, I would approach him that way. I would give him what he understood before I introduced what he felt he could not. And maybe then those two things would come together for him and create something new.

Something that was only ours.

Something that he could see and touch and feel.

I was afraid.

Like I had been afraid that first time we'd been together down on the beach.

But I was also determined. And I knew what I wanted. I knew who I was.

I could only hope that Hercules would come to understand the same way that I did.

Because if he did…

If he did, then he wouldn't want to accept less either.

But there was no way for me to know. So I had to step out in faith.

I had to be brave.

CHAPTER THIRTEEN

Hercules

I HAD DONE my very best to throw myself into the leadership of Pelion. It was difficult when I was obsessed with erotic thoughts about my wife. I knew that she was unhappy. The few times that I had seen her since we had returned from the island, she had been a bit sullen with me. At dinner she had been quiet, and the air had been filled by chatter coming from Lily, and I knew that I had been disengaged with that as well.

But I had to rule. I had to be King. There was no scope for me to be distracted by my family.

My family.

Marissa and Lily were my family.

Such a strange and foreign concept to me.

I couldn't remember having family dinners when I was growing up. No, I ate in the nursery; my mother was usually away. By the time my sister was born, I was nearly grown.

I didn't remember saying that we could have family dinners, but one evening Marissa, her mother and Lily showed up and sat at the table. The staff brought dinner to all of us, and so it had continued on every night since.

But even as we had those dinners, and Marissa would respond to the things I said with brightness, I could sense that beneath it she was unhappy.

I didn't like that, but I didn't know what else she wanted from me either.

I was the leader of a nation. I had concerns I had to put above all else. Including the two of us.

From everything I'd been told by my staff, Marissa was adapting beautifully to her role as Queen. And yet…

She was different than she had been on our honeymoon.

But then, so was I. Of necessity. I had allowed myself to be distracted by her there. I had broken there. I had shown weakness, and that could not be allowed. If my father had died, and I had not had a soft spot to land in the form of Marissa's arms, how would it have gone?

Instead, I had splintered, and I had allowed my darkness to pour out, to spill onto my wife, and that was unacceptable.

I knew that.

And so, we would continue to be separate. We would continue to have separate rooms. Until such time as I felt that I had a grip on…everything. From the running of the palace to my emotions.

My emotions. The fact that I had them at all made me feel weak.

I despised it.

Even in the form of rage I was beginning to find them unwieldy.

I disliked it.

It made me wonder if I was closer to my father than I had ever anticipated.

I liked to pretend that I was something else. Something different entirely, but I wondered.

Was there any way to fully escape being like your maker when he had fashioned you in his image? It was not something I knew the answer to, and I feared that only time would tell.

But in the meantime, I would not affect Marissa and Lily.

It was the one good thing I knew I could do. Keep my distance.

I had been spending every night in my office, staying up as late as I possibly could to ensure that I fell into bed in exhaustion that would prevent me from going down the hall and taking Marissa again and again.

She was a temptation that I was finding difficult to resist, and that was yet more reason to resist her.

I couldn't allow her to have control over me.

I couldn't allow anyone or anything to have control over me. Not my base desires, not my lust and certainly not my wife.

Those things made for a weak king, and I refused to be weak. Had I not spent my childhood trying to demonstrate my strength? I would not falter now.

My father was wrong. You did not have to be a monster to rule. I would show that until my dying day.

But in order to do that, I had to make sure that I did not falter.

When work didn't help, I went to the gym. And I exhausted myself there. Tonight, thankfully, I was exhausted without punishing my body, and when the time was past midnight, I finally went to my quarters.

The palace was quiet, dark and empty, the obsidian halls glittering bleakly in the blackness.

It felt all too close to what was going on inside of me.

I pushed the door open to my chambers, and the lights were on.

The flood of brightness was a shock after walking down the long, dark hall.

But not as much of a shock as the sight that greeted me.

Marissa, lying on the bed, completely naked.

She did not look defeated now. She did not look shy or innocent. She was bold. There was nothing on her body, and she reclined across the pillows in a way that emphasized her curves. The glorious plumpness of her breasts, the indent of her waist, the round swell of her hips.

And those nipples… Dusky berry and tight, begging for my attention. That dark thatch of curls between her thighs that I wanted to bury my face in.

I had spent days resisting this very thing, and now I wasn't certain I had it in me to resist any longer.

"What are you doing here?"

She moved her hand, and the only thing that adorned her body—our ring—glimmered there.

"I missed you," she said softly.

They were not the words of the siren, and they were not the words that I had expected. They were emotional, spoken with a sweetness that truly stunned me.

"Did you?" I asked.

"Yes," she said softly.

"You could have simply told me over dinner."

"I don't want to talk," she said.

The words were a male fantasy, and not ones I could quite credit coming out of Marissa's mouth. Because if there was one thing we had always done, it was talk. Even when passion was hot between us, we always spoke.

"You don't want to talk?"

"No," she said, shaking her head, her glossy mane shimmering in the light. "I can talk to anyone. You're the only man that I can do this with. The only man I've ever been with at all. The only man I will ever be with."

Something twisted hard and low in my stomach. "The only man you've ever been with?"

"Did you imagine that I was entertaining lovers these last few years?"

"You would have been forgiven for doing so. You are human, after all. And humans have needs."

"But you ruined me for everyone else."

"You see," I said darkly, "you ruined me for everyone else as well, but that did not stop me from…" I began to remove my shirt, and I questioned my own resolve and strength the entire time. Still, it didn't prevent me from doing it. "That made it all the worse. It was hollow. The promise of a feast, but when I reached out to take it in hand, it just turned to ash. Bitterness in my mouth. It was never what I wanted. Because I had tasted…paradise. I tasted paradise on your skin, Marissa, and then it was gone. I knew what making love could be, and it was never that, not after you."

"Well, I was just smart enough to know that I didn't want to substitute."

I felt humbled by that. Because I hadn't been. I had been angry and filled with thwarted pride, and I had tried to erase her from my body, from my skin, in the beds of other women. I didn't like the way that made me feel. I didn't like the shame. Didn't like the heavy, hot emotion that stabbed me in the chest and seemed to twist my heart into strange and unnatural shapes.

She was twisting me into strange and unnatural shapes inside, and I didn't know what the hell I was supposed to do about it. I was supposed to be supreme and sovereign ruler, or something like that, and yet... And yet.

I shoved my trousers off, left them down on the ground, and the rest of my clothes along with them.

I was past the point of pretending that I was going to resist.

It was one thing to keep separate when she was across the palace, but it was quite another when she was naked and in my bed.

I had to ask myself who this man was that he couldn't control himself around a woman. Ever.

That she had been my downfall there on the island, and I had learned nothing in the time since.

But she said she didn't want to talk, and she said she only wanted me, and why couldn't I take her like I did any other woman? She was still paradise, still Marissa, and I should be able to have whatever sort of physical relationship with her that I desired. It would feel the same.

I'd had any number of emotionless sexual experiences, and there was no reason she couldn't be the same. She would have to be. If we were going to continue, if this were going to continue, then we would have to.

And I couldn't live with her, not in the same sphere and resist her. So we would have to.

She moved, getting up on her knees and sliding her hand slowly across my chest. She was angling to kiss my mouth and I grabbed her chin, stopping her. "No."

"Why not?"

"You said you didn't want to talk," I said. "So don't talk."

A fire lit behind her eyes, but she didn't speak.

I pinched her chin between my thumb and forefinger and guided her slowly downward. She knew what I wanted.

She parted her lips, the expression in her eyes bright. And then she dragged her tongue along the head of my arousal, and I let my head fall back, luxuriating in the soft, slick pleasure as she took me deep into her mouth, making low, satisfied sounds as she did.

We hadn't had the time to play at such things when we'd been younger, desperate to couple together out in the open, and with no time for extras in case we might get caught.

I had thought about this, though. With her. So many times that I'd lost count.

She had no experience, and I could see that, but what she didn't have in experience she made up for with her very clear desire for it. For me.

She wasn't timid; she wasn't uncertain. She took me in deep, wrapping her hand around the base of me and tasting me slowly and thoroughly.

It was heaven and hell, all contained in this woman. It always had been.

She lowered her head, her dark hair falling over her

face, and I tried to force myself to pretend that she was just one of the substitutes that I'd had in the years between our coming together again.

That she didn't matter.

That she was no one.

But I couldn't, and I didn't want to. Because the minute that I tried to imagine it was anyone other than Marissa, the spark was gone. She mattered.

I gritted my teeth. I arched my hips upward, and she accepted me, took me in deeper.

I was getting close to the edge, unable to hold myself back any longer, and I guided her away. She made a soft sound of protest, but I wouldn't hear of it.

"That isn't how this is going to end," I said. "On your knees."

She looked at me. "I already am."

"Turn around," I said, and she obeyed.

I looked at her, the long line of her elegant back, moving down to the full curves of her ass. Her glossy hair was draped over her shoulder, exposing all that skin. And she was exquisite. More than beautiful.

Desire coursed through me, hot and hard as I approached her. I put my hands on her shoulders, slid them down her back, around to grip her hips hard, watching as my fingers left impressions in her skin. Then I reached between her legs and stroked her until her wetness coated my fingers, until her desire was all over my skin. She whimpered, gasping as I pushed two fingers inside of her, rocking her hips back and begging.

I had control. She might have come in here to seduce me, might have come in here to prove some kind of point, but the point would be mine in the end.

I would have her, however I wanted, whenever I wanted, and she would allow it, because she was mine.

Maybe I couldn't pretend that she was someone else. Maybe I couldn't make it carry less weight, but I could stay in control of this.

I commanded; she obeyed.

That could work.

We could work.

Because God knew I couldn't stay away.

She made a little kittenish cry, arching back, the motion pushing my fingers deeper into her body, and my arousal pulsed with need. I pulled away from her, positioning myself at the entrance to her body, teasing her, sliding my length through her folds before moving back to her opening and pushing in just slightly, before repeating the motion again.

She was panting, near to crying, when I finally gave her what we both wanted.

I gripped her hips hard and pushed in, rough and deep.

But she didn't seem to mind.

No, if her cry of pleasure was any indicator, she was more than happy with my desperation.

And that meant that I would have hers.

Because this could not be a meeting of equals. I had to make sure that she was the one who was desperate. She was the one who was reduced. Because I could not afford to be.

I pumped into her, chasing my release, chasing our end. She whimpered, and I pressed my hand between her shoulder blades, pushing her chest down flat on the bed, keeping her hips raised up. Then I grabbed hold of her arms, wrapped my hand around her wrist and pinned it to her lower back, then the other. I held her tight as I thrust into her, over and over again, the angle letting me go deep, the way I had her pinned keeping her motionless.

"Please," she whimpered, "please."

But I refused to end it. I kept it going, torturing her, torturing myself, the bright, brilliant flashes of pleasure that consumed me a torment that I didn't want to end. I knew what she needed. I knew that she needed me to touch her between her legs so that she could come. Or that she needed to touch herself, but I had her captive.

She began to shake, she began to weep, and I moved harder inside of her, until we had slid up the mattress, until I had to brace myself on the headboard, so we didn't collide into it. I freed her hands when I did, and she used the opportunity to shift, wiggling and putting her hands between her legs as I continued to pump inside of her.

"Don't," I bit out. "Not until I say."

"I need to," she said.

"You are my wife," I said. "My Queen. Your body belongs to me."

She went still. "Yes," she whispered. "But your body belongs to me."

She reached between her legs, beneath us, and stroked me at the point where our bodies met, and I shuddered, cursing as she did so.

"Witch," I said, finally agreeing to give her what she wanted.

I put my hand where I knew she needed me, and I pinched her gently, before stroking her, keeping time with my thrusts.

And then there were no games, no more fights for

control, because there was only pleasure. Wrapping around us, binding us together.

And when we both found our release, it was together, the violence of it shaking us, shaking the bed, shaking the very stone the palace was made of.

Shaking what I was made of.

And when it had ended, she curled up against my chest, and I couldn't play games any longer.

I hadn't won anything. I hadn't distanced myself.

When her fingers traced delicate shapes over my chest, I couldn't pretend she wasn't Marissa, couldn't pretend that it would ever be anything but heavy.

"Hercules," she whispered, "I love you."

Marissa

And that was when the walls fell down around us. My heart was still beating hard from my release. But more than that. From the admission that had just fallen from my lips. I wasn't afraid, though. There was no place for fear here. Inside my body. How could I fear when I was in his arms?

Hercules was my husband, the father of my daughter. He was the man that I loved. And with him I had always felt an absence of fear. With him I had always felt strong and solid in who I was. And what I knew from talking to my mother was this: what you allow will continue.

And I could allow for us to continue on in unspoken words. I could allow for us to stay in a world where I let safety mean more than truth.

But I didn't want that. And I didn't have to allow it.

"I love you," I repeated, again.

He shifted. "No," he said, simply, definitively.

"Hercules, I don't know who you think you're speaking to, but I am neither your daughter nor one of your subjects. I am your wife. And you don't get to tell me *no* as a response to *I love you*."

"I… No. I cannot accept."

"It wasn't a gift. It was a statement of fact."

On some level, I wasn't surprised at his denial. On some level, this didn't shock or wound me. Because how could it? This was who he was. A man made of rock, and for some reason he seemed to need to cling to the facade.

I knew that I would have to break the walls down. I knew that I couldn't simply walk up to the door and ask for entry. No. I had asked for entry, and now I would have to be willing to do battle.

"You don't understand. There is no room in my life for these kinds of emotions."

"Why not? What about Lily?"

"This has nothing to do with Lily."

"Do you love her?"

"But that is a foolish question. I have known her for a matter of weeks."

"She's your daughter. That's… That's not how that works. I've loved Lily from the moment she first came into the world, and I can tell you I didn't know her then. With children, it's not a matter of knowing them, is it? It's a matter of knowing that their lives are in your hands. That you must protect them, that you must care for them. That without you they won't know anything of the world. You're meant to be her conscience, her guidance. Her place of protection. And that… Let me tell you, Hercules, that produces feelings of love faster than knowing someone ever could. So do you intend to never love your daughter? Because you will be the only father that she ever has."

"I didn't need love. I didn't need love—it was weak, and it did nothing."

"Your father didn't love you. At least, not in the way that a normal person should. He didn't demonstrate love."

And then Hercules exploded. "Not my father. My mother. My father never said that he loved me. My father never lowered himself to tell such a lie. He never would. It was her. *I love you.* She would whisper that. Over my bruised body, but she would never do anything to stop it."

"Hercules…"

"She couldn't, and I understand that, but what did her love get for me? It meant nothing. She would go off, because she claimed she couldn't stand to see the way that he treated me, but she left me here with him. She had another child for the sole purpose of having one that she could…that she could love in the way that she wanted. Because she had to surrender me to him. So, you tell me what love ever did for me. You tell me how love makes a family. Because it never did in mine."

"Hercules," I said softly. "Your mother was wrong. Your father was wrong."

"That's a lot of people who were supposed to love me being wrong, Marissa. At a certain point a man must acknowledge that the problem might be with him."

"I love you. You think I would allow you to be submitted to torture? Do you think I wouldn't die for you?"

"No," he said, the admission ferocious. "Never offer such a thing to me. I don't deserve it. I am not worth that. Don't you ever say something like that to me again."

"Why must you reject it so?"

"Because I am last—do you understand me? That is how I must see myself. My father saw himself as first. Above all else, above anything, sovereign to the entire world. And look at the things he did. To me. To my mother."

"Hercules, your parents were broken. Undeniably. I am sorry if your mother had a difficult time of it, but that doesn't give her an excuse to allow her child to be abused. She had money. She could've fled with you. The UN would have taken care of you, something. There must have been a way that you could have escaped."

"It would have created a national incident. And I was not worth that. The chaos would've thrown the country into…"

"No. It would have healed your country years earlier. Your mother could have exposed him for the madman that he was, and what purpose did it serve for her to protect him? All it did was protect her position as Queen. That's what it did. Your parents loved themselves more than they loved you, and on that score you're correct. But love isn't what created the brokenness in that scenario. It was the lack of it. Surely you must see that."

"In any case," he said, "I don't know how to love."

"That isn't true. You do know how to love… You do…"

"No. I am not the right man for that. I'm a broken vessel, and if you pour into me, it's all going to leak out, and I won't hold a drop of it in the end. I'm not worth it, Marissa."

"You're worth everything."

"No. No."

And then he stood and walked away from me, walked naked out of the bedroom, as if he weren't a king and we weren't in a palace full of other people. I knew the hallways would be empty, but still.

I ran out into the hall, without bothering with clothes myself, but I didn't see which way he'd gone.

Then I returned to the bed and sank to it in misery.

He didn't love me. He didn't want to love me.

And I had the feeling that something permanent had happened just now. That he had closed the door on something with a finality that would break us both.

I had given up on Hercules once, and I had cast him as the villain before. But I could see him now. See him for what he was. The wounded boy who was afraid.

Because his mother had offered him love but not protection.

Because she had given him words and not actions.

It scared me. Because my mother had been faithful to my father, she had demonstrated love every day, and she had given him as he asked, and he had taken advantage of it, and nothing had changed.

But I would have to trust that Hercules was a different manner of man, and that our love was different. That it could be bigger, that it could be better.

And that I could change him.

I knew that it was ludicrous. I knew that there were multiple self-help books on the topic.

But if he didn't want me, I was better off leaving. Demanding everything or taking nothing.

I would have to have faith. Faith in that first moment we had ever met.

In that certainty I had felt then.

I had lost that faith over the years, but when the truth had come out, it had become clear that Hercules hadn't been the villain.

And I had to trust it would bear out again.

But, oh, that trust would take a leap. The bravery to remain open when all I wanted to do was close in on myself...

I got beneath the covers, not caring that I was in his room. And I curled into a ball and dissolved.

Because in the morning I would have to emerge whole. I would have to do it for Lily, for Pelion and for the future of my marriage—such as it was.

But for the first time in my memory, the hope wasn't there. That little bubble had burst, abandoning me when I needed it most.

I had an answer to the question of what remained when you were plunged into darkness, what remained when the last vestige of hope was extinguished inside you.

It was love.

When everything else failed, love remained.

And that was simply where I would have to place my trust.

Because love never failed.

It was a truth that I believed, and it was one that I would hold to. I had no other choice.

CHAPTER FOURTEEN

Hercules

I HAD NOT spoken to Marissa in days. And I told myself that it was for the best. I told myself that I was doing the right thing.

Love.

She loved me. What did love mean?

Do people abandon you often?

The words that she had spoken to me stuck now, stung. I couldn't get them out of my head. They were like a barb in my heart.

I love you. My mother had said that, every time she had left the palace. Every time she had left me there.

But she had never taken me with her.

She loved me, but I was the heir.

She loved me, but I was Xerxes's son, not really hers.

I had been her obligation to the Crown, and I had given her freedom with my very existence.

That was why she loved me.

But she loved her freedom more, and she had gone her own way, flitting about the world as I was tortured.

Going about her life as I was broken and reshaped into a weapon for the throne of Pelion.

For my father's own satisfaction.

What good were words of love if there was nothing behind them?

What was wrong with a child that his mother could speak those words so carelessly and then leave him to be devoured by the wolves?

I didn't know.

I didn't understand.

All I knew was that those words felt like they had fractured something between us. Because they reminded me of the ache that I had felt in my soul when she had spoken them.

No.

I would not allow emotion, words, to create that kind of pain inside of me.

What could I reason? What could I see and touch? Certainly never my mother's love.

Those words were useless.

And yet I craved them.

For Marissa.

And I thought of Lily…

Lily, my own daughter, who I was avoiding like a true coward, because…

What if I gave her the words and failed miserably in the execution of them?

I didn't even know what love was supposed to look like.

The bloodline of my family was poison. And that was all it was. A bloodline, and not a family.

It was all I knew. All I understood.

I had taken to prowling the halls at night, because I couldn't sleep. My need for Marissa was like a sickness, and I didn't trust that I wouldn't go to her in a moment of weakness. This was what she had reduced me to. A man who did not trust himself. A man who wandered the halls of his own palace, questioning his sanity and trying to breathe around fractured pieces in his heart.

It was then I heard a sound. A whimpering sound, and I stopped for a moment, trying to figure out the source of it. It was the sound of a child, and for a moment that struck me as strange. Because for a moment, I could only think of myself.

I had whimpered like that in this palace, reduced to such a thing at the hands of my father. I couldn't move. Not then.

But I was jarred back to the present, and I knew it could not be me, for I was standing on my feet, and I was a man, not a child. And I was not helpless, which meant I had to move toward the sound, whatever it was.

I stopped at the door, and her name slammed into my mind.

Lily. Of course it was Lily.

I had been pushing her away in my mind, pushing Marissa away, and there she was, crying out.

And I could not turn away from her. That much I knew.

I pushed the door open slowly and saw her lying there in the bed, turning over and over fitfully, wrapping herself up in the blankets.

Her dark hair covered her eyes, and she looked distressed.

I crossed the room, feeling like anything but a king,

feeling like the lowest of men. Because I didn't know what to do, and none of my power, none of my money and none of my status would give me insight into what the best course of action should be.

But I couldn't abandon her.

"Lily," I whispered.

I went to the bed and sat on the edge, pressing my hand against her forehead. "Lily," I repeated.

"Daddy!" She sat upright and nearly crawled up my body, wrapping her arms around my neck. "Daddy. I dreamed that we were taken away from you. From here."

I was stunned into silence by that. That Lily's worst nightmare would be to be taken from here.

"I don't want to not know you," she said. "I remember when I didn't know you. It wasn't as good."

She clung to me with trust, this child, with helplessness and sadness, and I felt undone. Because who was I to deserve this?

She was so vulnerable…so helpless…

She felt her life was better for having me in it.

She didn't know. She didn't know who I was, how broken I was inside.

And she didn't care.

She loved me with an openness that had nothing to do with knowing me and everything to do with what I represented, and I kept thinking of what Marissa had said to me.

This was the love of a child.

A love so freely given, a love that didn't even have to be earned.

No, a love like this had to be stripped away.

And my parents had done that to me.

To me, when I had been like Lily.

When I would have happily crawled into either of their laps and offered them all my small heart.

Because that was what children did, and it was how they were made.

They came into the world with innocence, and it was taken.

"I can't sleep," she said.

"You haven't tried," I said.

"I know I can't. Will you sing me a song?"

"A song?" My heart thundered in my temples. "I don't sing."

"Everyone sings," she said matter-of-factly, and I didn't know how to argue with that.

I tried to think if I knew any songs that were suitable for children. The only thing that came to mind was something my nanny used to sing to me when I was a child. Back when I'd had a nanny…when there had been one soft person in my world.

The words were in Greek, so I clumsily tried to translate them along with the tune.

"Dear child, dear child, you've no need to cry.

Dear child, dear child, count the stars in the sky.

Dear child, dear child, rest your sleepy head.

Dear child, my child, rest in my heart.

For it is I who will love you even in your dreams."

"Promise?" she asked, her voice small and tired.

"I promise," I said.

And I meant it.

I would love her. I would protect her. I would fight armies for her.

And that no one had done it for me...

It was their failure, not mine.

To see myself through the eyes of a parent was... stunning.

My father had taken me when I was as young as Lily and put his hands on me to hurt me.

I touched Lily's cheek. I could not imagine harming her, let alone ordering that others harm her.

I would kill first. Anyone who dared harm a hair on her head.

My eyes felt dry.

Marissa had looked at me with trust and love once. And it was only there as I sat on the bed holding our daughter that I realized it.

The first time she saw me. A full acceptance of what was happening between us, even though it made no sense. Just implicit love. Implicit trust.

And I had thrown it back at her. She had been alone and pregnant, thrown out on her own. She had been wounded in my absence, and what had I done when I'd found her again? I had condemned her the same way so many others had.

And then...she had married me. She hadn't punished me by withholding Lily. She had given me my daughter, given me what I needed to run my country.

And then she had given me her body.

Given me her love.

I was suddenly overwhelmed by all this love that I knew for a fact I would never be able to earn.

This love that I wasn't being asked to earn.

Love.

I had been so convinced that it wasn't real, because I couldn't reason it out.

But that, I suddenly realized, was the beauty of love.

You might not be able to reason it out, but you could see it. You could touch it. You could feel it. And anything you couldn't see, touch and feel wasn't love. It was just words.

Hollow words that lacked any action.

And I was shamed, because I had not seen what was right before me. The gift that had been Marissa for the last five years.

When I was certain Lily was asleep, I dropped a kiss on her head, and I went down the hall.

I knew it was midnight. I knew that Marissa was probably sleeping, but this couldn't wait. It couldn't.

What good was being a king if you couldn't wake people up in the middle of the night when you were having an important revelation?

I didn't knock; I opened the door to her bedroom, and I realized that it couldn't be her bedroom anymore.

We needed a bedroom, together.

Because we were one, after all.

She and I had spoken of souls, and I had rejected the notion of them, but I knew now that they were real. And mine was tied with hers. The match, the mate. All manner of mystical things that I hadn't believed in before.

But didn't they come back to faith?

I had never believed I was a man of faith, but Marissa had shown me different.

"What are you doing here?" She was not asleep; she was perched on the edge of the bed in a white nightgown, looking confused. Though I imagined she had not been looking confused before I came into the room.

"We need to talk."

"It's after midnight."

"I know, but you are not sleeping."

"No. I haven't been. Not since…"

"I know," I said, moving to where she sat on the edge of the bed. Then I dropped to my knees, debasing myself for a second time in such a short period. But it would always be for them. For Marissa and Lily, and it would never be anything less than they deserved. For they were my life, my heart, my mission. And everything good that I did in the kingdom of Pelion would be an extension of that.

Of the love that existed between us.

"Lily had a nightmare," I said.

"Oh no. Is she okay?"

"She's fine. She's… She's beautiful. She's perfect. Marissa," I said, her name broken. "Marissa, I… I didn't realize. I didn't realize how love worked. I didn't realize how a child could love a parent, because I'd forgotten. I'd forgotten what it was like. They stole it from me. They tore it away from me, stripped it right out of my body. They hurt me. Abused me, abandoned me. And I thought something had to be broken in me, but when I looked down at Lily, so vulnerable and small and crying like that… The unspeakable wickedness of someone who could harm a child, who could tell them they love them and then leave them. It was not me. And you and Lily… You showed me what love really is. You are unwavering, Marissa. You gave me more than I've ever deserved. I sure as hell didn't earn it.

"All this grace that you bestowed upon me. This un-merited, unearned, unasked-for favor… It is like salva-tion, and I was too afraid to admit that I needed it. But I was in the darkness without you."

"Hercules… I… I have loved you, from the moment we met, but I'm sure that you loved me since then as well. I know you have."

"I have," I said, my voice rough. "I have loved you. It took hold of me that first day, and I didn't recognize it, because I didn't know a connection with women that was about something other than lust. What we had grew into lust, after we had a friendship, and I'd never ex-perienced anything like that. Someone who loved me after they knew me. Someone I wanted to speak to and sleep with in equal measure."

"You feel like your mother abandoned you," she said softly. "That's why it hurt you so much when you thought I'd left."

"I thought you cared about me. And I never put the two things together, because I did not think about my mother and her own fault in what had happened to me, because I could not bear to hate them both… But… Yes. That is why. Because I finally thought that someone cared for me again and then… And then that."

"I would never have left you," she said. "Believe that. And I won't now. No matter what. What we have is real. And it's worth fighting for. It's worth clinging to. Even if neither of us are perfect. Especially if neither of us are perfect. Because this was never about *perfect*. I grew up thinking that I had to be perfect. That I had to try to live up to this impossible thing. But my father left out grace. He left out joy. He left out love. And we'll fill our lives with that, surround ourselves with it."

"I never knew what it was, not really," I said, my voice rough. "But I would very much like to have a lifetime of discovering it with you."

"So would I," she said. "I knew that I found something special the first day I met you. And it scared me. Because I also knew that it would change everything. That you could ruin all of me. But I needed to be ruined. That old me, she needed to be ruined, so that I could be made whole."

"We will be whole together," I said. "I know that I told you I didn't believe in souls. That I didn't believe in things I could not see. But I see you. I see you, Marissa. And I feel that you love me. And I feel… I love you too. I have, from the beginning. I just didn't know what it was. I didn't know what to call it. I didn't know what to do with it."

"Neither did I," she said. "And I could never have known that we would end here. What a road that we walked. Separate for a while, but I'm ready to be together."

"And you know… With my father dead, we don't have to stay married. I have the throne. I have made Lily legitimate."

"You're not suggesting that we…get divorced."

"Never," I said. "But what I do want you to understand is that I'm not staying married to you for the bloodline. I'm not bound by anything. My country is not in peril. You are free to go, and I'm free to ask you to leave. But I won't ask that. I hope that you'll stay."

"You know I will," she said, scooting closer to me and grabbing hold of my face. "You know I will forever."

"I love you," I said.

And it was the first time I could ever remember saying those words to another person. "I love you," I said again. "And I love Lily." Suddenly, desperation filled my chest. "I need to go tell her."

She laughed. "No, you don't. It can wait until morning."

"It doesn't feel like it can. Everything feels desperate. So... I've never felt like this before. I love you. I love you so much."

"If it feels desperate, then perhaps we should explore that. Together."

And this time when she took me into her arms, and took me into her bed, it was not merely as lustful young people on a beach, not merely as husband and wife, but as a man and woman who were desperately in love.

And I knew that we would be that forever.

"I pledge myself to you," I said. "And I pledge to love you above all else."

"But you must love the country," she said.

"Everything good that I am comes from my love for you. My love for Lily stems from that, and what you taught me. My desire to be a good king in a richer, deeper sense than what my father was comes from loving you. I will love you above all others, above all else, for as long as I shall live."

"And I shall do the same."

EPILOGUE

Marissa

IT WAS A wonderful blessing, watching Hercules gaze at our son in the private nursing wing the day I gave birth. Lily was thrilled to have a little brother, and her excitement was difficult to contain. My mother had finally taken her home a few hours ago, exhausted. And that left Hercules and myself.

"I'm very glad that you got to see this. That you were part of it this time."

"So am I," he said, his voice rough as he gazed down at Leonidas.

Such a big name for such a tiny creature.

"You have a son."

"And a daughter," he said. "And I will protect both of them with every breath left in me. They will never question my love for them."

"No," I agreed, "they won't."

Our lives had been filled with love that no one on earth could ever question these past months. Hercules was the best King, the best husband, the best father. I was blissfully happy in a way I hadn't known it was possible to be. And it all seemed to just keep expanding.

That was the beautiful thing we were both discovering about love. It had no limits.

I looked at him, and I was cast back.

I'll never forget the first time I saw Prince Hercules, standing there on a beach.

Hercules, who was now King. Who bore a name fit for a god but who, blessedly for me, was a man. A man I loved.

And I never could have guessed that it would lead here, to a maternity ward in a hospital halfway across the world, to me being a queen, us being married, us being so blissfully in love neither of us could see straight.

I had been so certain he was my downfall. But in the end, I hadn't fallen. I had grown wings strong enough to fly. And now we flew together, my King and I.

It would be easy to call it fate, and perhaps whatever had brought us together was fate. But what kept us together was love. A love more powerful than all the pain the world had given to us.

And it was love that would sustain us.

Always.

* * * * *

CONFESSIONS
OF AN ITALIAN
MARRIAGE

DANI COLLINS

To the stars of *Murderball*, who made me think,
'those high-octane alphas would make a great romance hero,'
one of whom who patiently simmered in my head
for fifteen years until bursting to life in Giovanni.

And to my editor Megan, who nudges my stories in
directions I hadn't considered and always makes them better.

PROLOGUE

HELL HATH NO fury like a woman whose husband faked his own death.

Freja Catalano smiled with appropriately bedazzled delight as she took a selfie in the mirrors that surrounded where she stood on the small, carpeted dais in the back of Milan's most exclusive bridal boutique.

"I can take the photo," offered the designer, Teresina. She paused in her reverent arranging of the abundant and infinitely delicate chiffon overskirt. Every inch was tastefully embroidered with white flowers and swirling vines, seed pearls and sequins. The train puddled out for six feet behind Freja's reflection.

As Freja ran her image through different filters, a tiny prickling awareness swept across her scalp and into her shoulders. She lifted her head and glanced toward the closed curtain across the archway into the front of the shop, but there was no one there, just the sound of a bridezilla complaining about a swatch of organza.

"This is fine, thanks," Freja replied absently as she tapped out her selection and started typing her caption to post online. Her stomach remained full of unsettled butterflies, though.

#FinalFitting #BigDay #OneMonthAway #CantWait

As Teresina pinched seams and took in the narrow band of pearl-bedecked satin that formed the waistband of the gown, she asked around pins in her mouth, "Is the photo for your mother?"

"My social feed. My mother passed when I was young." Freja added several more hashtags about bridal nerves, first love and winter weddings in New York.

"I'm so sorry. I presumed she was in Sweden and would be attending the wedding."

"No, both of my parents are gone." And the wedding that had crushed Freja's soul for them to miss had already happened. Freja had worn a simple ivory sheath and held tulips stolen from a public garden. It had been perfect.

Or so she'd believed at the time.

And since that had been a short four and a half months ago, and since her first groom had "died" three weeks later, Freja's name was dominating the click-bait headlines with variations of *Gold-Digger to Grave-Digger* troll droppings.

Not that Freja's notoriety had bothered Terasina. Freja had earned Terasina's undying loyalty by stating, "Everyone knows Milan is superior to Paris." The fact Freja had taken possession of her husband's wealth and could buy this boutique thousands of times over didn't hurt either.

Freja didn't mention she had only come here because she was confident Giovanni was in his home country.

This is what I'm spending your money on. Do you

like it? She didn't write that, just finished tagging Teresina, the boutique and—

"Does your fiancé follow you?" Teresina asked with concern. "It's bad luck for him to see the dress before the wedding."

"I guess it is, isn't it?" Freja finished tagging Nels and hit Post.

Nels was a recent graduate of business law who was drowning in debt and firmly in the closet for family reasons. In exchange for stepping into Giovanni's non-existent shoes, Freja had promised to assure Nels's terminally ill grandmother that she loved him passionately and eternally.

It was a match made in screamingly civilized practicality.

"Tell him not to peek," Teresina suggested as she straightened and gently tested the hidden banding that secured the off-the-shoulder sleeves. The bodice was made of Venetian lace exquisitely crafted to plunge in both front and back, painting Freja's torso in white flames that danced down both arms to her wrists. "I can't imagine any man seeing you like this could resist you, though."

Freja smiled weakly, not revealing that the one man she had hoped to get a rise from had very firmly resisted.

She completely ignored the agonized whisper in the back of her head that asked, *What if he's really dead?*

He wasn't. Snakes of anxiety slithered in her middle over his continued absence, but she had plenty of reasons to believe he was still alive. Okay, more like a handful of subtle coincidences and one decent piece of evidence that wasn't solid enough to prove anything, not even a robbery. When she had tried to tell Nels she thought there was a chance her husband could be alive, however, he'd given her a look of pity and suggested she was stuck in the denial stage of grief.

Maybe she was. She had fought seeing Giovanni's true feelings toward her, right up until that final conversation.

Do you love me? Do you even want to be married?

You're behaving like a jealous shrew. Wait for me in my hotel room. I'll join you when I've finished my meeting.

He hadn't. And dead or not, Giovanni had left his fortune in her hands. She was wholly unequipped to manage it. Nels had lived on her floor when she'd been at university and had been kind enough to look over her book contract and, later, her prenuptial agreement. When she'd gone to him with the volumes of legal documents that were coming her way as a result of her husband's supposed demise, he'd been alarmed by the overreach some of Giovanni's top executives were attempting.

Freja was a millennial with pale blond hair, blue eyes, and no formal schooling until her degree in creative writing. Obviously, that meant she was a certified bubblehead who couldn't so much as recognize when a fast food outlet was trying to upsell her a supersize of fries. Her knowledge on running a multinational corporation was zero, but she was smart enough to see phrases like "irrevocable power of attorney" as the horrendous red flags that they were.

Another woman would have snatched up the reins

and stared down the sexist pigs trying to take advantage of her. Freja might have, if she hadn't been brittle with grief. Meanwhile, every meeting had been full of vultures making advances, baldly trying to flatter her into a relationship as a shortcut to Giovanni's money. It was exhausting. She didn't have the stomach for it, especially not for a fortune she neither wanted nor needed.

Nels had trusted her with his secret back when she'd shyly asked him on a date because he felt so unthreatening. He had minored in corporate ethics and longed to effect change at the highest levels. Remarrying would offer her protection from the vultures, so their grand bargain had been struck.

Was it bigamy if her first husband was secretly still alive and the second marriage was only on paper? She had asked Nels, but he had given her that pitying look again and said, "I need to know you're of sound mind or we can't do this."

Giovanni was the only person who could prove it was illegal. If he wanted to burst in at the last second to stop it, fine. But she wouldn't hold her breath. She really would be the clichéd dumb blonde if she failed to get the message that her husband didn't want to be tied to her after he had *staged an explosion* to end things.

No, she accepted that their whirlwind romance had fizzled as quickly as it had flared. If that left her feeling as bleak and wraithlike as a wisp of smoke, well, she only had herself to blame. She had known there was no such thing as forever, but she'd gone ahead and fallen for him anyway. Her heart had been broken into a thousand pieces for her trouble.

"Bellissima." Teresina finished her fussing and kissed the tips of her fingers. "Shall we try it with the veil?"

The muted ping of the bell at the front silenced the squirrel-like chatter out there. It happened so abruptly, Teresina and Freja both looked toward the closed curtain. Freja's stomach clenched with apprehension.

A male voice asked to see the manager.

The hair on the back of Freja's neck stood up. She didn't know that voice precisely, but she'd been on high alert since Giovanni's "death." The explosion had been reported as an accident, but she was convinced it had been a deliberate attempt to kill him. She understood that meant she could be a target, too.

Maybe she was paranoid. Maybe it was just a salesman. She had no reason to believe that authoritative voice was here for her. Any man who wanted to meet with her could make an appointment through her agent or Nels or any number of other channels. They wouldn't hunt her down in a wedding boutique.

But as the clerk said, "I'll see if she's available," and the silence remained absolute, a cold layer of perspiration burst onto Freja's skin.

Teresina smiled an apology and started for the curtain.

Freja forced an unbothered smile as adrenaline poured into her extremities, clenching her lungs and tightening her hand on her phone.

As Teresina slipped past the curtain, Freja moved without second-guessing her instinct. She scooped up her miles of skirt and ran silently on the toes of her five-inch heels past the door into the changing room, where she'd left her clothes and purse, past the powder room, into the administration office, where she'd first met with Teresina and seen the—

Porta di emergenza allarmata.

That's what this was. An emergency. She was alarmed.

She shoved against the lever and burst into the narrow cobblestone alley. A loud bell began to ring within the shop. The door clattered closed behind her, muffling the sound. It grew fainter as she raced toward the street, where traffic honked in its usual chaotic madness.

She was only thinking she needed witnesses. Getting arrested for stealing a dress she'd only half paid for was better than facing whatever *that* man had in store for her. She could call Nels from the police sta—

Behind her, she heard the door slam open again. Shouts sounded.

In front of her, a black SUV swerved into the sidewalk, forcing her to pull up short at the mouth of the alley. She started to pivot in hopes of squeezing past it and down the street, but the back door flung open.

"Get in," Giovanni said.

The sight of him struck like a gong, leaving her quivering. He had a shaggy black beard and dark glasses, and his black hoodie was pulled up to hide all but his familiar cheekbones, but his legs stopped above the knees and she recognized the tense line of his mouth.

Alive. Her heart soared so high, it should have shattered the sky.

At the same time, a thousand furies invaded her like a swarm of killer bees. There was no triumph in learning she was right. There was only a crippling heartbreak that he had abandoned her. If he'd been truly dead, she would have been angry, but she wouldn't have blamed him.

This, though? He had put her through horrifying hours of actually believing he was gone. She had endured his gut-wrenching funeral, convinced it was a sham. Then, two short weeks later, she'd suffered another unbearable loss that would never heal.

He'd forced her to go through all of that *alone*.

For every minute that had passed since that awful day, she had longed for him to reveal himself, but now her feet only carried her forward so she could bitterly hiss, "Go to *hell*."

"Where do you think I've been?" he growled.

"I'm calling the police!" Teresina yelled from deep in the alley. Two of Teresina's employees were recording everything on their phones.

A man in a suit was running toward her. She instinctively moved closer to Giovanni, heart jamming with fear.

Giovanni's hard arm looped around her and he dragged her into the back of the car. He clutched the door frame for leverage, but his strength was as annoyingly effortless as always.

She didn't fight him. In fact, once he grabbed her out of her stasis, she helped, kicking against the edge of the door to thrust herself inside, desperate for whatever sanctuary he offered.

They wound up in a heap on the back seat while the man who was chasing her came up to the open door and reached for her leg.

She screamed and kicked at him with her sharp heels.

He dodged her shoes and threw the yards of silk in after her, then slammed the door before he leaped into the passenger seat in front of Giovanni.

"Go," Giovanni said to the driver, and he pushed himself upright.

As the SUV sped into traffic, Freja rocked deeper into the seat, stunned to her toes.

CHAPTER ONE

Six months ago...

"ARE THOSE THE MUSHROOMS?" a woman asked, catching Freja's attention as she circulated with a tray of canapés.

Freja paused at the clutch of guests perched on sectional benches in the reception hall, waiting for the ballroom doors to open. Everyone wore beaded gowns and tuxedos and one man was in a wheelchair—

"Oh, my God!"

The tray and its contents would have slipped right off her hand if he hadn't caught it with an effortless reflex.

Giovanni Catalano. She'd checked up on him through the years, so she knew him instantly. His father had been an Italian ambassador, his mother a well-known heiress. Giovanni had been left in a wheelchair by the same car crash that had killed his parents and older brother. He'd become a Paralympic athlete, then later developed software apps that had earned him obscene amounts of money—as if what he'd inherited hadn't been enough. He had since broadened his investments to become a billionaire at thirty-two.

His wealth and power cloaked him in authority and

an air of earned arrogance, but she hadn't expected him to project so much sheer magnetism.

He was ridiculously handsome and compelling. His tuxedo didn't have to do any work, but its pleated shirt and white bow tie accentuated his tanned, clean-shaven jaw. His jacket was beautifully tailored to his wide shoulders, and the crisp trousers were neatly hemmed to drape a few inches past where his legs stopped above the knee.

His bone structure was to die for with his stern brow, sensual lips and heavy-lidded bedroom eyes. It was impossible to tell the color of his irises in the subdued lighting of the reception hall, but she knew them to be stormy gray.

She belatedly straightened while he continued to hold her dumbfounded stare, absently offering the tray to the group as he did.

Someone tittered about him missing his calling.

Freja was only dimly aware of the world beyond their sustained eye contact. Her heart was racing as though she'd run up ten flights of stairs. A flush of something like shyness or embarrassment was washing through her along with strange tugs and a tremendous sensual awareness throughout her entire body.

She tried to dismiss it as the silly vestiges of an infatuation that was so far in the past, it shouldn't affect her now. It hadn't even been *him* she'd had a pre-pubescent crush on!

That wasn't what this was, though. This was far more intense. Physical.

Was it *lust*? How mortifying.

He swiveled the empty tray back to her and cocked one eyebrow. "Do I know you?"

"No!" She nearly choked on her tongue. "I mean, I met y— I thought you were someone else." Not true, but her very brief history with his brother wasn't something she wanted to blurt out in front of strangers. Far too many questions followed when she spoke about her childhood.

"We've never met," she hurried to affirm in a sputter, but her discomfiture made him narrow his eyes. Butterflies invaded her stomach. "Have a nice evening."

She took the tray and walked away with a dizzy stagger. It took everything in her not to look back over her shoulder as she fetched more canapés and continued serving.

Nearly a full hour passed in which she tracked back and forth, waiting for everyone to filter into the ballroom and find their seats. She forced a smile and concentrated on not becoming clumsy when her limbs didn't feel as if they were her own.

Giovanni Catalano stayed on her radar the entire time.

Was it her imagination or was she on his? She didn't catch him looking at her, but she experienced the sensation of being observed.

She lost track of him once everyone had finally entered the ballroom, though. Still disconcerted, she busied herself with gathering abandoned napkins and dishes from the reception hall. The sense of being watched returned and she spun around.

His wheels had made his approach nearly silent, but

there he was. An intense zing of electrical awareness went through her, so sharp it hurt.

"Come." He neatly pivoted and rolled down the hall.

Her heart lurched and she glanced to see the people in the ballroom were watching screens flashing to life with a presentation. Her colleagues would be looking for her to help serve shortly, but she could slip away unnoticed for a few minutes. Pulse racing unevenly, she followed.

Giovanni ducked down a corridor, turned the handle on a door, and led her into the empty cloakroom. A handful of light wraps and jackets hung on the racks, but the shutters were closed and the attendant absent.

He swiveled to confront her and nodded for her to close the door.

She did, still astonished to be in his presence.

"*Have* we met?" he demanded.

"No. I mean, I know who you are." Freja wished she'd kept her tray, needing a shield of some type. Not that she felt unsafe, but nor did she feel completely safe, either. Something about him struck her as dangerous in ways she couldn't articulate. Not that he wanted to hurt her, but she suspected he *could*. He was so muscled and had that air of power.

She was breathless in his presence for no explicable reason, completely beyond her depth—which was odd for her. She rolled with punches and was almost always ten steps ahead of most people around her.

Nevertheless, she found herself sinking into the single wooden chair tucked beneath an empty section of a rack, weakened simply by the force of his personality.

A brief flicker of surprise went across his expression as she came down to his eye level.

"Why did you give those people the impression we've had sex?" he asked bluntly.

"I didn't. Did I?" She pressed into the hard rungs of the chair back. "No one thought that! Why would they?"

"They not only thought it, they judged me a cradle robber." His turbulent gaze took her in from crown to toes. "You're what? Twenty-two?"

"Twenty-three." Not a young twenty-three, either. At least, she knew a lot of people her age who were far less capable of looking after themselves. He made her feel positively juvenile, though. Like those perfectly sensible students who spouted feminist doctrines, then grew flushed and got all high-voiced around the football quarterback. "I'm really embarrassed for reacting like that." She fought to keep her voice steady and clear. "I didn't mean to."

"Why did you?" His demeanor was both compelling and faintly ominous. "Who did you think I was?"

"No one. Well… It was a prevarication. I knew right away that you're…" Oh, God, she was touching her hair. Playing with the fine hairs beneath her ponytail, where the hollow at the back of her neck was prickly with heightened awareness. Exactly like a flirty cheerleader. She clasped her hands in her lap. "I met your brother once. When I was a child."

His head went back and his whole body bunched as though preparing for a fight. His hands closed into fists and his jaw hardened.

She understood that reaction. It happened to her sometimes when people mentioned her father. Years of carrying grief didn't mean it no longer had the power to knock the wind out of you, especially when it arrived out of the blue.

"He made an impression," she continued gently, understanding, too, that there could be a gift hidden behind the sucker punch. A new memory could bring that person to life again, if only for a brief, intangible moment. "It was a fencing class for children."

"In Sicily?" Another raking glance filled with skepticism.

"I was there with my father. He often enrolled me in local activities while he worked. Stefano was teaching with a girl named Paloma."

Giovanni's head jerked slightly at the sound of his brother's name. He offered her a three-quarter profile under the unforgiving fluorescent light. "You would have been very young. Seven?" he calculated.

"He said I had potential." She smiled with nostalgia for the little girl who had developed instant hero worship from being noticed by such a dynamic young man. "I thought I would go on to become an Olympian like him."

His cheek ticked. "Did you?"

"No." Laughably, she wasn't much of anything, not even a proper US citizen. One day she might become a schoolteacher. At best she could call herself an author, but she wasn't even published yet and was riding on her father's coattails. "No, that swashbuckling fantasy went the way of my equally delusional dream that I would grow up and marry him."

His choked-off laugh could have been actual humor

or a measure of outrage that she would dare to aspire to marry such a man.

"He was always flirting with Paloma during class," she explained. "He was so dashing and full of compliments, he became the ideal against which I judged all other boys when I grew old enough to have an interest in them. None had much chance after that." She sighed wistfully, laughing at herself before she sobered. "I was devastated when I heard he'd been killed. It was the first time I understood that people could die before their time."

He was staring holes through her, leaving hollow spaces, but she said what was in her because she knew she would regret it if she didn't take this chance to express her sincere condolences when she had this chance.

"He talked about you with fondness. I was worried about you after the accident. Sad for you losing your brother and your parents. I always wanted a sibling myself." She shrugged self-consciously at having such depth of compassion for a complete stranger. "I've looked you up over the years—which makes me sound like a stalker, I suppose, but I only viewed public things like your events at the games and read up on the apps you developed. That's why I recognized you and acted so strangely. I'm sorry I made you uncomfortable."

Uncomfortable? Giovanni snorted. He had thought his cover was blown.

Maybe it was. Freja—why had she only given him her first name?—was setting off all sorts of alarms on his internal gauges, from self-preservation to the sexual ones he did his best to ignore.

She was too beautiful to disregard out of hand, though, even in a cheap, ill-fitting catering uniform. Her black vest hugged her slender waist, emphasizing the thrust of her hips and breasts. She wasn't tall, but he'd watched her for an hour and she moved like a dancer, graceful and light. There wasn't a speck of makeup on her face, but her translucent skin looked soft and luminous as baby powder. Her lashes and brows were nearly invisible, glinting pale gold, same as the hair pulled back into a simple ponytail. Her blue eyes bloomed like cornflowers and her pale pink lips looked smooth as rose petals.

That impression of absolute innocence was an illusion, though. She possessed an underlying maturity that allowed her to hold his gaze with disconcerting confidence—and imbue their stare with a pulse of male-female awareness.

Proceed with caution, he warned himself, even as he rationalized that he had no choice but to proceed.

"Have dinner with me tomorrow."

She blinked, appearing startled by the invitation, which didn't line up with his apprehension that she had approached him for the sole purpose of nurturing a better acquaintance.

Her hesitation could also be an illusion, he reminded himself, but it caused a surprisingly brutal clench of disappointment in him. "No?"

"If I can switch my shift, yes," she said with a shy smile. "Thank you. I'd like that." She was looking at him much the way he was studying her. *Who is this person? I must find out.*

He couldn't allow her to see beneath his surface,

of course, but oh, did he want to dig beneath hers. He took her number.

"I should get back," she said with a glance to the closed door, but she didn't rise. She studied him with an expectancy, as though she was waiting for something more.

To hell with it. The manufactured shell of a persona he wore was necessary, but he was all man beneath. A nudge of his wheels and he was close enough to touch her. He didn't. Not yet. He managed to maintain some shred of self-control, but he wanted to. Unless…

"I'm not my brother."

"I know." Her brow quirked, dismissing the very idea. "That was a childish crush, not—"

He lifted his brows, confounded by her and fighting not to show it.

"Whatever this is." Her gaze searched his.

Yes, what was it? He wanted to know, too. He absently braked his wheels and dropped his hand on the edge of her chair. He felt the small jolt in her thigh against his inner wrist as he leaned in, waited a half second for her to decide if she wanted to reject him, then set his mouth against hers.

He'd been so focused on the job at hand for so long, he'd forgotten how satisfying it was to let himself feel. To *taste*. To experience the surprised tremble of a woman's lips. Hers were as smooth and soft as they looked, parting with welcome and moving in tentative response.

Hooks of desire snagged into him while a wind seemed to buffet them, making them sway. He lifted his free hand to her neck, drew her forward a fraction more so he could deepen their kiss, suddenly ravenous

for all things sexual. For *her*. His blood became fire
and she was the rain.

She made a noise that was pleasure and surrender,
gorgeous and evocative. She leaned into him. One of
her hands found his arm, the other touched his shoulder.

Without breaking their kiss, he gathered her and
dragged her into his lap.

She gasped, eyes blinking open with surprise before
her arms went around his shoulders. She set her mouth
against his and made another of those blissful humming
noises as her breasts mashed against his chest.

She was making this too easy. He knew that objec-
tively, and he wasn't so desperate for female company
that he took it where he found it. He shouldn't allow this
seemingly unfettered response of hers to fuel his, but he
was racing past normal checkpoints. In another instinctive move, he dug his fingers into her hip and pressed
her deeper into the cradle of his thighs, wanting the
weight and pressure of her in the places he could feel it.

Her hands went into his hair as if she knew how sensitive his scalp was. The tingle of pleasure was so acute,
he had to bite back a ragged groan. He buried the sound
in her throat as he ran his mouth down to her collar, suddenly starving, wanting all of her, right here, right now.

A pair of women walked past the far side of the
vented panel that was the only thing hiding them from
view. Their gossipy voices yanked him back to an
awareness that he and Freja were essentially in public.

She stared at him the way a stranger might who had
blindly stepped in front of his car, her whole life flashing in her eyes while her shiny lips quivered in astonishment that she was still intact.

He felt the same, which was sobering enough to steady his galloping heart.

"Tomorrow," he promised, forcing himself to remember that she might be a plant. He helped her to her feet, determined to use the time between now and then to find out.

And even though he would need every minute of that time to assess whether he could trust her, he was already urging that time to pass quickly.

Freja walked briskly to the Manhattan restaurant from the gallery where she'd been working a few blocks away.

Her catering uniform was in a bag over her shoulder. She had already changed into a tweed skirt over knee-high boots with red leggings and a red turtleneck. She'd topped it with a brown motorcycle jacket mined from a thrift store. When she had combed out her hair, it had immediately lost the waves she'd hoped to retain by keeping it in a plait all day. No such luck. As always, it was fine as spider silk and arrow-straight. She had plopped a newsboy cap over it and called it "good enough."

The busy street was carpeted in cherry blossom petals from the trees that lined it. It made a snowy carpet for Giovanni where he had parked his chair beside the wrought iron rail that surrounded a massive oak. He was reading something on his phone. The collar of his white shirt poked from his gray pullover, and the end of a pale blue scarf flicked in the breeze like the tip of a cat's tail. He was casual and stunningly elegant, definitely not wearing anything that had been purchased secondhand.

Both road and foot traffic were heavy and noisy, but he lifted his head and looked straight at her as she approached, as though he'd been aware of her from the moment she turned the corner at the end of the block. His black hair was charmingly ruffled by the breeze, his tanned face naturally stern, yet lit with probing curiosity.

"You've written a book," was his cryptic greeting. "It's very compelling."

"How—"

She cut herself off as he lifted a hand, leaving her in the awkward position of rebuffing his invitation to embrace and kiss in greeting or bend to accept it. She'd been reliving last night's kiss nonstop, so she set her hand on his shoulder and leaned in.

Something flashed in his gray eyes—humor, surprise—then an inferno of heat before he steadied her with one hard arm and captured her mouth with startling greed. Her heart leaped and her feet seemed to leave the ground. All of her felt suspended and floating as she abandoned herself to the wonder that was his mouth playing over hers.

She could have kissed him forever, here in the street, while strangers brushed by them. *He* was a stranger, she reminded herself distantly, but he didn't feel like one. She felt as though he'd been calling to her for her entire life and she had finally caught up to him.

He let their kiss dwindle to a series of briefer tastes while a rumble of deprivation sounded in his throat. He kept her hand in his own as she straightened. She locked her soggy knees, trying to remain upright.

"I was offering to take your bag, but thank you."

His mouth curved with amusement, while his heavy eyelids transmitted a smoldering beam of sensual appreciation. "I've been thinking about you and wanted to do that again."

"Oh, my God." She ducked her brow behind her free hand, flustered at having read the situation so wrongly.

He released a soft chuckle across her knuckles and kissed the back of her hand. "Give me your bag and we'll get out of this wind."

She slid her bag from her shoulder and set it in his lap, then obeyed his wave that invited her to walk down the ramp ahead of him. Inside, he passed her bag to the maître d' and she gave up her jacket before they were shown through the intimate dining lounge.

From the outside, with its small street-level windows, she had presumed this was a midrange Italian restaurant. It was far more impressive and exclusive. Subtle lighting lent intimacy to the sumptuous furniture arranged in private pockets and alcoves. A harpist in the middle of the room plucked a soothing mood into the air. A woman in a corner wore an epoch's worth of diamonds, while the man sampling wine was a famous American with a full complement of EGOT awards. His companion was a well-known human rights lawyer.

"Am I dressed all right?" Freja asked in a whisper.

"You're perfect," he assured her.

Moments later they were settled at a discreet table. His chair was armless and streamlined, but still too bulky for the space on the opposite side of the table. He slid into the spot on the side, close enough that only the corner of the table separated them.

She self-consciously set aside her cap and dropped

her phone into it, then flicked her hair behind her shoulders, aware of him watching her as he ordered a bottle of wine.

When they were alone, she cleared her throat and said, "I was going to ask how you learned about my book." She'd only given him her first name yesterday, partly because it tended to prompt the conversation she could feel building right now. "I'm even more interested in how you have a copy? It doesn't come out until the fall."

"I'm extremely well-connected." His mouth quirked as though that was an understatement. "I received it an hour ago, so I haven't read all of it. You're still in Mongolia. My sense is that it gets worse before it gets better." He grew somber.

Various accounts of her story had been excerpted in the news when she was first freed. Throughout her recent four years at university, while writing the book, she had read aloud sections in class or circulated them for feedback. She was used to a reaction of sheer disbelief or dismay that she wasn't more disparaging of the people who'd held her.

Giovanni only waited patiently for her to respond.

"I think we've established that loss is as bad as it gets," she murmured.

"True," he agreed in a grave tone. "Is that why you wanted to write it? As an homage to your father? I'd heard of him, but only vaguely as a travel writer. I had no idea he'd been such an avid blogger. And so political."

Something in that leading statement caused her a brief flashback to those early days of arriving in America, when government types had interrogated her incessantly. Giovanni was the son of an ambassador, she reminded herself. His interest was likely ingrained from his early life observing the highest level of world governments, not suspicion that she was a cog in such things.

"Pappa didn't take sides so much as document blatant injustice when he came across it. His true interest was culture and history and the beauty of nature that we too often overlook. That's what his fans wanted from him—escape from the clamor and nonsense of their own lives into the reassurance that we're all part of the same human fabric. And yes, there was a part of me that wanted to give his readers his final chapter. They did, after all, pay for my upkeep most of my life."

They still did. Many of his books had gone into reprint after the story of his death broke. She was his sole beneficiary.

"I imagine they feel invested in you, being his companion through all his adventures."

"You'll laugh, but I honestly had no idea how famous he was. My publisher told me to join social media to promote my book, and my phone exploded. I hadn't even read any of his books cover to cover until I was at university. Why would I need to? I was there. And in the places we visited, he was only seen as a nosy tourist."

His attention was fully on her as though he examined and weighed every word she spoke. It was disconcerting, causing her to blush with self-consciousness.

"Now that I've started my own blog, and realize how much work it is to find interesting content, I realize why he exploited me so shamelessly."

"Does that bother you?"

"Not really. He was always very good about asking which photos he could post or whether he could quote something I'd said. He would flag pages in his manuscript and let me veto anything I felt was too personal or didn't reflect well on me. I rarely pushed back because it never occurred to me that people even read what he wrote or cared about me. At best, I imagined they were reading for snippets of history and odd mishaps like arguing with a donkey on a muddy track. I didn't realize they came to believe they knew me, not until I was brought to America and the reporters wouldn't leave me alone."

"Why America? You're Swedish, aren't you?" Again, she had the flickering sense she was being debriefed, but this was how her life had gone since her father's death. Her notoriety gave people the impression they had a right to ask personal questions.

"I have distant relations in Sweden, but we only returned to renew our passports. My mother died when I was four and my father took me with him on his travels."

"He educated you himself?"

"He was a teacher in a previous life." She nodded. "He enrolled me in local schools at different times, mostly for language and socialization. You must know a little about that sort of upbringing?" She tried to bat the conversation in his direction.

"I do," he said after the briefest of pauses. "While my father was alive, we lived wherever he happened to be assigned. I resented being uprooted every year, forced to say goodbye to my latest batch of friends, then having to assimilate into a new culture. Above anything, I wanted to stay in one place. Be careful what you wish for," he said with an ironic nod at his chair.

"Is New York your home now?"

"My complex business interests keep me traveling. I have many homes."

"You've become your father," she teased.

"It appears that way." He said it lightly, but his face smoothed to unreadable and he sat back, popping the fragile bubble of connection they'd briefly shared.

The wine arrived, distracting her from examining her distinct impression that he didn't want to talk about himself. Giovanni ordered appetizers and they clinked glasses.

"How did you come to settle in New York instead of Sweden? School?"

"You could read the book to learn all this. You didn't have to buy me dinner," she pointed out.

"I want the raw data, not the polished prose. Unless you'd rather not talk about it?" That penetrating gaze of his made her heart stall each time it landed on her. There seemed to be a degree of challenge in it, as though refusing to talk would be seen as a sign of weakness or guilt.

"I don't mind," she lied.

She'd told her story enough times it was something she could usually do while holding herself at a distance so the facts didn't hurt too much to revisit. With him, however, her typical confidence was butting up against a level of self-assurance she had never encountered. She felt overpowered, which made her defenses shaky. She had to remind herself that she didn't need his approval for any reason, but it didn't stop her from wanting it and she didn't understand why.

"You might have seen in the book's acknowledgment the mention of my father's editor? Oliver was instrumental in getting me out of North Korea. It's why the US took over negotiations from the Swedish officials. Oliver worked tirelessly for two years to learn whether I was alive, locate exactly where I was, and petition for my release. He brought me into his home afterward."

"Because he felt responsible for sending you and your father there?"

"It was my father's choice to go. No, Oliver regarded himself as a surrogate father after such a long friendship with Pappa. He and his wife, Barbara, continue to be very kind to me, but I was nineteen when I arrived. I didn't want to be a foster child or a houseguest." Not again. "I had several offers for ghostwriters to tell my story, but Oliver suggested I write the book myself, as part of a creative writing degree. I had some money from my father's estate for tuition, Oliver made some calls to his alma mater. I thought university would be a good way to integrate into Western society, that I would meet people my age and expand my mental horizons."

"Oh? How did that go?" Giovanni's mouth pursed knowingly. "I'm guessing your horizons were already stratospheres beyond your peers."

"Pizza, sex, binge drinking… That's all they cared about." She sighed. "The people who had traveled hadn't really traveled. They had spent summers on a yacht in the Greek islands or went on a spring break rager through the Caribbean. Even my instructors seemed stunted, hammering at me to draw a thicker line between black and white. They couldn't understand why I wasn't angrier. *They* made me angry, trying to force me to rewrite my own experience to fit the narrative they thought it should have."

"It's a sensational story. Why wouldn't you sensationalize it for profit?"

"Exactly. I couldn't possibly have affection for the people who had held me. That would make them *people*."

She waited for the questions that usually came when she got this far, the ones that probed for salacious details. Had she been mistreated or assaulted? What horrible things had she done to survive?

"Were you not given an advance for your book? Why are you working in catering?"

That almost sounded as though he was more interested in how she'd come to meet him at the hotel last night than how she'd been pried from the clutches of a notoriously uncooperative government.

"I used my advance as a down payment on a small flat, but I have a mortgage and living expenses. Oddly enough, a creative writing degree isn't at the top of HR managers' wish lists." She shrugged. "So I tutor ESL students, and a friend got me in with this catering company. Once I get my book tour out of the way, I'll start a teacher certification program."

"You want to shape young minds?"

"Open them, at least." She made a more determined effort to steer the conversation in his direction. "May I ask you a question?"

"Never married and currently uninvolved," he said

promptly, maintaining his intense stare, though it held a shadow of self-deprecation at what he was implying.

"I wish I could say the same," she threw back, deadpan.

His face abruptly fell with shocked dismay.

She burst out laughing.

"I didn't expect you to be so gullible." Freja's laugh was so merry, her expression so incandescent, he was spellbound.

Giovanni's only thought should have been to question how his team had missed something as vital as romantic associations, but her remark had prompted a far more visceral reaction. Involved? *No.* He wanted her for himself.

Which was not only an uncharacteristic thrust of unjustified jealousy, it was the sort of emotional reaction he had trained himself not to have. The fact she had so easily slid past his well-fortified shields against any sort of manipulations, intended or otherwise, told him exactly how dangerous she was.

He tried to neutralize all of that firepower of hers with some heat of his own.

"You're nothing like I expected." He picked up her hand and brought it to his mouth to drop a kiss in her palm. "Which is why I have such a strong disinclination to share you."

She blushed, and he felt her hand twitch in nervous reaction, but she left it trustingly in his. Her brow pulled into a small frown. "You're possessive?"

"I'm Sicilian, *bidduzza.* I'm incapable of being anything else."

Each breath he drew was laden with the scent of her—spring and berries and something sweet like almond cookies. He wanted to continue nuzzling along her wrist, but contented himself with tracing his thumb along her love line.

This isn't real, a voice in his head reminded him. She might not be as innocent as she projected. Even more concerning, she might be, in which case he definitely shouldn't allow himself to sink into any sort of involvement with her.

How was he to know either way if he didn't spend time with her, though? It was a convenient rationalization for pursuing a woman he couldn't have. What the hell was he going to do?

"What was your real question?" he prompted, still caressing her palm with his thumb.

"Do you still fence?"

Ah, yes. He had confirmed that small detail, at least. An online search had unearthed a passage from one of Hugo Anderson's earliest books about his "young companion," as her father had referred to her, taking fencing lessons from an Olympic hopeful. For weeks after, every stray piece of driftwood had become a weapon until a nasty sliver had forced her to find other amusements.

"These days I stay fit in ways that allow me to watch the market numbers or take a conference call. Fencing requires complete focus."

"And world domination via cell phone apps doesn't?"

"That was dumb luck," he said with uncharacteristic frankness—and a hint of disparagement that she leaped on with an incisive frown.

"What do you do with your downtime, then? Inspire me. My pastimes are all very tame."

He scratched his cheek, stalling. "You don't yearn to fill your time with the obvious? Marriage and a family?"

She let her mouth hang open before she accused, "Sexist."

"How is that sexist? Many people want those things, gender notwithstanding."

"Do you?"

She wasn't afraid to put him on the spot. It was as annoying as it was refreshing. Given his wealth and position, most people jumped at his every whim, rarely challenging him on his opinions or what he did with his life.

His response to her question should have been a quick and firm no. He'd buried any youthful assumptions that he would one day have a family when he'd buried the one he'd had. Part of that reaction had been bitterness. Lately it was simply a matter of priorities. Close relationships of any kind were a vulnerability he couldn't afford.

But he had a sudden vision of her in his bed, gaze sleepy and filled with infinite possibilities. His heart lurched in warning. Or was it masculine craving?

"Marriage isn't a priority for me," he said in an implacable signal. "I've always been focused on other things. My physical health, athletic training, my education. My investments." Not to mention unraveling multinational conspiracies and political corruptions without getting himself further maimed or killed in the process.

"Same." She nodded thoughtfully. "I've been focused

on my book and finding my feet. In many ways, I feel as though I'm still waiting for my life to start." She looked at the hand still in his warm grip. "This is the first date I've been on in ages. The handful of friends I made at school have moved on to careers and other things. I know a lot of people, but I've always moved around so much, I've never connected deeply with anyone."

Her thumb tentatively caressed the backs of his fingers. His hair damned near stood on end, the sensation caused such an acute reaction in him.

At the same time, the wistful yearning in her voice reverberated off the steel shields he'd erected around his heart, making her words echo inside him as though they were his own. He had an overpowering urge to mute that inner vibration with the press of her body against his.

All his good sense flew out the window. Before he realized what he was saying, his voice rumbled from the depths of his chest.

"Come home with me."

"Now?" Her pupils dilated and a visible quake went through her, one that leaped so quickly onto the suggestion, his honed instincts of self-preservation tingled in warning, but a responsive ripple of pleasure rolled through him. How could he resist her when this was how they reacted to one another?

Don't let her see how desperate you are, he cautioned himself.

While his mouth affirmed, "Right now."

CHAPTER TWO

"This is something I'm still getting used to," Freja admitted nervously as they left the elevator into his penthouse. Recessed lighting kept the lounge dim enough that the view of the city lights was like a carpet of stars beyond the darkened windows. She trailed her hand over the buttery leather of the overstuffed sofa. "I thought Oliver and Barbara lived like kings in their two-bedroom walk-up. This…"

There were no words for the kind of expansive luxury surrounding her. Until moving to New York, she'd only seen this sort of wealth in historic palaces. Catering had sent her into a few high-end hotels and penthouses, but even those paled next to what appeared to be a mansion atop a skyscraper. The floors were a gleaming hardwood, the drapes silk, the art on the walls a colorful mix of modern impressionists. Beyond the value in such things, the real luxury was in how the entire space was tastefully customized for a man who moved in a wheelchair instead of on two feet.

Something introspective shadowed his expression as he hung her jacket. He paused.

"When I asked you here, I was only thinking that I

wanted to be alone with you. I didn't consider the way you've been forced to live in the past." His mouth pulled with consternation. "If you have second thoughts—I hope you feel comfortable here, but leave anytime if you don't. Or we can go back to the restaurant." He turned to regard her as though she were a complex puzzle he was trying to solve.

"I like to believe I'm a good judge of character."

She had believed it until meeting him, at least. He was hard to read, though. She continued to finger the soft leather of the sofa, soothed by its texture as she considered his contradictions. Bold enough to state what he wanted, compassionate enough to anticipate her hidden apprehensions. Open about his attraction, completely closed off in other ways.

"I wouldn't have come here if I thought you were planning to attack me."

His expression eased into a smoldering one that pulled her insides tight with anticipation. "Only in a very sensual sense, *bidduzza.* And with your explicit consent, of course." He rolled forward. "Come. Sit," he invited, nodding at the sofa.

She hesitated behind it.

His expression cleared, but his mouth tightened briefly. "That's fine," he said evenly. "I presumed you'd have questions."

"I do, but not— Well, that too, I guess." She hadn't even considered whether he had full sexual function, only thinking that she wanted to be alone with him, too. "It's more…" She could hear herself stammering and wanted to die of mortification. "I've never done this," she blurted.

His shoulders relaxed and one of his dark eyebrows lifted in self-deprecation. "This is considerably faster than I usually move, myself."

"No, I mean…" She nervously linked her hands before her. "I've never had sex."

His head went back in astonishment.

She wrinkled her nose. "I knew you'd think I'm odd." Her fellow students had. "That's why I mentioned it."

"It's not odd." He tilted his head, conceding, "Okay, I'm surprised. I didn't expect someone as worldly as you are wouldn't have taken a lover somewhere along the line." He studied her again in that way that picked over her bones, but left small fires in its wake.

She was used to being a curiosity. People disbelieved things she said about herself and her life. For the most part she didn't care what others thought of her, but Giovanni's skepticism was different. That shadow of doubt he wore provoked a small outrage in her along with a clench of something more defensive. She wanted him to see her exactly as she was. To know her and like her and want her despite all the nicks and dents that life had left upon her.

"There wasn't at least one young man at university who tempted you?"

"They all seemed very one-track and immature." The one she had thought had potential turned out to play for another team. She shrugged self-consciously. "No one made me feel like I wanted more than coffee and kisses."

"But I do?" His face was impassive while the line of his shoulders had turned to granite.

"Why is that hard to believe? You invited me here.

I thought that meant we were mutually attracted." She crossed her arms protectively.

"I'm very attracted to you," he assured her in a voice that curled her toes in her boots. "It's still a big step for you to take with someone you barely know."

She hunched her shoulders to her ears. "Growing up the way I did, always moving to a new place, I learned that I don't often get second chances. If there was a place I wanted to see or something I wanted to do, I had to take the opportunity when it was presented or we would be in the next town or across a border and I couldn't go back."

"I'm a unique experience you don't want to miss?" His voice chilled with warning.

"Am I not for you?" she asked with a spark of tetchiness. "Because if I'm a run-of-the-mill hookup, then yes, I would prefer to take my jacket and bag and find my own way home."

His cheeks hollowed and his mouth pursed in doleful humor. "You're definitely unique, Freja." He absently ran the backs of his fingers under the angle of his jaw.

The silence drew out until her stomach was so tight she could hardly breathe. She looked to her bag where he'd set it on the table by the door.

"I'm trying to make myself say that this isn't your only opportunity to sleep with me," he said in a voice that went gritty and thick. "I know I should tell you that if you're feeling pressured, we can back off. We can date and wait for a time that feels right." He shook his head, jaw clenched. "But I'll be leaving for Europe next week. Which is another reason you should be sensible about this decision. I'll be there through the summer, possibly longer. I wouldn't expect you to wait for me."

And wouldn't invite her to come with him. He was warning her this wasn't the beginning of anything serious. She absorbed that as a clash that rang through her whole body. But as she weighed little against nothing, there was no contest. She would take what she could get.

"If you want to leave, go. I'll call you tomorrow. If you want to stay the night, then I want you in my bed."

That declaration was as weighty as a thick wool quilt, a little abrasive, but strangely comforting. She warmed under it. Fast.

"I want to stay." Even though her stomach was nothing but butterflies in anticipation. "That's why I'm here."

His breath left him in a jagged laugh. "That frankness of yours is going to be the death of me. Come here." In a well-practiced shift, he used the arm of the sofa to transfer himself onto the cushions. He held out a hand to her.

She came around and let him draw her to sit next to him. He set one arm along the back of the sofa and angled toward her. His light touch encouraged her to angle toward him and drape her legs across his thighs.

"You won't hurt me," he assured her, but it was the way his touch played across her knees that made her twitch in reaction. He pointed to what was left of his right leg. "This one is completely without sensation. I can't control it at all. Sometimes it spasms. This one I can move a bit and feel some pressure, but no heat or pain." He thwacked his finger against his meatier left thigh. "I don't feel anything at all right here." He drew a wide band from his spine around his rib cage to the middle of his chest on the right side. "Sensation is patchy through here." He waved his hand over his abdomen and lap. "If I move your hand when you're touching me, that's why." He picked up her hand and played with her fingers. "Go ahead and do the same with me. I want to touch you where you enjoy it most."

Her fingers flexed in reaction at the idea of setting his hand in intimate places.

The corners of his mouth deepened knowingly. He set a tiny kiss on her knuckle, melting her thought processes one brain cell at a time.

"My shoulders and scalp and earlobes are really sensitive. My left nipple." He shrugged at that incongruity. "I may not finish the way you expect. Don't take that as a reflection on you or my level of enjoyment."

"I don't know what to expect," she reminded him, trying to keep the moment light while she quaked internally at the enormity of what they were discussing so calmly and naturally.

"Right. I should have said, everything that happens between us is a completely typical experience exactly as you would have had with your able-bodied university nits."

She chuckled dryly, but her smile faded as he trailed his reverent gaze over her face.

"Or not." He picked up a tendril of her hair, letting it sift through his fingers. "That is sleek as a satin ribbon, isn't it? I've been dying to know." He did it again. "Smooth and cool. Like you," he added in a tone that maybe was supposed to be whimsical, but she was having trouble tracking.

Her scalp grew sensitized and a shiver chased down her spine. She reflexively pulled from his light hold on her hand to cross her arms and rub away the goose bumps that rose beneath her sleeves.

"Am I making you shiver? I want to." He stroked a light touch from her shoulder to her elbow and back, reigniting the prickling sensation she'd tried to erase. His touch firmed into a warm massage that was equally inciting. "Don't hold back any of your reactions. Your pleasure is my pleasure."

"Really?" Her experience with men was…not that. More like, *Go farther, faster. Why aren't you into this?*

"I want to know you're as excited as I am." He tucked her hair behind her ear and played his fingertip along the whorls he exposed, caressing behind and into the hollow beneath her earlobe.

Why that made her nipples stand up, she didn't know, but she felt them tighten and sting. She bit her lip and wanted to lift her hand to erase that sensation, too, especially when his gaze dropped. She looked down and yes, her nipples were poking against the soft red knit of her pullover.

"I want it to be so good, you can't bring yourself to leave my bed." His voice grew husky and intimate, his concentration wholly on the vision he created as he slid his hand to her side. He pressed the knit of her turtleneck taut so her breast was blatantly outlined, nipple standing firmly against it. "No bra?"

"I don't like them," she confessed faintly.

"Neither do I. Not anymore."

She had never experienced such a strange euphoria simply by being near someone, barely touching.

His light caress through her clothing was feathery and wonderful. She liked being snuggled close to his solid warmth, able to discern his strength and take in his scent of wool and outdoors and faint aftershave and a more intimate, personal fragrance that was spicy and musky and all him.

His touch slid back to her shoulder, encouraging her to lean in as he did, closer and closer, gaze on his mouth. He didn't kiss her, though. He touched light kisses along her jaw, then stole a very brief kiss. Started to come back for more.

She drew back slightly. "Shouldn't we go to the bedroom?"

He frowned with insult. "I'll have to turn in my Italian citizenship if I don't seduce you."

"But I already said yes."

"You agreed to the sensual attack I promised you." He grew serious. Maybe faintly suspicious. "Why the hurry?"

"I'm nervous," she admitted with a sheepish wrinkle of her nose.

"Then we should take it slow."

"But I feel…impatient." Her low-grade blush increased until she was so hot, she probably glowed, fully embarrassed by how urgent she felt. "I want to be naked and feel all of you and know how it will be when we're…together."

He gathered her in his strong arms and his chest muscles flexed as he pulled her to sit fully in his lap, so they were nose to nose. His big hands moved over her lower back and hips, waking her up to swirling sensations that expanded into her inner thighs.

"This is how it will be," he told her, opening his mouth against her throat and licking at her flesh. "Better and better with every minute that goes by."

He really did attack her senses. She caught her breath at the onslaught of sensations, gasping when his hands hardened on her, holding her in place.

"I'm dying to have you naked and spread out on my bed, weak with need for the release I give you." His hot breath wafted against her nape. "I'm going to take liberties that are liable to shock you. I'm as impatient as you are for all of that."

"Are you?" He seemed in such complete control.

"Do *you* lack sensation below the waist? What do you think that is against your ass? A penknife?"

She chuckled shyly and glanced down to where a stiff ridge dug into her cheek. She gave a small wriggle that made heat flare in his eyes.

Oh.

She did it again, testing her newfound feminine power.

"You *will* be the death of me," he said in a rasp and rocked to shift his legs open a little farther, nestling her deeper into his lap. "Can we lose these?" He tugged the zipper on the inside of her boot.

She nodded, wondering how the slow relaxing of her boots and their loose drop could pull such an erotic sensation from her loins to the arch of her foot.

He caressed her calf and invited, "Kiss me."

She did, sliding her arms around his neck while she worked her mouth over his, dabbing her tongue into the taste of him between his parted lips. Trying to slake a greedy hunger she'd never experienced—or expressed—in her life.

Gradually, she became aware of his arms firming around her. His hand was in her hair, his other one soothing along her rib cage while he took control of their kiss. He was unhurried about it, but she slowly became aware that they were fully involved. He was thoroughly ravaging her and it was *fantastic*. She curled into him with a groan, pressing her thighs together to ease the growing ache between them. When his touch crept over her breast and he molded the swell while sweeping his thumb across her nipple, she moaned into his mouth.

He drew back and his heavy-lidded gaze was fixated on where he was fondling her. "Let me see," he said in a thick voice and gave a tug against the back of the turtleneck.

"Yes, I'm so hot," she breathed anxiously.

"Me, too." He swept off his own pullover first, then helped her do the same. He swore as she twisted her naked torso back toward him, stalling her with his wide hands against her shoulders, still balancing her on his thighs.

"You're so beautiful." His palms went down to cup the sides of her breasts. His thumbs shaped the swells to plump them and tilt her beaded nipples higher.

She trembled as she tried to work his shirt buttons loose. It wasn't easy. He dropped his head to set the sweetest kisses across her shoulders. His light touch grazed her stomach and ribs and tickled the curves of her breasts. It was such a tease! Her breasts grew heavy with anticipation. Everything in her wanted to sit still for the lovely sensations he was causing with those clever fingers and damp lips, but more than that, she wanted to *feel* him. His hair against her jaw made her turn her nose in to his scent, but she finally had his shirt undone enough to push it open and—"Oh!"

She thrust her arms beneath the edges, hugging his sides. The scrape of her naked breasts against the silken hairs on his chest sent a glorious, electrical excitement through her. He made a growling noise and caught her into a passionate kiss. As they devoured each other, tongues tangling, they moved against one another, skin against skin in hedonistic friction.

It took her a moment to realize her perception of falling was real. He was tipping her onto her back on the cushions, but coming down with her. He leaned over her, mouth finding her throat and taking soft, wet bites.

"Giovanni," she moaned.

"Say it like you mean it." His expression was so stark and intensely masculine, it should have been intimidating, but his touch as he cupped her breast was reverent. He looked at her naked flesh, licked at her nipple, then blew softly. Her loins pulsed in reaction.

"Giovanni," she said with all the yearning in her, tone ringing with plea and command.

He rewarded her with a delicate suction that had her tangling her fingers in his hair, arching up to offer more. She was going insane, she was so aroused, but he moved from one breast to the other and back until instinct drove her to slither herself more completely beneath him. Her body screamed for the weight of his. For his thighs between her own.

As they rearranged themselves, her skirt rode up, allowing her to bend her knees on either side of his hips.

He balanced on one elbow over her. "Tell me if I'm too heavy."

"I like it." She pulled his shirt from his waistband and slid her palms all over his back.

He had the torso of a power lifter, thick chest and shoulder muscles rippling under her touch. When her fingers grazed his left nipple, he sucked in a sharp breath.

She lifted her hand. "Hurt?"

"No," he said on a jagged laugh. "It feels really good."

She touched him again, watching his eyes drift shut as she very deliberately played her thumbs across his nipples. His breathing grew uneven and her own arousal intensified as she watched the way he was reacting.

He suddenly snapped his eyes open and dragged her hand to his shoulder. "I'm going to lose it if you keep that up. Ladies first." He kissed her parted lips and settled his weight on her.

When she felt the pressure of his erection through their clothes against the juncture of her thighs, she tilted her hips to increase the pressure.

"What do you need?" He rolled onto his elbow and pressed the heat of his palm against her mound. "This?" He rocked his palm firmly.

"Yes," she moaned in anguished relief. "Was I hurting you?"

"Quit asking that." He nipped at the edge of her jaw. "The only thing that's hurting me is that I can't feel more of you." He searched beneath her skirt for the waistband of her leggings and worked his hand inside, fingers cleverly getting into her underwear.

He watched her expression as he did. She bit her lip, shy, yet dying of anticipation. She never let men get this far. It had never felt right, but now she dearly wanted to know how it would feel.

One long touch parted the wet seam of her folds, intimate and lovely. He returned to the swollen bundle of nerves he'd only grazed, as if he'd known exactly what he was doing all along. One firm circle and such an exquisite streak of pleasure went through her, she clenched her eyes shut to savor it while a decadent groan filled her throat.

"Hurt?" he mocked with a hot chuckle of his breath against her cheek. He did it again.

She groaned again and met his kiss with a flagrant offer of her tongue while she rocked her hips to match the slow rhythm of his touch firming and gliding away, returning and easing, dipping lower and deeper, invading so that she clung to him with all her might, driven by sheer desire to cast off propriety and seek the pinnacle that suddenly loomed.

And there it was, quick and sweet and expansive, bathing her in a rush of tingles while her cries of satisfaction were muffled by his carnal kiss.

His touch stayed under her skirt, but eased to a proprietary hand on her belly while he let her break their kiss and catch her breath.

"You very nearly took me with you. That was incredibly sexy." He circled the tip of his nose against her own, kissed her temple, then her cheekbone. Through her haze, she thought he might be shaking.

She wished he had climaxed with her. She'd never orgasmed with anyone else in the room and she felt incredibly vulnerable right now, having done it by his hand. Letting him draw that from her gave him a power over her that she didn't know how to take back. He had broken down barriers in her before she fully understood how much protection they offered.

Even knowing that, however, latent desire throbbed in her blood. She was still aroused. She wanted more and the depth of want in her—for more of his touch, his kisses, and the pleasure he gave her—was genuinely painful. Her need for him felt as basic as breathing or eating. It was unsettling to become so carnal within the space of a few minutes.

"*Now* I want to go to the bedroom," he informed her smokily, setting one short, suggestive kiss on her mouth.

Her lips clung to his and she felt obvious in her desire. As though he knew her better than she knew herself. As though a single feel-up on the sofa had turned her into a slave to the lure of his touch.

Which it had. Her legs barely worked and she wound up in his lap, kissing his jaw and neck as he bumped them down the hall into the master bedroom.

One lamp glowed next to a huge, low bed. The floor-to-ceiling drapes had been drawn shut, but judging by the two walls of them, the entire corner was nothing but glass overlooking the city.

He nodded for her to sit on the bed while he opened the drawer of the nightstand to withdraw condoms. "I don't ejaculate, but I always wear one."

She perched nervously and watched as he threw off his shirt and moved onto the mattress beside her. He dropped back and opened his fly, worked his pants off and pushed them to the floor. Then he stayed propped on his elbows, letting her look her fill.

She tracked her gaze from his alert expression to his powerful shoulders and flexed biceps to his flat abs. There was a distinct tan line above the band of his snug blue briefs. His erection pressed a line against it. Below that, his thighs were visibly different sizes, the right one thinner and amputated higher than the left. There was more scarring on the right one, too, and a nasty bruise.

"What happened?" she asked with concern, gently touching the blue-green smudge.

He glanced and dismissed it with, "I stumbled during gait therapy."

"You can walk?"

"I can balance on crutches and one prosthetic leg while dragging the other. It's not practical for daily life, but it keeps my good leg from atrophying and helps with other functions." He settled onto his back, one arm curled behind his head to reveal the tuft of hair beneath. He angled his head to study her. "I'm regretting taking off your boots. I would love to see your foot right here while you unzipped it." He patted the mattress next to his hip.

If he was feeling a fraction of the self-consciousness she was experiencing, there was no evidence of it. He radiated confidence and patience.

She stood, but she was so befuddled, her fingers couldn't find the zipper on her skirt.

"Please don't laugh at how awkward I am." She turned the skirt. Her hair fell across her face, blinding her as she tried to work the catch free.

"On the contrary, I'm turned on by the fact you're as

excited as I am. Let me help." He pushed to sit up and she nervously edged closer. With no clumsiness whatsoever, he opened her skirt and brushed it off her hips.

He brought her twitching hands to his shoulders and pressed one palm to his neck so she could feel the rapid slam of his pulse. "I'm so aroused, I can hardly breathe."

His skin was faintly damp with perspiration, his nostrils flared and tense.

Yet he was in complete control. She stroked her fingers through his hair, as though she'd been given the gift of petting a tiger. The strength and power in him awed her and the flare of excitement in his eyes excited her. It was reassuring to know he was reacting so strongly. Heady. He began to roll her leggings down and she pushed her panties off with them, kicking them away as she stood before him, still nervous, but driven by that urgency again.

A primordial noise rumbled in his chest as he looked at the thatch of blond over her mound. His splayed hands grasped her hips and drew big circles to her butt cheeks and the backs of her thighs, nudging her closer to the edge of the bed between his open thighs until her knees and shins rested against the side of the mattress. His hands lingered to caress in slow circles that were driving her mad while he blew softly on her curls.

A helpless noise left her and she dug her fingernails into his shoulders. Her inner muscles clenched while the rest of her went taut.

"Shy?" He dragged his gaze upward as if it took supreme effort. "Or something more?"

"Shy," she managed in a paper-thin voice. "I've never— No one—"

He set a light kiss against her mound and she forgot how words worked. Every single nerve ending throughout her body pulsated.

He was a ridiculously patient man, teasing her with another small kiss into the crease where her thigh met her pelvis, then the other side. When his tongue traced a barely-there caress along the seam of her folds, skating a not-quite-fulfilling touch across the bud swollen with yearning, she moaned his name. Her fingers moved mindlessly in his hair.

He groaned and heat enveloped her flesh. She had thought what they'd done on the sofa was a type of paradise she could never again live without, but *this*. This was the sort of rapture that would induce her to do nearly anything to keep experiencing it.

He proved it, too. Just as the last vestiges of control were abandoning her, when she was so aroused she was relying on the hard hands under her butt to keep her upright while she pushed her hips into his lascivious kiss, he dropped his head back to look at her from beneath heavy eyelids.

An unconscious noise of loss throbbed in her throat.

He smiled, wicked and dark, then twisted to throw pillows into a pile against the headboard. He dragged himself to sit against them and met her gaze as he rocked to get his briefs down, revealing his thick erection. He took himself in hand, squeezed.

"You're going to decide how much you can take." He sounded as primal as she felt. He unwrapped a condom and rolled it on. "I can still feel heat. Pressure. Let me feel how hot and tight you are."

He invited her to straddle his thighs. There was no

modesty as she splayed her knees on either side of his hips, but given what he'd done to her already, inhibitions were moot. He held himself steady for her to position herself and she began accepting him into her. It was deliberate and overwhelming, both physically and emotionally, but she had never wanted anything so much in her life.

The pinch of his broad shape entering her was sharp enough to startle her. She steadied herself by gripping the headboard.

"Take your time." His voice was gruff, his skin pulled taut across his cheekbones. He watched her with such intensity, she ought to have caught fire.

She *was* on fire. The pressure between her legs burned, but he shifted his touch and caressed her, using her own moisture to lubricate his penetration, enticing her to chase that capricious flutter that promised such exquisite pleasure.

He was saying things in Sicilian. Dirty things, maybe, but his tone was filled with praise and encouragement. Earthy pleasure. He didn't seem to care that she was being tentative. He groaned in suffering, but the fingers that dug into her hips didn't force her to take any more of him than she was ready for.

His intrusion hurt, but the internal stretch seemed to amplify her growing arousal. He kept caressing her, soothing her taut flesh with gentle fingers where they joined, then heightening her desire with circling touches across the straining button he'd anointed so mercilessly with his tongue.

She could hear herself making noises that bordered on distress as she hovered in the space between acute pain and profound pleasure. Such exquisite torture. How did anyone stand it?

"Give me your nipple," he coaxed in a voice that resonated from deep in his chest.

She did, leaning her breast closer to his mouth. The movement caused him to shift inside her, alarming her with the stinging sensation. She gasped, but as he suckled, she grew wetter and found herself sinking and lifting, seeking that hot friction. She was afraid to take all of him, but oh, it felt lovely to have the tip of him moving inside her.

This was the mysterious primeval knowledge she'd sought. This was the ethereal world she had heard existed between the poetic descriptions of sensual magnificence and the corporeal reality of sex. She had never understood how another's touch could be more gratifying than her own, but his hand and mouth and penetration became her entire world.

This man, with his head dropping back to watch her, somehow heightened everything about this experience into something exalted. His scent permeated the air she breathed and his lips tasted of her own essence. She sank all the way down, taking him fully inside her, and dazzlement turned his eyes silver. She could feel their sweat mingling, and their noises of pleasure were a perfect harmony.

She had never felt so connected to anyone. As they moved like this, they were essentially one being, experiencing together something that could not have happened apart. Not with anyone else, ever, anywhere. Only them. Here. Now. Like this.

As she rode up and down every last inch of him, her

arousal contracted to a tight point inside her. She stilled, fighting to hold back from the paradise she longed for, hovering on the brink of losing control.

"Giovanni," she breathed. "I'm—"

"Do it," he growled.

She moved with unfettered greed, thrilling at the feel of him buried deep inside her, and the euphoria of climax crept up on her. In a mindless need to have him with her, she scraped her thumb across his nipple and sucked his earlobe while her orgasm engulfed her, flooding her with shuddering ecstasy.

He locked his hands on her hips and his whole body clenched right before he released a ragged cry of gratification.

CHAPTER THREE

"MISSION ACCOMPLISHED," FREJA murmured next to him, pulling Giovanni from his postcoital doze.

He didn't want to come back to full consciousness. He would have to start picking apart exactly how unwise this had been, from the dinner he'd been urged to cancel to...*this*.

He shouldn't be feeling this smug when she had so completely destroyed him, leaving him more sated than any sexual experience he'd ever had.

Still, her odd choice of words penetrated his haze.

"Mission?" His voice had to be dug out of the depths of his chest and barely arrived above a graveled whisper. He turned his head on the pillow.

A decadent smile touched her lips. "I don't want to leave this bed."

He didn't want her to leave it, either. Ever. Realizing that was one of those moments when his life went out of focus and came back with finer edges and starker contrasts. It was sobering because he couldn't pretend things hadn't changed. *He* had.

"Not even to eat? I'm starving." He kept his tone light so he wouldn't betray how deeply affected he was.

"I'll make a call, order in. Stay here." He had to make more than one call, but food was a good excuse to gain some distance and perspective. He sat up on the edge of the bed.

"I might shower if you don't mind?"

He looked over his shoulder. "Run a bath. I'll join you."

"Do you remember where my bag went?"

"*Bidduzza*, I'm having trouble remembering my own name."

She chuckled throatily and rose to hug him from behind. The cool swells of her breasts were against his back and her bent knees bracketed his hips. Her arms slithered around his neck and she gave his earlobe a light nip.

"Ouch." He protectively pinched it. Definitely a bath and a tutorial on his most sensitive erogenous zones. Sucking? Great. Biting? Not so much.

Which implied they would be doing this again.

Since when did he have such weak self-discipline?

"Sorry." Her soft breath wafted against his nape while her hair fell across his naked shoulder in a sensuous tickle. "I'm trying to thank you. That was wondrous."

"It was." Recognizing that, admitting it, increased his growing caution. He was very good at compartmentalizing, but needed to catch up on the filing. "I'll find your bag."

"I can." She rose and picked up his shirt, shook it out and pushed her arms into the sleeves. "Do you mind?" she asked with a glance as she did.

How could he? Not only was she a splendid picture

of debauchery, rosy curves and shadowed nipples visible beneath the fine linen, he experienced a Neanderthal-like thrill at seeing her in a garment that belonged to him. Not that he was such a throwback as to see *her* as a belonging, but he was aware of something inside him locking into place. The kind of possessiveness that came of discovering something priceless and resolving to shelter it close. Protect and cherish.

Damn, that was unsettling. He had sexual affairs, but always kept them as simple and casual as possible, yet here he felt the tug to follow when she moved out of sight into the bathroom. The water started running.

He pulled on his briefs and settled in his chair, picked up his pants, but his phone wasn't in them. On the table by the front door, perhaps.

"What do you feel like?" he asked when he found his phone and she joined him in the lounge. "There's a Thai place that's quite good." He thumbed through his contacts. "The vegan place is better, but it takes longer."

"You're vegan?"

"I have teams of people dedicated to my physical health. I eat what they make me. I should check the refrigerator. There's probably something there."

"Whatever you want is fine." She picked up her bag from the table and started to dig through it. "But I need lip balm before I eat. My lips feel like they're starting to chap. How do you think that happened?" She tucked her chin and elevated her brows in a scold.

"I have no idea. Let me kiss it better," he offered.

"Nice try. Not until—" She frowned. "Someone has been through my bag."

A guarded shiver chased over him, making him wish

he'd put on more clothes. This was what came of letting sex make him complacent.

"Is something missing?" he asked with a suitable level of concern, even though he was damned confident nothing would be. "I can't imagine anyone at the restaurant went into it, but I can make a call."

She set the bag back on the table while she took a thorough inventory. "Everything seems to be here." She counted some bills, rearranged the order of them before she folded them back into a pocket.

"How do you know someone's been through it?" Only spies like him tended to set up little traps to betray those who might enter where they weren't invited.

"I've lived out of a suitcase most of my life. I arrange all my bags so I can get what I want without looking and can always tell when a maid or customs agent has rummaged through. I *never* put my lip balm in that pocket." She tsked. "Maybe tell the restaurant to be on the lookout for pickpockets?"

"I'll call them after I order the food. Join you in a minute," he promised.

She disappeared and he tapped to call Everett.

"You left early," was Everett's abrupt greeting. Perhaps that was the reason his minion had been so sloppy in the search of Freja's bag.

"Anything?" Giovanni asked.

"Two passports. American and Swedish."

That fact had been in the dossier Everett had provided on Giovanni's request, the one that had included her extensive debriefing after her two-year stint in a North Korean village, the names of her contacts at university, and the particulars of her book deal. The general consensus among government agencies was that she *could* be a foreign operative, but no one had been able to prove it or determine who employed her.

"That's it?" Giovanni prompted.

"She was prepared to spend the night with you." Everett's tone held a warning.

Giovanni dismissed her changes of clothes with a meaningless grunt. Freja had been coming from work. Plenty of women were veritable tortoises, carrying their entire boudoir everywhere they went.

"I have a car waiting to take her home," Everett said.

"Unnecessary." Giovanni didn't even pause to think about it.

A potent silence on the other end told him he ought to.

"Do you mind if I have dessert?" Freja asked, jolting him with her sudden reappearance. "I have a hideous sweet tooth. Chocolate?"

"Done," he assured her, saying to Everett, "Did you get that? Add dessert to my order. Something with chocolate. Leave it with the doorman."

"Do you know what you're doing?"

"Absolutely," Giovanni lied dismissively. "Good night."

The massive triangular jetted tub was set into a corner of the palatial master bath. The tiled edges were set at a height that made it easy for Giovanni to transfer back and forth from his chair. The windows fogged from the steam off the water, but otherwise offered a clear view of the city.

"I'll have to tell the doorman he can eat the Thai delivery," Giovanni said as they finished what his Sicilian nutritionist had left in the refrigerator.

He hadn't bothered to heat the chickpea fritters or saffron risotto balls. They'd gobbled them down cold with antipasto and scoops of savory pistachio sauce. He'd even brought a handful of chocolate chip cookies from the freezer. They tasted amazing with the rich red wine they were sipping from stemless glasses.

As he reached to set the tray on the floor beside the edge of the tub, the jets went off. She realized he'd put on music when he'd lowered the lights. Feathery strokes of guitar played over the soothing breaths and lazy keys of an accordion.

He settled back with a sigh of repletion and invited, "Come here."

She shyly drifted from her seat opposite and he drew her in front of him. She reclined upon him, head pillowed by his shoulder as he stretched his long arms along the tub's edge and absently adjusted the handheld spray washer in its holder.

"What if we fall asleep like this?" she asked, eyelids heavy.

"Then we will wake up very cold and wrinkly."

She smiled and they were quiet for a few minutes.

"Will you tell me about your time in North Korea?" he asked.

Her defenses were so low, she felt thin and fragile as his question penetrated. Hot emotion rushed into her eyes and she turned her face against his bicep in an instinctive flinch.

"Can't you just read it?" Telling him the story, when she was this defenseless, felt too hard.

"You don't want to tell me?" Subtle tension hardened the body that cradled hers.

"It makes me sad. And no one will let me *be* sad. They want me to be angry. And grateful that I was rescued."

"Aren't you?"

"I'm grateful to be in a country where I can talk and move freely, obviously. But I'm equally grateful to have had a home there. I wasn't as miserable there as people want me to be."

"You said your father's editor didn't send him there. What were you two doing there? Why did he drag you into the farthest reaches of China, never mind North Korea?"

"That was his job," she defended her father for what felt like the millionth time. It amazed her how many people criticized him for taking his daughter into remote parts of the world when his tales of parenting while trying to avoid yellow fever, Zika, and old-fashioned travel tummy were the reasons for his great appeal. "Taking impulsive side trips was very normal for us. We were visiting the crater lake in the nature preserve on the border between China and North Korea when the opportunity came up to join a tour to see the other side. Pappa was always trying to make a point that people are just people and that nearly every place in the world is safe to visit if you're respectful. It was, but we were hiking in the foothills of the mountains when he had the stroke. The guide had to run to ask villagers to come back with a vehicle to carry him down. He had passed by the time they got us to the clinic."

"I'm so sorry." His voice was a grave, reassuring

rumble against her back. His arm slid under the water and around her waist, holding her comfortingly close. "That must have been terrifying. You were seventeen?"

"Yes. And the rest of our tour had to move on. Our guide left me at the clinic with my father's body. I saw the guide hand my passport to an official in a military uniform. I thought, *That's bad*, but there wasn't anything I could do."

"Could you speak the language at all?"

"Only rudimentary words like 'please' and 'thank you.' Byung-woo was the doctor who wrote out Pappa's death certificate. He and his wife, Sung-mi, lived upstairs. I was a wreck, obviously. She brought me a cup of tea and I could see her pretending not to listen to the men. She was being very stoic, but I could tell whatever they were saying was bad. I did the only thing I could think of. I tried to hand all my money to Sung-mi."

"Bribery," he said with disdain. "That quaint and reliable solution to any problem."

"I pretended I was trying to finance a proper burial for my father."

"And?"

"She took it into the room where the men were talking and they closed the door. A little while later, the official left and Sung-mi and Byung-woo brought my father's body into a special room and helped me lay him out. Villagers came by over the next few days, sat with me while I grieved. Then they took him back into the mountains and we buried him in a small graveyard."

"So he's still there."

"Yes." And she thought it somewhat appropriate that

he rested as he had lived, an interloper accepted in a land that wasn't his own.

"Did you try to leave at that point?"

"Foreigners aren't allowed to use public transport. There was no internet. Things like booking a flight or online banking… All those things people take for granted weren't available to me. My cash was gone. The few times Pappa and I had talked about what I should do if he passed, Pappa always said that Oliver would help me settle his affairs, so I went to that same official. I gave him a letter to mail for me. Open, of course. I made sure it said how well I was being treated and that I only wished to leave because I felt I was a burden on my hosts—which I was."

"He mailed it? You said earlier that the Swedish government was the first to get involved."

"Oliver never got the letter, but the guide made a report about my father's death. More officials turned up. That's when I realized I was being officially detained, but I guess my letter reassured them. They left me in the custody of Byung-woo and Sung-mi instead of sending me to a work camp or jail."

"Why would they risk taking in a stranger? One from the West no less?"

That cool, inquisitive tone of his bothered her. She started to sit up, but his arm stayed heavy across her waist. After a disgruntled moment, she sank back into him.

"When Sung-mi brought me upstairs that first night, she put me in a tiny room under the slant of the roof. It had a single bed with a handmade quilt. There was a chair with a doll in it and a pair of child's glasses on the table. There was a box of puzzles beneath the bed."

"Ah," he said with solemn understanding.

"Yes. Their daughter was sick her whole life and died when she was twelve. Sung-mi talked about her a lot. That's how I learned Korean. She taught me to cook and took me to the sewing circles where the local women made uniforms for the army. In many ways, she became the mother I'd missed all my life. Byung-woo was kind, too. He took me fishing sometimes. We barely spoke, but we sat by the river for hours."

"Sounds idyllic."

"Not really." Her wandering gaze landed on the square head of the handheld shower nozzle. She realized it perfectly reflected his face in its gold surface.

"No? Why not?" His voice lazily encouraged her to confide, but she jolted as she realized he was looking right at her in that tiny reflection.

He casually turned his head so his mouth nuzzled into her hair.

"I, um…"

She didn't know what disconcerted her more, the realization he might have been watching her the whole time she'd been talking or his languid return to assaulting her senses. Beneath the water, he cupped her breast and gently massaged.

"What were you saying?" He nibbled along her nape.

"Hmm? Oh. That I had to be very careful," she recalled dimly, tilting her head to expose more of her neck. "We were under constant surveillance." Her nipple tightened to stab into his palm. "My classmates at university didn't understand how I cared for my hosts and wanted to protect them as much as myself. They said that sort of thing makes me a traitor."

"Are you?"

"No." She twisted to face him.

His eyelids were heavy, but his gaze keen beneath. All he said was, "Good." And he pressed his mouth to hers. They didn't talk again until he said, "We should take this to the bed."

Giovanni had been fifteen when the car his father had been driving was broadsided and sent over an embankment, rolling three times before coming to rest. Everyone else had been killed instantly. Giovanni had spent a year in hospital, enduring endless pain and surgeries that culminated in amputation of his remaining leg when a stubborn infection had forced him to choose between his limb or his life.

He'd always been stubborn and competitive, but it had taken two more years of grit and effort before he felt comfortable in this new body, learning how it worked and ultimately achieving the independence he craved.

He'd never stopped hitting on girls. Charm was a quality Sicilian men possessed by law. He'd become sexually active around the same time as his peers, but there'd been a steeper learning curve for him when it came to giving and receiving pleasure.

Until a few days ago, he'd been satisfied with the frequency and quality of lovemaking he engaged in and thought he had it all figured out.

Freja was rewriting his entire scope of experience.

He kept telling himself he was only continuing to see her for investigative purposes, but as day four dawned and they'd barely been out of each other's sight since dinner that first night, he had to admit it was the sex. He couldn't keep his hands off her.

He had tried to take her home. Their first lazy morning had turned into an indolent afternoon, but she'd been scheduled to work that evening. His driver had parked outside her building and their goodbye in the back seat of his town car had turned into a steamy suggestion that she call in sick.

She'd left him long enough to run up to her flat for her laptop and to pack a small bag. She'd been here ever since, coaching a couple of her Korean students over video chat, helping with their English pronunciation and offering feedback on some writing assignments. She had made no effort to hide any of it while Giovanni answered emails on the other side of the room.

Yesterday, they'd strolled through the park, but the rest of the days they had stayed in. They worked, ate, swam, and waited for his small army of aids, therapists, assistants and housekeepers to leave so they could make love and lounge around half-dressed.

They had intimate encounters constantly. A light kiss turned into heavy petting that turned into an intense, inventive interlude. Other times he woke from a lengthy debauched session that had left him wrung out and supremely satisfied. His sense of contentment lingered into those moments when he turned his head to find her beside him, blinking awake and smiling through a yawn.

Those unguarded moments were the best and the worst. They convinced him she was exactly as she seemed—unusual, but ultimately harmless. For a woman who hadn't had a lover until a few days ago, however, she was taking to it like a duck to water. That forced him to ask himself if he was being played by a champion manipulator.

Even Everett was starting to worry, sounding impatient when Giovanni accepted his call. "She's still there. *Why?*"

Giovanni bit back asking Everett if he'd ever gotten laid, because he definitely should try it sometime.

"I'm in the pool." Despite the April rain spitting from the overcast sky. "What do you need?"

"Leave early and plan for a week in France in June," Everett said in crisp tone.

Giovanni didn't ask why. Everett would have a contact he wanted Giovanni to intercept or a party he wanted him to observe. It was the work he'd signed on for, but as he watched Freja continue to lap the pool in a graceful crawl, Giovanni resented Everett's claim on his time. He wasn't ready for this liaison to end.

Which was the most compelling reason it should.

"Sure," he muttered and clicked off his phone, sliding it into the pocket of his robe where it hung next to his pool lift. He pushed away from the ledge and windmilled a backstroke until he crossed paths with Freja.

She stopped to catch her breath. They both hooked an arm on the ledge.

"Is everything okay?" She pushed her wet hair off her face. "You look annoyed."

"Details about my trip. I'm leaving early." He had deliberately mentioned this trip their first evening. He was always clear with women that he wasn't looking for anything but a brief, enjoyable dalliance.

That same evening, Freja had called him a sexist for suggesting she aspired to marry and have children. Inexperienced she might be, but she wasn't immature. There were no unrealistic fantasies dancing in her eyes. There was no guilt trip that he had been leading her on. She expressed exactly the right pout of disappointment, then turned it into a rueful smile.

"Probably for the best." She wrinkled her nose. "The owner of the catering company asked if I should be admitted to hospital, I've called in sick so many times."

He slid his free arm around her waist, floating her into contact with his chest. Swimming always aroused him, but the desire sizzling in his wiring was all for her. That and the tendrils of possessiveness that were becoming barbed hooks within him as their time together drew to a close.

It was a potent combination that charged what was supposed to be a leisurely kiss into one with more ferocious greed than he intended.

She stiffened in surprise, then melted into him, greeting his tongue with her own as she moaned and coiled her limbs around him.

This was why he still had her here after four days. This response of hers was addictive.

He flexed his arm on the ledge to secure them at the edge of the pool and slid his other hand into the bottom of her suit, palming her bare ass. He'd had time to learn what she liked, and that always made her squirm. She tightened her thighs around his waist and rocked her hips against him.

She knew his triggers, too. She swooped her lips

across to suck his earlobe until he could hardly keep their heads above water.

The strings on her bikini were too much bother. He caught the neck strap and stretched it to bring it up and forward, dropping it away under the water between them. Her pale breasts with their pink tips sat just below the surface, pretty and tempting.

He scooped his arm under her butt and lifted her enough that he could suck her nipples, each one going cold and hard as a pebble in the brisk spring air.

"Giovanni," she gasped, hands scraping through his hair and roaming restlessly over his shoulders. "Let's go to the bedroom."

"So impatient," he teased grittily, even though that eagerness of hers never ceased to thrill him. Hell, he was right there with her, feeling so damned ravenous he didn't want to let her go for the time it would take to dry off and get to the bed. How would he go months without her when he couldn't bear to wait five minutes?

"I want to feel all of you," she said with a pang in her voice and a drift of her touch to delicately pinch his nipple.

He shuddered in reaction, nearly losing his grip on the ledge.

She chuckled softly as she dropped back into the water with a slosh. They were nose to nose again, mouth fusing to mouth with insatiate need. He shoved his hand in her bottoms again, squeezing her cheek and sliding his touch under her thigh. There. His long fingers reached the plump folds and fine hairs. A sweet noise throbbed in her throat as he found the heart of her response.

"If you want all of me, take me," he said against her mouth. Distant warning bells sounded in his head, but he ignored them. "I want to feel you, too." He deepened his touch, shaking with want at the idea of being naked inside her.

"H-here?" She blinked dazed eyes at him. "Without a condom?"

He wore them to protect his health. "I don't ejaculate," he reminded her.

Her hand dropped into the space between them. She pushed the front of his bathing suit down, freeing his erection. The cool of the water did nothing to chill his ardor. He pulled aside the crotch of her bathing suit, his thumb lingering to coax another jagged noise out of her.

She guided the head of his erection against her folds. Slowly he was enfolded in heat, a sensation so acute his whole body felt as though he was thrust into a furnace.

His one rational thought was that he shouldn't let them drown, but— He tilted his head back and swore his gratification at the overcast, spitting sky. "You're so *hot*."

"You feel good, too," she gasped, curling her arms and legs around him, clinging as they kissed and kissed.

The suspension of the water gave him more ability to thrust than he usually had. He used his arm to cushion her against the hard, tiled wall, but gripping the ledge, he was able to use his whole body to make love to her. It was incredibly exciting. The water swirled around them, further stimulating him, while Freja moved in response, making those gorgeous noises that told him he was giving her great pleasure.

He wanted to slow down and make this last forever,

it was so impossibly good, but the intensity was more than he could control.

"Giovanni," she gasped in the fractured breath of approaching climax.

"Come," he coaxed, speaking Sicilian because his own crisis gathered like a condensed ball of energy, ready to explode. "It's too good. I can't hold back."

He didn't want to. Ecstasy beckoned.

As the last of his discipline shredded, she released a cry of elation and convulsed against him. A ragged, "Freja," tore from his throat as his entire body shuddered in a way he hadn't experienced in years.

CHAPTER FOUR

FREJA WAS FEELING very subdued as she and Giovanni showered off the salt from the pool.

The shower was enormous with a dozen heads and nozzles and taps. He had a special chair he used in here, but there was still plenty of room for her. He'd even had his housekeeper purchase some organic, vanilla-scented body wash and shampoo, making it super easy to linger in the warm spray.

Or maybe she was seizing the excuse to draw out her last few minutes with him. Once she dried off and dressed, she would have to say goodbye and she didn't feel ready.

Not that she could say so. Giovanni was a sophisticated man. This was the sort of transitory affair that consenting adults engaged in. She kept reminding herself that this was a rite of passage on her part. It was her first tumble into physical intimacy, one that was paired with deep infatuation with a dynamic man. Getting her heart bruised was all part of the process.

If anything, she ought to view the termination of their affair as a healthy end point. They were ending things in a civilized and, frankly, necessary way. In recent years, she'd grown used to being autonomous and making her own decisions, but these last few days, she had found herself accommodating his presence in her life, trying to maximize the limited time she had with him. That was fine for a weekend, but arranging her world around a man had its pitfalls. She knew that.

Nevertheless, the sense of abandonment that engulfed her as their goodbye loomed threatened to crush her.

"You're being very quiet," Giovanni noted, turning off the sprayer he was using.

"Hmm? Oh." She tilted back her head to give her hair one last unneeded rinse, not wanting him to see the morose expression on her face. Her worst nightmare was to behave like some gauche teenager at the last minute. "I'm thinking of all those very compelling things like whether I need to pick up milk on my way home."

She turned off her showerhead and accepted the towel he handed her. She stayed in the shower to dry off while he rolled out to the spot under the heat lamp.

She realized he was being very quiet as well, sitting up straighter to saw the towel across his back, but watching her closely. Anxious for her to leave? She wrapped the towel around herself and stepped out with a meaningless smile plastered on her face.

"Freja." He reached out as she came even with him and tugged the bottom corner of her towel.

She scrabbled to secure it, letting out a laugh only to sober when she realized he wasn't trying to playfully steal it, only to get her attention. The gravity in his expression made her heart lurch.

"What's wrong?" Her hand instinctively tightened on the towel.

"Do you realize that I may have made you pregnant just now?"

"What?" She stumbled back a few steps, bumping into the edge of the sink.

"Are you going to faint?" He pushed forward and set a hard hand at her hip.

She kept one hand clenched in the towel, the other gripped the sink. "But you said—"

"I know." He gave a slight shrug that only hinted at sheepish because she didn't see a lot of embarrassment or remorse in him. "It was the last thing I expected and I could be wrong. The way it felt in the pool, though... I can't explain it, but it was different. I'm pretty sure I came inside you."

"But..." Maybe she was going to faint because her gaze couldn't seem to land on a stationary spot in the room and everything seemed to be spinning. "What should I do?"

"Come here." He nudged even closer and drew her into his lap.

She kind of collapsed, joints not wanting to support her.

He caught her, of course. She'd watched him do pull-ups while strapped into his workout chair, lifting the combined weight with what looked like effortless ease. His upper body was insanely strong, his arms the most secure place she could ever be.

"I feel so stupid," she mumbled. "The one thing I didn't want was for you to think I was naive just because I've never done this before. Unprotected sex is *such* a rookie move."

"Tell me about it. I know better myself."

She met his gaze hoping for humor, but the austere lines in his face dug into her heart like a shard of broken glass.

"I guess I take one of those morning-after pills?"

He didn't answer right away and she didn't look at him. She didn't realize she was chewing her thumbnail until he took her hand and eased it into her lap.

"It's possible nothing will happen. Paraplegic men have all sorts of fertility issues. Low counts…"

"Do you?"

"I have no idea what my count is. I've never been tested for it. Having children was always something I shelved in the back of my mental cupboard. I didn't imagine I could reach it without medical intervention." His thumb was wearing a restless circle into the back of her hand. "Obviously, it's your body, your choice, but I would like to wait and see what happens."

"What?" If he hadn't been holding her so firmly in his lap, she would have tumbled out and onto the floor in a splat of shock.

"I'm asking you not to take any pills. The chance you'll conceive is really low, but…" Huskiness crept into his tone. "I'd like to take that chance."

"Just…wait?" She couldn't make sense of any of it. That this was a thing that could happen, that he wanted her to *let* it happen. "But you're leaving," she reminded him, as if she needed him around to "wait and see." His part in such things was over.

"Well, you'll have to come to Europe with me," he stated as though that was obvious.

"I can't go to *Europe* with you!" Now she did find her legs and stood on both of them.

She realized he was still naked in his chair and entirely too confident and powerful in his natural state. He sent a circumspect look up at her.

"Why not? If it's a passport issue, I have people who can sort that very quickly."

"My passport is fine." She was pathological about keeping both of hers current. "But I have a job. Bills."

"It's catering." He dismissed it with a flick of his fingers. "They'll give your shifts to the next person on the list."

"And skip me in future because I'm unreliable. They'll fire me outright if they find out I'm seeing you. We're not supposed to fraternize with guests."

"That's not even an argument." He went through to the adjacent closet and found a pair of blue boxers, staying where he could see her as he pulled them on. "Catering is hardly a career you love or planned to do forever."

"I still need it. I have a flat to pay for."

"Lease it."

"Oh, just like that," she scoffed. "I'm not going to hand my keys to the first stranger who answers an ad. It takes time to find someone suitable."

"It takes a phone call to my property agent. She'll have someone with impeccable references in it tomorrow. And before you bring up your blogging or tutoring work, you've done both from this apartment. You can do them from anywhere with a Wi-Fi connection."

"Wow. Must be nice to solve all your problems with your bank account."

"It is," he assured her as she came into the closet, where he had pulled on a shirt and was working on his pants.

She found her own underwear in the drawer his housekeeper had allotted her. "Well, excuse me for pointing out the obvious, but my blog and tutoring income won't cover first-class airfare, let alone support me at your standard of living." The monthly cost of heating his rooftop pool was probably more than her mortgage payment. "I can't afford the type of hotels you stay in, either. Don't say you'll pay my way," she warned with a pointed finger.

"I travel by private jet," he said pithily. "One more body on board is a name on a manifest, no extra expense. Same goes for the hotels. Much of my stay will be in properties I own. I prefer spaces equipped to suit my needs. Feel free to cook if you're worried about the cost of food. I'm not."

She stood there feeling impotent, damp hair causing runnels of water to tickle irritatingly down her back. "I can't just—"

"Why not?" he cut in with a lift of his arrogant brows.

"Frankly?" She gave her wet hair a flick. "After spending most of my life following a man around the world, I'm not that keen to do it again."

She stepped into a pair of jeans and a light pullover, then looked for her empty suitcase to pack it.

"I've reached the part in your book where your father had the stroke," he said quietly. "It's difficult to read. Your writing is beautiful. Poignant. But it put a knife in my stomach that is twisted by every word. I had to stop."

She dropped her hands to her sides. He was the most disarming man!

"Thank you?" she mumbled, eyes burning white-hot.

"I keep thinking about that tour you're expected to do. I don't want to see your heartache exploited for book sales. Are you sure you want that?"

"No. But it's different when it's strangers. I don't care what they think." She hugged herself and gave him a disgruntled side-eye. "I worry what you think, though."

His stormy gray gaze was too intense to hold. "Why? Do you have something to hide?"

"No."

He left an expectant silence for her to fill, but she didn't know what he wanted her to say. Her heart panged with unexpected and acute inadequacy. And yearning. He was even more of a mystery to her than she was to him.

This was the crux of her worry about his effect on her, she realized. He touched her as though she was delicate china, brought her to the heights of pleasure and gave her free rein to explore his body. He let her sleep in his bed and share his bath and gave her his Wi-Fi password, but there was an invisible wall between them. He kept himself deeply guarded and impenetrable, but expected her to somehow reveal her whole self to him.

When she didn't say anything, he rolled close and encircled her wrist with his loose grip. "You said you were struggling for blog content. Wouldn't traveling help?"

"I could take a trip on my own if I thought that was the answer."

"Would you please quit arguing?" His eyes turned pewter with molten emotions. "If you're pregnant with my child, I want to look after you both."

And there went her knees turning to gelatin again.

"What happens if I am? We've known each other *four days*, Giovanni."

"Then things will accelerate even more."

Her choked laugh was more a sob of helplessness.

"Many couples have unprotected sex for years and don't conceive." The stiff defensiveness in him cut through better than anything else might have. "This is very much a long shot, Freja."

"It's not that I don't *want* your baby, Giovanni. Only that I'm still figuring out my own life. It makes it hard to imagine being responsible for someone else's, especially one so vulnerable."

"You won't be doing that alone. That's why I want you to come with me."

She shook her head, unable to believe she was doing this, but she knew she would regret it if she didn't take this chance to spend a little more time with him, to see if it could turn into more.

"Okay," she agreed.

Pregnant?

It shouldn't be such a shocking possibility for a woman who was having regular sex, but Freja was completely unprepared for the idea. She fell inward as she processed it, existing in a sort of meditative state, barely participating in the real world beyond the necessary preparations for travel with Giovanni. She quit her catering job and advised her students their schedule would be changing. She leased her apartment and put a few things in storage.

Giovanni told her not to pack more than one case, which was hilarious because she always traveled light, but he added, "My people will ensure you have everything you need."

Even her father hadn't been that arrogant. He'd paid her for odd jobs and photos, then sent her along to the local shops to find her own feminine products and shoes that fit. She had saved up for her own laptop as a teenager, rather than using her father's castoff, but that was as materialistic as she got.

So relying on Giovanni and letting his schedule dictate hers felt both natural and challenging. When she tried to imagine adding another body and personality to the equation, her brain shorted out and wandered down impractical paths of potential baby names instead.

Not that she could resent Giovanni for turning her life upside down. He might be formidable, but he was also remarkable. He commanded respect not just for his wealth or the confidence that carried him along so well, but for the person he was beneath.

He might not reveal much about himself, but she was catching glimpses. He made dry remarks that had his physical therapist snickering and came up with fresh solutions over conference calls with his development teams. He even generously shoehorned a last-minute charity event into his packed schedule.

"You're on board with that?" she dimly heard him ask. His voice firmed. "Freja?"

"Hmm? Sorry, I thought you were talking to someone else." She was barely tracking what was going on in his stylish, contemporary villa on the outskirts of Milan. She'd slept on the plane, so she'd been awake half the night. Now the stylist was turning her in circles, taking her measurements while someone else made notes. Another assistant flashed swatches while yet another was in a huddle with the young man who seemed to be charged with organizing Giovanni's calendar. She kept hearing color-related questions like, "Red carpet? Black tie or white?"

"*Ciau.* Welcome back to the conversation," Giovanni teased as she blinked at him. "I know I said we would use today to recover from jet lag and get your wardrobe started, but I'm accepting an invitation for this evening. It's a good cause. A sport program for child amputees."

"Oh. Yes, I heard you say that. So you're going out tonight? Of course. Do whatever you normally would. I'll probably be asleep before dinner."

"*We* are going out," he said dryly. "But you can nap this afternoon if you need to. Can you have something ready by then?" He directed that to the stylist.

"Of course. Shall I book one of my technicians to help with hair and makeup?"

"Thank you."

Freja would have argued that she was capable of putting on her own lipstick, but someone else came in with a call for him and they weren't alone again until several hours later. By then, they'd flown to Monaco.

The flight was less than an hour, but it added to her sense of disorientation. They were given a penthouse in the hotel. It was very swanky and staff were buzzing around, shifting furniture and taking orders.

Giovanni caught her stifling a yawn, and said, "Go lie down. I'll join you as soon as I finish my calls. The desk will wake us when your dress arrives."

That was indeed what happened, tying her up for another hour. By the time she joined him in the lounge, she was more scattered and overwhelmed than ever.

His head went back and he raked his gaze down the one-shouldered dress in a color the stylist had called "Egyptian blue."

"I thought you were beautiful in a catering uniform that did you no favors. This…" His attention came back to her face and his brows snapped together. "Are you unwell? If this was too much for you, you should have said."

"It is too much, but not in the way you mean. This is an *evening* gown, Giovanni!" She plucked at the beaded silk, accidentally opening the slit that climbed to midthigh.

"Call me old-fashioned, but when I'm on a date, I prefer to be the one wearing the tuxedo."

And he looked amazing in his dove-white jacket over a white shirt and scrupulously tailored black pants. His bow tie was black, as was his satin pocket square.

"Is the dress not comfortable? You look fantastic." His appreciative gaze took a second, slower tour down to her silver gladiator heels. "I'm regretting that we're already late because I would love to see you in *just* those." His gaze lingered on her shoes.

"What about these?" She gave the earrings dangling off her lobes an askance bobble. They were exquisite cascades of blue sapphires and white diamonds, and had to be worth a small country's GDP.

"Those, too," he said throatily. "Now I'll be hard all evening, picturing you in only those earrings and those shoes. Thanks."

"That's not—" She almost stamped her foot. "The stylist told me they're *real*."

"As opposed to imaginary?"

"As opposed to costume. When you said we were attending a casino fundraiser, I thought that meant a casino *theme*. That we would go to a bingo hall or the back of a pub where you wager with vouchers and bid on prizes like movie tickets in a bucket of flavored popcorn." That was the sort of fundraiser she'd attended at university.

"Ah. No. Real casino, real money."

She suspected he was laughing at her as he moved to press the button for their private elevator. It was small, so she let him back his chair in before she joined him.

"I'll stake you fifty thousand euros, though," he added.

"I'm not going to gamble your money!"

"You don't like gambling? No worries. There's a silent auction. I'll stake you fifty thousand for that, too."

"I'm not going to throw your money away on silly prizes, either!"

"Should I just write the check and we'll stay in the room?" His tone cooled. "It's a very reputable organization, Freja. They're getting my money either way. I thought we'd enjoy a proper date and let them have the scoop on announcing our relationship, to get them extra exposure. I'd rather we were old news by the time I finalize my acquisition of the airline later this week."

The elevator stopped and she rocked on her heels, realizing she had underestimated him in the most bizarre way. She had known he was rich, but it hadn't penetrated that he was "acquire an airline" rich.

The doors opened and she made an effort to rearrange her flabbergasted expression, but how was she supposed to process any of this?

He lifted a brow, waiting for her to make up her mind.

"Are you calling our first date *im*proper?" she finally asked.

The corner of his mouth twitched. He scratched his upper lip and said, "One could argue either way, I think."

He waved for her to precede him out of the elevator.

It was a short walk through the mild evening from the hotel into the casino. The lavishness of their hotel suite hadn't prepared her for the opulence of the casino. She tried not to gawk as they were shown through a massive hall where a stained-glass dome dominated the ceiling. Ornate gold filigree framed what had to be hand-painted frescoes, and crystal chandeliers sparkled over the various gaming tables.

She had barely caught a glimpse of the spinning images on the slot machines before they were shown through a passageway between marble columns, into a private salon.

If she had thought the main hall a monument to luxury, here was where indulgence met taste in all forms. The clatter of tourists and seasoned gamblers was shut out by a small orchestra providing a refined background to the smooth conversation and cultivated laughter. Men and women in stunning evening wear milled around gaming tables and hovered near the bar, all casually flashing jewels and gold watches, tiaras and even a ceremonial sword hanging off the hip of a decorated military officer.

"Giovanni!" A lovely blonde with a soft British accent greeted him warmly, bending to kiss each of his cheeks. "You're too good to us, flying in at the last minute like this. Hello. I'm Clair. Thank you for coming." The woman offered to shake Freja's hand.

"Freja Anderson, Clair Dmitriev. Clair is on the board of several charities that benefit children, this one included," Giovanni explained. He asked after Clair's children and husband.

"Oh, everyone has teeth either coming in or falling out, but otherwise we're all well."

"Aleksy, too?" he asked dryly, making her chuckle with enjoyment.

"Not unless he's losing his gold fillings at the poker table." She glanced toward the back of the room. "I told him you were coming. He's looking forward to catching up with you. Don't you dare outbid him on the necklace in the auction. It's to die for," she told Freja with a sigh of admiration. "An amazing goldsmith out of Budapest donated it. I'm so sorry for rushing away. I have to straighten out a mix-up with the presentation, but I'll check in with you again as soon as I can."

"That's how she does it," Giovanni said with laconic amusement as Clair hurried away. "If she wanted the necklace that badly, her husband would have already bought it for her. But let's see if we can start a bidding war over it."

The necklace was beautiful and Giovanni doubled the current bid, earning a frosty look from a woman in a sea-green gown. He offered a small fortune for a rare bottle of cognac and another for a hand-blown vase.

"Ah. You need luggage," he said as they paused before the designer set.

It had a vintage carpetbag look trimmed in brown leather with gold clasps and hinges. The ensemble included four suitcases of various sizes, a steamer trunk, a shoe chest, a jewelry case, a garment bag and a hatbox. It claimed to have a value of eighty thousand euros.

Giovanni put a one in front of that figure.

"What are you doing?" she hissed, appalled.

"Winning."

"I need *a* suitcase." For underwear. "All the eveningwear is on loan, isn't it?"

He sent her a look that asked if she was missing several marbles. "This is why I find you endlessly fascinating. I can never tell if you're feeding me a line like you did about being married, or if you're actually that naive."

"Are you serious?" Her stomach dropped to the middle of the earth. "Please tell me these are loans." She pointed at her ears.

"I thought they would suit you and they do. This says they'll monogram each piece." He nodded at the bidding sheet. "That's a nice touch, don't you think?" He scratched off his bid and increased it, then rolled along, leaving her speechless.

She was still trying to come to terms with the idea

she could, however unlikely, be pregnant. Now she began to understand what it would mean if she was. She would be part of Giovanni's life. Part of *this*. The high fashion and high rollers, the titled and the privileged.

Freja had spent her whole life as an odd duck. She had learned to embrace her status as an outsider and press forward on that left foot so she wouldn't be shunned completely. She didn't expect to be accepted into the different cultures she encountered, but it meant she'd spent most of her life feeling apart from everyone around her. She'd had her father for company and later Sung-mi, but even they had eventually fallen away. She had never found "my people, my home."

Then she'd come to America and encountered the strangest culture shock of all. In New York, everyone stuck out so no one did. She hadn't realized how comfortable she'd been there until she failed to blend in again.

She didn't belong here! This crowd drowned odd ducks in orange sauce and ate them with roasted beets.

She didn't even want to belong here. She had grown up on a shoestring, not living in poverty, but often a witness to it. She still lived very frugally, not liking to see waste when she knew how hard some people worked for the little they had.

"I'm going to try my luck at the craps table," Giovanni said.

She nodded. "I'm going to read the…" She gestured absently at the display of framed stories about children the charity had helped.

It was an excuse to steal a moment to catch her breath, but soon she was losing herself in each of the success stories. Children hurt by land mines or illness or pure bad luck were all finding purpose and achieving bigger things than ribbons and bronze medallions. They wore smiles and pride and confidence. Each photo lifted Freja's heart a little more until she was smiling to herself with happiness for them.

Darn him, this *was* a good cause. She couldn't be angry with him for being wretchedly generous in supporting it. She went to his side and set a hand on his shoulder.

"I'm losing. Give me some lady luck." He showed her the dice in his hand.

She blew on them and he threw.

A roar of approval went up around the table.

It was the beginning of a hot streak that had people betting in an increasing frenzy. She blew each time while Giovanni stacked up chips before him. She couldn't help holding her breath, then bursting with a cheer of laughter with everyone else when the sevens kept coming up. She was completely caught up in the play as the stakes rose higher and higher.

Suddenly Giovanni said, "That's a million." He pushed his stack of chips toward the stickman. "Donate it to the foundation."

There was another loud reaction from the spectators, this one a mix of shock and approval with a few moans that their luck was changing as someone else moved in to throw the dice.

Freja and Giovanni ran a small gauntlet of congratulations before settling into a quieter area of the room to sample the canapés and enjoy complimentary champagne sent over by Clair.

"Please don't ever put me through a roller coaster like that again. I don't think my heart can stand it." Freja set her hand on her chest, still breathless. "I thought you were here because you're a big softie who can't resist helping injured children, but you're actually an adrenaline junkie who enjoys risk, aren't you?"

"Aren't you?"

He might have meant it as light banter, but she heard the edge in his voice that invaded sometimes, the one that made her feel as though he saw something in her that wasn't there. The crash of his gaze into her own made her heart stutter and trip.

Every time she thought she was coming to know him a little, he had one of these mercurial shifts that disoriented her again. He did have a taste for risk. For one second, he let her see there was an atavistic barbarian in him willing to fight to the death if he had to.

She ought to have gone cold with premonition, but something in her leaped toward that Neanderthal the way a stray fleck of metal latched on to a magnet.

She was so shocked by her reaction, she yanked her gaze from his and tried to steady her breathing, but she was left teetering upon an intrinsic difference between them—as if they needed more proof beyond this enormous wealth gap.

"No," she said quietly but firmly. "Some people enjoy the tension of a haunted house, but I don't put myself in scary situations if I can avoid it. I've been genuinely frightened and I braved it out because I wanted to survive, but I don't like it. I'm here *in spite* of my fear."

"You're afraid right now? Why?" His steel gaze kept swooping into hers, catching like talons into her heart.

"It's obvious, isn't it? We're very different, but we might wind up tied to each other for life."

"I'm not frightened of that."

"Of course *you're* not!" She laughed, but there was mild hysteria in it.

He narrowed his eyes. "What does that mean?"

"It means it's one thing to lower into a cage and admire the shark. It's quite another to swim in the open water with him. I'm not a shark." She tapped her breastbone.

"You want me to believe you're a goldfish? I don't."

"And you want me to believe after that display—" she pointed in the direction of the craps table "—that you'll be happy stuck in a bowl with me and a guppy you didn't ask for. I don't."

"You don't know me," he bit out.

She choked on the irony of that while he sat back, mouth pinned flat with frustration.

After a moment, she sighed and leaned forward to set her hand on his sleeve.

"The fact that my experience is strange enough to write a book about it makes people think I'm a lot more interesting than I am. I don't actually want to be the most interesting person in the room. There's a lot more security in being exactly the same."

"Is that what you want? Security?" A muscle in his cheek ticked. "Because I can definitely give you that."

"Financial security is important." There was no denying that. "But I'm talking about emotional security." And neither was likely to be found in a casino, she thought with a droll observation of the fortunes on the table and the straying eyes on the faces.

Or him, she acknowledged as she brought her attention back to Giovanni and fell into the turbulent eyes of a creature far more dangerous than a shark. Not the merciless stare of a predator about to pounce, but the calculating intelligence of a man.

So compelling and so inscrutable.

"Do you mind if I go back to the room? Jet lag is catching up to me." Along with a deep sense of inadequacy.

He refused to let her cross the street alone and escorted her to the penthouse. He was restless once they got there, though, not removing his jacket or tie. He picked up the card on the tray that held a bottle of scotch and read aloud, "Compliments of the management."

He tucked the card into his pocket and helped himself to a pour, but only held it without sipping. His tension was obvious.

"You're realizing that I'm as boring as I claim, aren't you?" She was trying to make light of it when she actually regretted being so frank. "You don't have to turn in because I am. If you want to go back and gamble, please do."

"I missed speaking to Clair's husband." He set aside his drink. "We have mutual business interests that I'd like to discuss with him. I won't be long."

It sounded perfectly reasonable, but for some reason her stomach clenched with suspicion. She wasn't sure why. It made her feel like a jealous girlfriend to have this lurching reaction when she had no reason to mistrust him. She had just urged him to go!

But she was stung that he was so quick to leave.

Everything felt very tenuous all of a sudden. The

small connection they'd developed in New York was disintegrating, mostly because she was realizing exactly how far out of her reach he really was. Perhaps that sense of affinity had only ever been a conjured fantasy in her head anyway. She wanted to say, *Stay. Hold me.* But that seemed pathetic.

She made herself cross to set a hand on his shoulder. As she leaned to peck his mouth with a kiss, she murmured, "Good night."

He caught a firm hand around the back of her neck and held her for a long, possessive kiss that tasted of craving and frustration and conflict, further confusing her and leaving her breathless.

He reluctantly released her, gray eyes stormier than ever—which only reinforced her sense that something was amiss between them.

"I'll be back within the hour," he promised. "I'll try not to wake you."

She nodded and turned away, throat tight.

CHAPTER FIVE

"HAVE YOU LOST your mind?" was Everett's casual greeting when Giovanni let himself into the private salon with the card that had been propped against the bottle of scotch in his suite. "Why is she still with you? You're *working*."

Giovanni met the ice-blue eyes of his colleague. His boss, if one wanted to get technical. His *friend*, since there was no one else on earth who knew about this sideline job of his except the man who'd recruited him.

"The chancellor was there with his wife. His mistress was not, but he kept the napkin when his drink was delivered. The server was a brunette, midtwenties, five-eight or -nine with a mole on the left side of her throat. When she brought a scotch to the admiral, he tipped her *very* generously."

Everett sipped his drink, considering that in silence.

Everett had been born to a Swiss father who was a captain of automotive engineering and a French mother who translated at Interpol. He'd been at boarding school with Giovanni's brother and had come to the hospital often in that first year after the crash, as lost without his friend as Giovanni had been without his brother.

They had taken different paths for several years, but when Giovanni had uncovered a letter from a foreign government official attempting to blackmail his father into making certain concessions, he had realized it was evidence that his family had been murdered, not killed in a random crash as he'd always believed.

He hadn't known where to turn or who to trust, but given Everett's mother's connections, Giovanni had reached out to him.

That's when Everett had revealed he was more than the spoiled playboy he portrayed himself to be. He was employed by the American government and soon persuaded Giovanni to help him gather information and evidence for various ongoing investigations.

Giovanni had the ability to travel freely and infiltrate the highest industrial and political circles. It was amazing how nonthreatening a man in a wheelchair seemed to most people, or how quickly they opened up if they thought they could earn a favor from a wealthy man.

Giovanni had latched on to the challenge and inherent danger—Freja had read him correctly. There was an indescribable thrill in undercover work, avoiding detection while subversively righting wrongs and cleaning house at the highest level.

That side of his nature had made her uncomfortable, though, which left him questioning how badly he wanted to keep doing it.

"What of the waitress in *your* life?" Everett asked idly.

"You tell me," Giovanni challenged, hackles instantly rising. "Have you found anything?"

"No." Everett's mouth twisted with dismay. "All her

income streams are legit. The monitoring of her tutoring hasn't turned up anything except one young man who is faking bad grades so he can keep paying her to talk to him. You have competition for her affections."

Giovanni didn't find that funny. At all.

"I told you she was harmless."

"Harmless?" Everett scoffed. "In less than twenty-four hours after approaching one of my most valued and highly placed operatives, she was in your bed. She hasn't left it. I'm not suggesting that chair means you're dead from the waist down, but this is completely out of character for you. If she was the corn-fed milkmaid she resembles, I wouldn't bat an eye, but she spent two years in *North Korea* and came out without a scratch. *How?*"

"Have you read her book?" Giovanni had finished it on the plane and Freja couldn't be more wrong, calling herself boring. She was resourceful and resilient. Kind and warmly funny. Infinitely fascinating.

"Have I read a lengthy fairy tale that provides a comprehensive cover story for a sleeper agent? Yes. It stretches credulity. Her father could still be alive there. The authorities could be using him as leverage to keep her in line. Or holding those people she lived with. You can't risk having such a dark horse shadowing your every move. Send her back to New York," Everett ordered.

He debated briefly, then admitted, "I can't. We're waiting to see if she's pregnant."

Everett choked on his scotch.

"Screw you," Giovanni bit out. "I can get a woman pregnant."

Maybe. Hell, he didn't know, but from the moment

he'd realized there was a chance Freja might be carrying his baby, there was no question in him as to how he wanted to proceed. Of course she would stay with him. Of course he would marry her if a baby was on the way.

His reaction was primal and immediate, but he hadn't given thought to how that would look long-term, not until their odd conversation this evening when she'd pointed out how ill-suited she thought they were.

She was afraid to be tied to him by the child they might share. *Financial security is important, but I'm talking about emotional security.*

His ego was stung by the suggestion he would fail to provide everything she needed, but emotions were something he no longer used—like shoes.

"I wasn't questioning your ability." Everett gave a last cough into his fist. "I'm astonished you let her maneuver you into that risk. Can you be sure it's yours? You've known her less than a week."

"Screw you again. I'm not a victim. Sometimes things happen." The details were none of Everett's damned business. "I'm man enough to take responsibility for my own lapse in judgment so I will."

"Are you? Because this is sounding like a very big lapse." Everett was referring to more than a skipped condom. He meant getting involved with Freja at all.

"You've been doing this too long if you regard an innocent woman with this much cynicism, Everett."

"This cynicism keeps me and my people alive. You're one of my people, Giovanni, so appreciate it."

"Warm and fuzzy as that sounds, not everyone lives in this cloak-and-dagger world we occupy. *She* doesn't," Giovanni asserted.

"Yes, we do. *You* do." Everett sat on the edge of the sofa cushion, leaning forward. "If she is an innocent bystander, you're putting her in danger. If your cover is blown, she becomes a target. Do you realize that?"

"Of course I realize that!" Giovanni gripped the rims of his wheels so hard he should have bent them. "If she's not pregnant, I'll send her back to New York," he conceded in a snarl.

"That's the first intelligent thing you've said since you came in here." Everett sat back again. "What are you going to do if she is?"

"Marry her," Giovanni answered without hesitation. "And retire."

Everett swore. "I'll hope this is a false alarm, then."

Giovanni headed to the door aware he should be hoping the same thing. But he wasn't.

Despite her best efforts to quiet her misgivings and fall asleep, Freja was wide awake when Giovanni came to bed.

"Did you speak to him?" she asked.

He stilled with the covers still lifted by his upraised arm. "Who?"

"Aleksy."

"Oh. No." He finished settling on his back beside her. "He was tied up with someone else."

It was dark. She couldn't see his expression and he was a master at keeping any sort of emotional tells from his voice, but somehow that brisk "don't ask" tone left an impression that he wasn't being honest. She didn't know what the truth was, but that wasn't it.

A fault line cracked through her heart, leaving the

two pieces offset in her chest. Which scared her. She had been lying there thinking about how quickly and deeply involved they'd become, trying to convince herself it was an entanglement that had more to do with logistics and sex than her heart, but this sudden, acute ache wouldn't be happening if she wasn't falling for him in a more profound way.

Should she challenge him? What was the point? If he wanted to tell her the truth, he would already be doing so.

"Why are you still awake?" he asked. "I thought you were tired."

"I am, but I can't stop thinking," she murmured.

"About?"

When she hesitated to answer, he rolled to face her and dragged her into the spoon of his body, his bulky warmth at her back something she'd been missing as she lay here alone.

"You're not boring," he growled. "You're witty and intelligent. So self-possessed I forget you're actually quite young and new to intimate relationships."

"Well, that's it exactly. What if we wind up married and we don't even know who we're married to?"

"We'll cross that bridge when we get to it. Do you want me to help you sleep?" He nuzzled his lips through her hair against her nape.

Oh, he knew exactly how easily that caress distracted her. A pleasurable shiver slid down her back while his hand shifted the silk of her nightgown against her stomach.

"I believe that involves keeping me awake a little longer." Nevertheless, her hips wiggled an instinctive answer, nudging deeper into the bend of his body, seeking the growing firmness she found there.

He made a noise of satisfaction and stroked his hand down her hip and thigh, then gathered her nightgown against his wrist as he came back up. His light touch grazed the damp hairs between her thighs and lingered to explore deeper, making her draw a breath of deep longing.

Another rumble of erotic gratification vibrated his chest against her back.

"This is why you can't sleep, *tisoru*." He stroked his fingers into the growing moisture, bringing her to vibrant, gasping life. "I'll be back. Stay right here." He rolled away and she heard the drawer as he retrieved a condom.

Moments later, he settled behind her again. The thick shape of him prodded where she was swollen with longing.

"I feel weak," she said on a small sob as her body easily took him in. "You haven't even kissed me yet."

"I will." His stubbled chin moved the hair from her neck, and he opened his mouth against her skin. "I'll kiss you here if you need it." He drew her thighs apart, bracing her leg atop his thigh so she was open to his touch as he traced where his stiff shape filled her. "Tell me what you want. I'll give you anything."

"This," she breathed helplessly as she guided his caress. "I want this."

"Mmm. *Paradisu*," he agreed, taking his time with his luxurious explorations, not moving within her, but growing her arousal in increments while he dabbled kisses up her neck and suckled her earlobe. "Anytime you worry whether we will get along, think of how perfectly we fit like this, hmm?"

"I can't think," she said with a fractured breath. "You make me—" She gasped with shock at how quickly climax engulfed her.

He firmed his touch so he impaled her as deeply as he could while she shivered in orgasm. He hissed with pleasure at the way she convulsed in his arms.

Then he spoke only Sicilian, tone filled with praise as he stroked her all over, still barely shifting within her while he brought her to another peak of arousal before he joined her in the blinding ecstasy of release.

The next week passed in a blur. Freja enjoyed the mornings. She often joined Giovanni during his swim or physical therapy workout. Their breakfast was usually private. They would banter about the latest headlines and plan the rest of the day.

The rest of the day was mildly hellish. He would disappear for meetings while she was sent for fittings and spa treatments. Perhaps he thought he was spoiling her, but she didn't love strangers playing with her feet or using tweezers on her brows. Long nails made it hard to type and the polish made her feel vaguely suffocated.

Evenings were tolerable if lengthy events ranging from cocktail parties to white-tie galas. After the first two, Giovanni said, "You're very good at this."

"Talking to people? So are you. Everyone says you're so charming, but I've noticed all you do is coax them to talk about themselves. Sneaky."

He didn't laugh. He fixed her with his sharpened

gaze and noted, "You spoke with the countess a long time. What about?"

"Horses."

Giovanni wanted to know more. He nudged her along until she had relayed every word she'd exchanged with the pleasant if self-important woman.

"I didn't realize you were so into dressage." Was he *interested* in that other woman? "You should have joined us."

He must have heard the spark in her tone, but only said, "I thought you might have had a chance to mention your book. She does go on, though, doesn't she?" He changed the subject.

His curiosity stayed with her, feeding the tiny uncertainties in her that a dynamic man who had his pick among all these well-bred heiresses could remain interested in her.

A few days later, they had an even more disturbing encounter. They were in Frankfurt and Giovanni left to meet with automotive engineers. Freja was booked for a massage and a facial, but the sun was shining and she decided a walk along the river would relax her more.

She wound up crossing the Eiserner Steg, the iron footbridge. She was leaving a coffee shop, considering a visit to the museum up the block, when she saw Giovanni come out of it.

Her first instinct was to rush up and catch him. His car was pulling up to the curb, but two steps into her trot, she halted as it occurred to her that he might be with someone—a woman?

He moved toward the black sedan alone. The driver

opened the door and Giovanni took one casual glance down the block, as anyone might.

He stiffened. They were a full block away, but she could tell he saw her. She knew he could see that she was staring at him, but there was that split second when he almost pretended he didn't see her and considered leaving.

She stood there with her feet rooted by confusion. Betrayal. Absorbing that he had *definitely* lied to her this morning about where he was going.

He said something to his driver and swiveled his chair, rolling toward her. After a second, she managed to stumble forward, then stop at the corner and wait for the light. She met him on the opposite corner.

"What are you doing here?" was his crisp greeting, as if she was the one off course. He looked at the coffee in her hand then glanced behind her. "Are you meeting someone?"

"No. Are *you*?"

"No. How did you get here? You're supposed to be in the spa."

Supposed to be?

"I felt like a walk."

"You *walked* from the hotel? You need to text me when you decide to go out alone. What if you got lost or something happened to you?"

"Are you serious? I was seven when my father taught me to avoid the streets where girls in heavy makeup and short skirts stand on corners. The only crime in this district is how much they charge tourists for coffee." She lifted her biodegradable cup. "Maybe *you* should text *me*, since you seem to be the one who's lost."

Oh, this man knew how to use a stare to slice and dice. "Let's get in the car. I'll take you back to the hotel."

"No, thank you. I feel like visiting the museum." She really didn't. "Perhaps you'd like to join me? Oh, you've already been, haven't you? Shame."

"Don't turn this into something it's not," he said in a withering voice. "I had a few minutes to kill before my meeting. The display on the history of the financial sector is interesting. Use my ticket. You can probably get in for free." He offered it to her.

She wanted to throw her coffee in his face. She marched past him.

"Freja!" he bit out through gritted teeth.

They pivoted to face one another, a handful of paces apart, like duelists.

"It was nothing," he said quietly. "Go in and ask around. People will remember if the man in the wheel-chair was with anyone. I wasn't. We're fighting over nothing."

It didn't feel like nothing. Her chest was ready to burst with pressure. Her eyes were hot, but dry.

"We'll go in together." He came toward her.

"I don't even want to go. Not anymore." She looked back in the direction of the footbridge. It had been covered in love locks and she'd indulged a fantasy where she and Giovanni placed one. She should have been thinking about looking up flights to New York.

"If you're having second thoughts, just tell me," she said, refusing to play games.

He flinched. "I'm not."

"Because I told you we weren't suited for each other. I'd rather you were up-front—"

"I am not having second thoughts," he repeated firmly. "This isn't remotely what you're thinking." He sent a frustrated look toward the museum entrance. "Look, I'll walk with you. You're right. It's a nice day. We should enjoy it."

"What about your meeting?" she asked with suspicion.

"I'll cancel it." He took out his phone, sent a text and pocketed it again. Then he waved at his driver, signaling he didn't need him.

She stood there searching his expression, trying to process this about-face.

As he met her gaze, his shoulders lost some of their starch.

"I've been alone for a long time," he said without heat. "I've been making decisions for myself since I was fifteen. Major ones, like whether to have my own leg amputated." He waved at his stumps. "Answering to someone else does not come naturally."

He turned his chair and jerked his head to indicate she should walk with him.

"Telling people to fall in line is perfectly natural, however," she said, still sullen, but walking alongside him.

"It's like I was born for it," he said dryly.

"I didn't know that about your leg," she said after they'd crossed the street and were heading back to the river walk. "You don't have any relatives? A guardian who could have helped you with that decision?"

For a second, she thought he would do that thing where he deflected and turned everything on her. Instead he said, "I have some aunts and uncles who did what they could, but they had their own families. We weren't close because my father had traveled so much I'd rarely seen them. I kept up on my schooling with a tutor and when I was discharged, it was more convenient all around to send me back to boarding school. It was already wheelchair-accessible and there were nurses to monitor my health, physical education staff to assist with therapy and my athletic aspirations."

"What about school holidays?"

"I usually had a competition somewhere or I just stayed and trained. It was only a year before I moved on to university and would have left home anyway."

"It still seems—"

"Don't call me sad."

"I wouldn't dare," she mumbled against the lid of her coffee.

She caught his mouth twitch. He was a tiny bit amused.

The river walk was paved and offered lovely views of the water and abundant greenery between the buildings. She paused to take a photo of the skyline on the opposite bank.

"Did you come here with your father?"

"On this walk exactly? At least four times." She looked at the image, decided to take one more. "To the city, probably a dozen. If we're counting passing through airports and train stations, so many times I couldn't tell you. I took a photo of myself on the footbridge today, to match one he took of me for one of his earliest books. Oliver and my agent have suggested I follow in his footsteps. They said I could offer some of his most popular destinations a 'then and now' treatment, with the contemporary twist of a woman striking out on her own. This was my first stab at it, to see if I like it or if it makes me miss him too much."

"And?"

"Both. It's nostalgic, but makes me melancholy, too. I'll see what kind of hits I get on the blog, but I already know people prefer more colorful places like Marrakesh."

"You are not going to travel alone."

She sipped her cooling coffee. "Why not? Do you ever travel for pleasure? Or is it always business?"

One of those unreadable shields slid over his expression. "One could argue you haven't traveled for pleasure, given it was your father's occupation."

She sighed at that enormously typical deflection.

He heard it. "I don't like talking about myself, Freja."

"Is it too personal to ask why not?" she asked snippily.

"Because I have to give up enough personal information as it is." He gave his wheels an impatient push as they reached a slight incline. "I have to let people touch me as though I'm a dog at the vet. They take blood and write down what I'm eating and whether I'm following instructions. They're only trying to help, I know that, but it's still a loss of dignity, especially when they ask me to do something and I have to say I can't. And you wouldn't believe the things that perfect strangers have the gall to ask because I'm down here at the height of a child."

"Am I allowed to be mad on your behalf?"

"Don't waste your energy. But I'll have a sip of that coffee."

They passed it back and forth as they continued along.

"I won't pretend I'm an easy man, Freja. I will continue to be arrogant and uncommunicative, but I will never cheat on you. I promise."

He sounded so sincere, she had to believe him.

Giovanni was more careful over the next few days. By the time they settled into his penthouse in Paris, things between him and Freja had returned to what passed as their normal, but Everett was right. Much as Giovanni hated to admit it, this wasn't sustainable. The mere thought of sending her back to New York had him tensing his arm around her, though, accidentally waking her.

She drew a deep breath and stretched, warm curves shifting against his side while her hand made a lazy pass across his chest.

"Did I fall asleep? I didn't mean to," she said in a murmur and snuggled back into him, thigh coming up to his waist and lips turning into his shoulder. Her hair tickled under his jaw and her breath warmed his skin as she said, "We have to go out tonight, don't we?"

"We have time." He played his fingers in her hair, bordering on addicted to this simple pleasure of having her naked in bed beside him, all sated and warm as they dozed off their sex.

Ah, the sex. That wicked, exalted act that had gotten him into this predicament.

"Freja?" He discovered his voice wasn't nearly as steady as it should be. He cleared his throat. "When do you expect to know if you're pregnant?"

Just like that, the equilibrium they'd found after that difficult day in Frankfurt was sucked away, leaving a silence so profound, he could hear his own heartbeat in his ears.

"I'm a day late," she said in a small voice.

His heart lurched so hard, the sound in his ears kicked to life like a furnace bursting into action on a shot of fuel. His whole being was accosted by euphoria.

"A day," he repeated with wonder.

"Only one. It doesn't mean—"

"I know." He touched her lips to silence her. "Let me have this." He had told himself it wouldn't matter, that it was such a long shot he shouldn't project any anticipation into it, but he closed his eyes to savor this moment of possibility.

"You can't *want* me to be pregnant," she said against his finger.

"Why can't I?" He opened his eyes and tucked his chin to look at her, combing her hair off her face with his hand. "Who wouldn't want a little girl with your disarming blue eyes? Or a boy with my stubborn personality annoying the hell out of me? Or the other way around?" He closed his fist in the tails of her hair and drew it beneath her chin, tilting her mouth up close enough to set a kiss on her lips. "If nothing changes overnight, I'll book you a doctor's appointment in the morning. I want to know."

"I bought a test while I was out today."

Another thrust of shock went through him, this one edged with irritation that she was continuing to wander cities without mentioning where she was going or who she was with. Everett was the suspicious one, but Giovanni didn't need these slivers of doubt.

"Did you take it?" he asked.

"No. It's still early. It might give a false negative."

"Is there such a thing as a false positive?"

"Not really."

"Then—"

Sudden tears welled in her eyes. "*Please*, can I wait until tomorrow?"

Emotion tightened his chest. He wrapped his arms around her and tucked her head back under his chin. "If that's what you want."

He couldn't stop the race of his heart, though, as he contemplated what might be.

She pressed her hand to his chest and drew back, blinking up at him with amazement. "You're excited. You really do want me to be pregnant."

"So much that I'm afraid you'll run screaming. And I can't chase you," he said wryly.

"You're the most confounding man." She dipped her forehead against his jaw with a flummoxed laugh, then kissed his chin. "Okay, then." She rose and pulled on her light robe. "There are two in the box. If it says negative, I'll try again in a couple of days."

He came up on an elbow to watch her dig a purchase from her bag and disappear into the bathroom.

How long was he supposed to wait? He heard the toilet flush and water run. The silence after that was too much for him. He moved into his chair and went to the door, knocked.

"It's open," she said faintly.

He pushed in to see her sitting on the edge of the tub. There were tears and a wobbling smile on her face.

All the air was punched out of his lungs. He clumsily bumped his way closer and looked at the faint lines on the stick.

"I've never thought of myself as a lucky person, but…" The tears on her lashes were catching the light like glitter. "I feel really, really lucky right now."

"Me, too. Come here." He held out his arms and she scooted into his lap.

He didn't know how to process the awe that gripped him. It was too big. Bigger than anything he'd ever experienced.

"Marry me," he said.

She bit her trembling lips and nodded shyly.

CHAPTER SIX

Present day

FREJA SWAM THROUGH piles of rustling silk to sit up, fighting to catch her balance as the vehicle made a few quick turns. She grasped the armrest on the door to steady herself and flashed a malevolent look at Giovanni.

"I want a divorce."

"Lock the doors," Giovanni said to the driver as his incisive glance landed on her hand where she gripped the door.

The hard click of the door locks sounded and the SUV slowed for a light.

"Put your seat belt on," Giovanni instructed her.

She conjured her filthiest look. She didn't want him dead, not in her heart of hearts. She wasn't that kind of person. But with her eyes she urged, *Die.*

He released a short-tempered sigh and started to un-click his own belt.

She shot up a staying hand to hold him off and resentfully buckled herself. She refused to look at him. Not when he was over there oozing even more sex appeal than ever with that scruffy beard and his massive shoulders straining the fabric of his black hoodie.

She gave the catch of the door a useless, furious pull and let it thunk back into place.

"I know you're angry," Giovanni said in a tight voice, as though it pained him to say it. "You have a right to be."

"Do I?" Her choke of disbelief nearly spat her tongue onto the floor. What a colossal understatement! "It's so nice of you to give me permission to have feelings. Do you know what I give *you* permission to do? Only two guesses since it's only two words."

"You're not that surprised to see me, Freja. You knew I wasn't dead."

"Oh, that makes it all better then." She yanked every last inch of her skirt onto her side of the seat, gathering it all into her lap so not one stray bead or thread touched him.

"I was in a coma—"

"Until *today*?" She was being sarcastic, but concern clawed through her, forcing her to look at him. His color was good and he seemed as vital and healthy as always.

"For a week," he allowed. "Someone was trying to kill me. Everett—" he nodded at the man before him in the passenger seat "—had to make a decision about whether to let them believe they'd succeeded. There were other factors that kept me in hiding after that."

One week. That was the only thing that Freja processed. He'd been unconscious for one week. He must have known she'd been in hospital herself, but hadn't made an effort to come.

She looked out the window again, refusing to let him

see her tears. She swallowed back the agony that ached in her throat, ready to choke to death on it before she let him see how badly he could still hurt her.

"If they'd known I was alive, you would have become a target." Giovanni was using that awful tone that urged her to be reasonable. "I'll explain when we get where we're going."

"Don't bother. I don't care," she lied, looking at her small reflections in the sunglasses he was wearing. "You might not be dead, but anything I ever felt for you is. You feel the same or you would have turned up sooner."

"I'm here now."

"Yes, and I was assured it would be a quick, clean, no-fuss conversation to pick you up," Everett said with a testy smile over his shoulder. "Why did you run?"

"Gosh, I don't know. Fear of kidnapping?"

Despite the insulated interior, the sound of a siren penetrated. Before she could crane her neck to see whether it was the police and if they were in pursuit, the SUV ducked into the underground parking garage of a skyscraper. It stopped beside an open elevator flanked by two lean bodyguards.

Everett and the driver got out. The door was still locked beside her. She tried it despite the fact that the driver stood on the other side, ensuring she wouldn't get very far even if she managed to exit that side.

"I'm taking you to my safe house," Giovanni said. "We'll talk there."

"No, thank you." She curled her hand around the strap of her seat belt where it crossed her chest.

The back of the SUV opened and Everett removed Giovanni's wheelchair, then slammed it shut again.

"Look around you, Freja. You *are* coming with me. I'd rather it was your choice."

"Are you listening to yourself? You're not giving me one."

"I'm not asking you to forgive me, only to trust me that this was necessary. For both of our safety."

Her vision blurred with instant, furious tears. Helpless anguish. "I can *never* trust you. Do you realize that? How could you even suggest it?"

"Have I ever hurt you?" he demanded tightly, then swore and looked away, seeming to realize as he said it that he was inviting the vitriol that climbed like bile into her throat. "I meant physically. Look, I've been waiting for the right time to resurface. I need to know you're safe when word gets out that I'm alive. As of today's debacle, it's out. Please come with me and let me explain."

She realized the ache in her other hand was from gripping her phone this whole time. All those people inside this tiny rectangle, all those "friends" who'd been so sympathetic, eating up her grief like bitter chocolate bonbons. Where were they now, when she was in real trouble? *Not here.*

She fingered her pendant, thinking of Nels. He was a reliable friend, but they weren't exactly soul mates.

She didn't have anyone. That's what she'd come to terms with since Giovanni's disappearance. For a few short months, Giovanni had encouraged her to believe they were a unit. The kernels of a small and growing family.

That fantasy had vanished as quickly as it had formed.

"I'll go if you promise you'll divorce me. I'm not staying married to you."

A pause, then, "If that's what you want, but we might have to wait a few weeks."

"I'm not sleeping with you," she blurted.

"I don't expect you to."

As his flat response struck like an anvil, splitting her down the middle like a chunk of redwood, she realized she had been hoping for more of a fight. Apparently, that's not what this was.

The void of sorrow that had consumed her since his "death" closed in like a fog. Probably for the best. Giovanni had caused her too much emotional upheaval as it was. They needed closure and a clean break. Then she would finally stop crying over him. She would be able to speak without powdered glass in her throat. To breathe one breath that wasn't so heavy with loss it nearly crushed her flat.

"Take your money back, too," she said distantly. "I don't need it and it's just one more headache I don't want to deal with."

"Anything else?"

Oh, he thought he could take that sardonic tone with her? She blinked fast to see him through her matted lashes.

"Take off that ring. It's a mockery that you're wearing it."

"You want to talk about mocking our marriage with what we're wearing?" His pithy tone disparaged the meringue confection piled around her. "I promised you I would put it back on and never remove it again. I won't break that vow. So no, I will not take it off." He rapped a knuckle on the window and the locks were released. "Let's go."

Giovanni felt the familiar *tink* of metal to metal, his wedding ring grazing his hand rim as he rolled his wheelchair aboard the customized, unmarked, military-grade helicopter. He anchored his chair into its spot next to her seat.

He had insisted Everett retrieve the ring the minute he was conscious enough to comprehend all that had happened. He'd promised Freja he would put it back on his finger and never remove when she'd caught him without it. That had been minutes—twenty or thirty at most—before the explosion that had "killed" him.

Freja was watching Everett come in behind them and start to take the seat across from her. Her stiff profile was unnaturally ashen, not a version of her typical ivory skin tone, and not the clean, snowy white of her gown. She looked like bone china—delicate and translucent.

"Everett." Giovanni jerked his head toward the door.

Everett's face tightened, but Giovanni didn't relent. *Get me that ring and I'll do everything you ask.* He had. For three months he'd played dead, allowing Everett to identify the mole who'd set him up. That was over now. Giovanni had bought his freedom fair and square.

His promise to stay off grid had been a small bluff in the first place since he couldn't exactly hike out of the mountains on his nonexistent feet, but he would have turned himself into the most intractable asset anyone could have imagined if Everett hadn't done as he asked.

If I steal that ring and only that ring, she could become suspicious and deduce that you're alive.

That had been Giovanni's goal.

"I'll catch the next one, then," Everett said with caustic mockery.

"Collect Freja's things from her hotel," Giovanni suggested. "Settle up at the wedding shop. I'm sure they'll have questions."

Everett muttered something as he rose, but Giovanni had higher priorities than to worry about Everett's disgruntled cleanup of the mess his wife had made.

The doors closed and they were alone in the small cabin.

Freja nervously turned the flashy engagement ring she wore.

The dress, the diamond ring, the heart emojis beneath the professional engagement photos… Giovanni had seen all of her effusive posts as the acts of war she intended them to be. Every single one had landed like mortar shells in the middle of his angry, aching heart.

They'd both been wildly happy and gut-wrenchingly miserable in those weeks between their quickie wedding and their final confrontation. He had thought those strained days had been the limits of hell he could endure. He'd been proven so wrong.

"I should have come with you that day," Giovanni said gravely. Humbly.

Around and around the ring was going, faster and faster. "You sent me to your room to wait like a child."

He'd been in unstoppable agony over how badly he'd

handled that day. Impatience had been driving him. He hadn't wanted to wait for Everett's latest reports on the contacts he'd made. He'd wanted all of this over so he could properly devote himself to his marriage.

He'd taken a stupid risk and paid the price.

"I was coming after you. That's why I survived. I was supposed to meet someone, but it was a setup. The café was completely empty except for explosives, not that I knew it. After our argument, I suspected you wouldn't wait for me. I started back to the hotel instead of going in. When I turn to leave, they panicked and hit the detonator. Since I wasn't in the center of the blast, I only suffered a few broken bones and a concussion."

"And a coma." She kept her chin tucked as she sent him an appalled look, the first sign of concern he'd seen.

"Induced. They were worried about my spine. Once the swelling went down, they brought me out. By then, Everett had pronounced me dead."

He waited for her to say she was glad he'd survived, but he had a grim sense he would wait a long time to hear those words, if he ever did.

She folded her hands in her lap, very much the contained, enigmatic Freja he knew so well. She'd been kidnapped by her resurrected husband and she only wore a pinched thoughtfulness around her white lips and had her brow furrowed in thought.

The most hysteria she'd revealed today had been the moment when Everett had approached them as Giovanni had pulled her into the back of the SUV. Her fists had clenched into Giovanni's hoodie, whether seeking protection or refusing to be torn from him he didn't know, but he held tight to that instinctive reaction, desperate for it to mean she still felt something for him despite her claims to the contrary.

"I walked into that hotel room and saw the ring and I was so angry." Her voice panged. "I took it and left. Walked outside and a couple from Tuscany was leaving to catch the ferry back to Italy." Her voice grew dull and so empty he felt the cavernous chill in his chest as she continued. "When we got to the slip, everyone was talking about the blast. I realized it had happened close to where I'd seen you and tried calling. People were tweeting. There was a picture of a wheelchair lying in the street."

"Freja." He tried to take her hand.

She shook her head, elbows tight to her ribs, voice choking up. "I went to the hospital and was told a man with no legs had been brought to it, but he was expected to survive. Then someone else pulled me aside and said you were dead, but they wouldn't let me see you."

"If I had been conscious, I wouldn't have let them do that to you." Everett had been suspicious of her presence there, unsure who he could trust until he had Giovanni well away from the area and conscious enough to tell him what had happened.

"I guess I went into shock because I was lying in a bed when someone handed me a bag with your clothes and wallet and passport. I remember staring at it, saying I thought it had been the worst thing in the world that you weren't wearing your wedding ring when I saw you last. That man who'd brought it—he couldn't have been an orderly. I don't know who he was, but he was trying to be kind. He said you were wearing it. He swore he'd seen it himself, but said it couldn't be removed without cutting and ruining it. You would be cremated with it, he said, and he was sure you loved me very much."

Giovanni closed his eyes. "But you already had it."

"And all I could think was, *You liar*." She gave a broken laugh. "I asked what sort of arrangements I had to make and they were already made. Your things showed up from the hotel and I was flown back to Rome. It was all so very trouble-free," she scoffed. "But when I unpacked your things, your little kit of fix-it tools wasn't there. Which didn't make *any* sense because I'd seen it on the dresser next to the ring. One of the little screwdrivers had been left out, as if you'd made a last-minute adjustment before you left. Who steals an old, beat-up pair of calipers and a little screwdriver set? Your wheelchair showed up, rim bent and one of the small wheels missing, but the one thing *you* bring almost everywhere with you wasn't there."

"So you knew even before I had Everett get the ring." He wouldn't call it a relief, but he had hated that she had been lied to. That she had suffered. "I wanted to tell you, Freja. The minute I woke up and realized, I wanted you to know I was alive. Other lives would have been at risk, including yours. Taking back this ring was the best message I could send while also keeping it subtle enough it could be dismissed as a robbery if you decided to tell anyone."

She was turning the engagement ring again.

"Will you take that off?" he requested.

"No."

"Why not?"

"Because I'm marrying someone else."

* * *

Less than an hour later, the helicopter descended into a remote valley flickering with the reds and golds of autumn.

"Where are we?" Freja asked.

"Near the Swiss border."

Seemingly out of nowhere, a structure came into her sightline as they touched down. The floor-to-ceiling windows were overhung with a long platform covered in foliage so the house had been mostly indiscernible from the ground. It was a modern mansion built into the mountainside overlooking the snake of a silver river in the valley bottom.

The rotors stopped and Giovanni went out ahead of her.

A trim middle-aged man with a crisp white tunic over dark blue pants waited with a woman of similar age. Their smiles faltered with surprise when Freja emerged in her massive gown.

"Freja, this is Kurt. He's my physical therapist. His wife, Marie, is a registered dietician and keeps the house."

"Nice to meet you," Freja said with as much warmth as she could muster, shaking their hands. "I wonder if I could borrow a change of clothes?" she asked Marie.

"There's a full selection in the guest room," Marie said. "And fresh coffee and cake."

"We'll serve ourselves," Giovanni said. "Take some downtime."

The couple disappeared down a set of stairs to a lower floor of the pseudo-mansion.

"You've been staying here this whole time?"

"Yes."

The location was incredibly beautiful. Private and peaceful with only the sound of birdsong and rustling leaves now that the helicopter had fallen silent. A light breeze carried a hint of autumn briskness, but the air tasted of forests and streams and earthy wildness.

Freja followed Giovanni up the gradual incline of a covered zigzag path. She gave up trying to keep the dress pristine and only picked up the front of the skirt so she wouldn't trip, letting the rest drag behind her as she followed him to the veranda. A small dining table looked up the valley, and a collection of cushioned out-door furniture was positioned around an unlit fire bowl.

Giovanni slid open the screen door into the house. The wide entrance easily accommodated his chair. The sill of the door was recessed so he didn't even bump across it. Inside, the open-plan living area was arranged as most of his properties were, with airy spaces be-tween the furniture. The kitchen had two sinks, one for standing, one for sitting, with room against the lowered counter to accommodate his chair. Since the house was built into the mountainside, the upper cupboards had translucent panels in the doors with lights behind to give the impression of sunlight coming in from that angle.

"When did you have this built?" It couldn't have been thrown together within the last few months, not with this much tasteful attention to his specialized details.

"A few years ago. Before we met."

"It's not listed among your assets." She'd been through his portfolio of investments and properties umpteen times with Nels and lawyers and predators from his various corporate headquarters.

"As you guessed very quickly in our marriage, I lead—rather, I used to lead—it's over. I *led* a double life. About ten years ago, I discovered the crash that killed my family was deliberate. Someone had been trying to bribe my father. He refused so he was permanently removed from his post. Everett was a friend of Stefano's who had connections at Interpol. One thing led to another and I've been working with him ever since."

"Doing *what*?"

"Collecting intelligence."

"You're a *spy*?"

"That makes me sound as though I'm dropping from helicopters and kicking in doors. I talk to people, uncover hidden relationships and follow the money. If we're lucky, we compile enough evidence to expose corruption and make arrests."

She ought to be more incredulous, but it fit so neatly into all the strange prevarications during their short marriage. The private calls and the disappearing for meetings that weren't on his calendar. Maybe she was latching on to the explanation out of relief. It was a damned sight better to hear he was a secret agent than a cheating husband.

"But if you had all this to hide…why did you marry me?"

"You know why we married," he said gruffly.

They were only a few feet apart, close enough to see each other's eyes. His were bleak and gathering with questions, but a gulf opened between them. A chasm. A wide, throbbing wound that pulsed painfully in her ears and stung her nostrils and scorched her throat.

She wasn't ready to talk about that. *Couldn't.*

"I mean, why did you let it get that far?" she choked. "Why even ask me to dinner? Why...?" He had brought her home and told her to be the sensible one that first night. She hadn't had the confidence to drag him into a relationship. He had pursued her. He must know he had!

A muscle pulsed in his jaw before he said without emotion, "The way we met, the fact you mentioned Stefano, seemed suspicious. You had a full dossier in the system."

"What system?"

"*The* system. You'd been questioned about your time in North Korea. Everett and I thought you might still have connections there."

"You thought *I* was a spy?" Now she was flabbergasted.

"It seemed possible. Everett thought—"

"I don't care what Everett thought! *You* thought I could be a secret agent? Is that right? You thought that *I* knew you were a spy and I targeted you? You thought I gave you my virginity, got *pregnant* and *married* you because I wanted to—what? Expose you? Pump you for information? I'm not that complicated! I just wanted—"

Her throat locked over a lump of emotion as she contemplated the dreams that had died between then and now.

"Freja." His voice was ragged, his brow pulled with torture.

"I want out of this dress."

Freja flung around, skirt swirling. The silk fluttered behind her as she sailed down the hall and found the guest room.

Giovanni stayed where he was, head tilted against the back of his chair. His eyes were closed, but he still saw her face. The betrayal in her eyes, the anguish around her mouth.

He reflexively tried to push that image into a mental vault along with the ache in his throat, but it didn't work.

From the time he'd woken seventeen years ago, after a car crash that left him nothing of the life he'd known, Giovanni had become very good at compart- mentalizing. Rather than deal with the grief of losing his family, he focused on overcoming the physical pain of his recovery. Rather than resent his inability to live in his family home because it couldn't accommodate his wheelchair, he had focused on athletics that took him to far-off places. If his chair held him back from the wild pursuits of youth, he concentrated on making money. Doors were always thrown wide open for gold.

Then, when he took the reins of his father's business from the trustee and finally decided to face his past by going through old papers, he had found the evidence of attempted bribery.

Emotions had roared to life in him. Injustice. Hatred for the perpetrators. Intense bitterness at the personal injury he'd suffered for such paltry reasons as jockeying among energy sector bids. He should have blown open like a volcano. Instead, he had pushed all that emotion back inside him to use as fuel. He had gone to Everett and focused on proving the crime, naming names and dismantling that small tangle of venality.

Afterward, when he was still confronted with a life that was tormentingly empty, he had brushed aside any

soul-searching and leaped on Everett's request for as-
sistance with the next assignment and the next.

So he ought to be able to handle and dismiss the remorse he felt right now. He ought to be able to think
past it and know what to do, but no matter how hard
he tried to set aside his emotions, it didn't work. It had
never worked with Freja. He had been sitting here for
three months, tortured by what he was doing to her.

"Ahh!"

Her distressed scream had him flying down the hall
to the closed door of the guest room.

"Freja." He yanked at the latch, surprised to find it
unlocked, and pushed in.

She stood in the middle of the room, wild-eyed, face
flushed and hair mussed. Her hands were clenched in
the edge of lace across the tops of her breasts.

"I can't get out of it." She fairly shook with rage.

"I thought you were being murdered." His limbs were
shaking with the adrenaline that had sent him racing in
here. He rolled in far enough to throw the door shut behind him. "Sit." He motioned to the corner of the bed.

She plopped down, back still heaving with exer-
tion as she slumped with her elbows on her thighs and
dropped her face into her hands.

For one second, he just looked. He drank in the sad
slope of her shoulders, the fall of her scattered hair,
her ivory skin and the bow of her back and the slip of a
waist that was far too thin. The longing in him to pick
her up and draw her into his lap was so intense he shook
with the effort to resist it.

Very gently, he reached out to sweep her hair to the
front of her shoulder, exposing her delicate nape. Dear

God, he could live his entire life with his lips pressed to that sensitive spot that always made her quiver and sigh with bliss.

He wanted to pet his hand down her back, soothe her, draw her in. Make up and make love.

He forced himself to release the first tiny button, then the next. There were at least two dozen. It felt like hundreds, every single one too small for his big, clumsy fingers.

"You don't have to be so careful. It's ruined anyway."

There was a jealous, betrayed husband in him that wanted to rip this offensive dress right off her. How *dare* she spend his money on a dress for a wedding to another man?

But if he tore it in haste, he wouldn't be able to sit this close and watch that narrow strip of spine appear, would he? He wouldn't see her erratic breaths catch and her shoulder blades flex in reaction to his touch.

"Why all this pageantry if you knew you couldn't go through with the wedding?"

"I presumed if you let it happen then you really did plan to stay dead, so what did it matter if I was breaking the law? And my income depends on clicks, doesn't it? The bigger the dress, the higher the view count."

And the higher the chance he would see it? He allowed his fingertips to graze her warm skin.

She sat straighter, but he couldn't tell if that was reaction or rejection.

"Your blog says you knew him at school. I thought all the men there were twits who failed to impress you?"

"I couldn't help being impressed by Nels. He's very intelligent, but was always very focused on his studies. Now that he's written the bar, he has time for a relationship."

"So you're sleeping with him." It made him sick.

She jerked to her feet and spun to confront him, catching at the gaping front of her dress. "Do you have the right to question me on whether I was faithful when you were pretending to be *dead*?"

He narrowed his eyes. "You knew I was alive. You knew we were still married."

"But I didn't know where you were or whether you would ever show your face again. You were dead *enough*. For all I knew, *you* were sleeping with other people."

"Kurt and Marie are not into swinging. Aside from them, Everett and the pilot—neither of whom is my type—are the only people I've seen between leaving hospital and getting you today."

"Poor you. I've had nothing but offers. It's amazing how alluring a woman is when she has a billion dollars to her name. Nels is the only man I trust these days. That includes you."

"So you're marrying him for protection?" Not love?

"No one was coming to save me, Giovanni. *You* weren't. I had to look after myself and I have." Her chin came up and scorched flags of anger sat on her cheekbones. "I guess I'm being unnecessarily modest. If you were interested in seeing any of this, you would have shown up sooner."

She dragged her dress down, exposing her braless breasts. The pale globes jiggled as she worked the gown past her hips and left it as a mound on the floor, like a pile of melted snow.

He stopped breathing as he ate up her lissome figure. His entire being came alive as though he was feeling sunshine for the first time after a decade in prison. Her beige underpants looked paper-thin. They hugged her hips from her navel to the tops of her thighs, seamless as yoga shorts. He wanted to touch them, feel her warmth through the fine silk.

She turned to a drawer and shook out a lemon-yellow T-shirt. She dropped it over her head, then stepped into a pair of jeans from the next drawer. They were a little loose. She'd definitely lost weight.

"Nels has probably seen the video." She picked up her phone off the top of the dresser. "I should let him know I'm fine. What's the password to get online?"

"He'll see that you were with your husband. Since he's so intelligent, I'm sure he'll figure out the wedding is off."

She threw her phone onto the bed, temper instantly relit and now incandescent, beautiful in the way that the lightning strike that kills you fills you with awe at the same time.

"Or he'll activate the transmitter he suggested I wear because I'm worth a billion dollars and wanted to come to Europe alone." She picked up the pendant she wore around her neck.

How was he still underestimating her?

"Damn you, you always look so damned innocent and you're not!" He crashed his fist against his dead leg. "This is why I had to wonder if you were working for another government. You do these sly, underhanded things, hack my calendar and track my phone—yes, I know you did that. You followed me to Dubrovnik the very day I was nearly killed—"

"I thought you were having an affair!" she cried. "And that is a completely understandable suspicion when you were sneaking around as much as you were. You kept telling me you wanted to be a f—" She choked to a halt.

His heart clenched again, the way it had a few minutes ago in the lounge. He had never properly dealt with that pain because he didn't know how.

Freja turned away and flung open the drapes to reveal the glass doors that opened onto the fire escape. A full-spectrum bulb gave the impression of natural light, but it only led to a wide breezeway that terminated at the veranda.

"This is a stupid house!" She clattered open the door and stormed out.

CHAPTER SEVEN

FREJA HADN'T BOTHERED to put on socks or shoes. She was barefoot and even the paved passageway out of the bedroom had tiny pebbles that were sharp enough to cut into her soles. She didn't get very far on the cold path that wound down the hill.

With a huff, she stopped at the rail near the now empty helipad and brooded, rubbing one foot over the other to brush off the bottoms of her feet.

"I should have asked if you have any dietary restrictions," Marie said behind her.

Freja turned to see the woman was wearing gloves and a sunhat. She was pulling up plants in a small vegetable garden that was going to seed.

"I'm not fussy, but I'm not hungry right now, thanks."

Marie hesitated, then said, "It's nice to meet you in person. I've read all of your father's books and really enjoyed them."

Freja scrounged up the smile she turned on for her father's fans. "Pappa would be pleased to know they entertained you."

"I usually prefer romance, but they were here and there's not much to do in the evenings except read, so—"

"They're here?" *Oh, that odious man.*

"In the study," Marie said, but Freja was already charging up the path as quickly as her bare feet would take her.

She burst into the study to find Giovanni speaking to his open laptop. "—ensure he knows she's safe and—"

Giovanni halted and Everett's voice asked sharply, "What is it?"

In one sweeping glance, Freja took in the hardwood floors that Giovanni preferred. He sat at one of the modern desks he seemed to order in bulk because they accommodated all his different types of chairs. There was a small reading area in the corner with a recliner and a standing lamp. Bookshelves bracketed golden drapes that she assumed disguised another of those weird emergency exits.

Freja marched over and sure enough, there were all her father's titles in a tidy row at a convenient height to a man in a wheelchair. All the book jackets showed signs of wear, like library books that had been read several times.

"Giovanni," Everett prompted, but he was watching her.

She grabbed a handful and pulled them off the shelf, letting them tumble to the floor.

"I'll call you back," Giovanni said in a tone more weary than wary. "But yes, make that call and come for us in the morning. We'll return to Rome and have the press conference there." He closed the laptop. "Why are you angry that I have those?"

All of the books were hitting the floor with unsatisfying thumps. Year after year of her childhood, piling up after being consumed by him, secretly, over the last months.

"You could have asked *me*. How dare you hide out here, reading my dead father's words about me, rather than talk to me yourself? Do your covert information-gathering on anyone else on this earth, but not *me*."

"You looked me up online before I even knew you existed, Freja."

"I will never forgive you for any of this. Do you understand that?" She swept the last of the books onto the floor and stood there glaring at him.

"I know that!" he near-roared, temper snapping in a way that had her recoiling in shock. He had never yelled at her. Not once. "I knew it when I woke up and Everett told me he'd killed me." He snatched a book off his desk, one that had been set facedown, pages splayed open as though he'd been reading it minutes ago. "You think this has been easy for me?" He shook the book at her. *"This was all I had."*

"That was your choice!"

"No, it *wasn't*. For God's sake, Freja, step out of your own hurt and look at the big picture. Do you honestly think I would put both of us through all of this on a whim? People's lives were at stake. I got sloppy because I was impatient to retire from all of this." He threw down the book and pinched the bridge of his nose. "I've spent the last months thinking that if I'd only met you now, when I've done as much as I could, instead of when I was in the thick of an unfinished job, we might have had a chance. But I *am* out of it now. You and I can start fresh." His head came up. His gray eyes, dark as gathering thunderclouds, pierced into hers. "This is our chance for a new beginning, one that isn't overshadowed by anything in our past."

She shook her head. "Our past is going to follow us forever. I said I want a divorce and I meant it."

She spoke with guttural fervor, but it was reflexive defense. Fear of more pain. Even so, there was a faint flutter of hope in her that yearned for exactly what he was offering. She hadn't wanted to acknowledge it. That would mean he could hurt her anytime he wanted and she would forgive him for it. She couldn't do that.

Could she?

His expression tightened. He looked to his closed laptop.

"We will have to play the happy, reunited couple for the short term." There was no arguing with that implacable command. "I've been identified in the video and Everett is making some final arrests as we speak. You and I will both have to make statements. The helicopter is coming back in the morning."

Perversely, she was annoyed by that. She finally had him to herself and they were turning around and going back into the public eye? She crossed her arms and stared at the books tumbled around her feet. It had been childish to throw them around like that, but she was so angry. So filled with futility she had no means to express.

"You have always been a puzzle to me, Freja." He spoke more quietly. Gently. "You're completely unlike anyone else I've ever met. I was trying to understand you when I began reading those. If I hadn't had this double life, your quirks and contradictions wouldn't have fazed me, but you're this anomaly who picks up a language in minutes and moves through a foreign city as though you already know every street."

"I know I'm not normal!"

"Neither am I! That's what I'm saying." He sat back with a tired exhale and turned up a hand in a plea for understanding. "You slid past my very stalwart defenses the moment we met, made me your first lover on our first date. We happened *so fast*, Freja. You know that. I couldn't take you at face value, given what I was hiding. I had to keep my guard up."

"*You* made everything happen fast. That was your fault," she accused him, pointing at him.

"You didn't slow me down," he threw back.

"And that made me an object of suspicion? I'm sorry for being attracted to you, okay? I thought you were a better man than you are. I won't make that mistake again."

A muscle pulsed in his cheek. "You're hurt so you're trying to hurt me. It's working." His gaze pierced into her, so naked for a second, she forgot to breathe. So anguished, the backs of her eyes grew hot. "I will accept all those stones you're hurling because at least you're here to hurl them."

Her bottom lip pushed up into her top, and she had to pull it between her teeth and bite to keep from letting a sob of pain escape her thick throat. She looked away, still angry, still hating him, but now hating herself a little, too.

"This is who we are, Freja. I've had ample time to reflect on that. We happened too soon, too fast. Too *hard*. Our timing was off and our feelings were too strong. I've walked through every single 'if only' and

'I should have.' The truth is, I wouldn't have done anything differently. I wanted you in my life, even though you weren't supposed to be there. There were times you could have made different choices, too, but you didn't. Because we're inevitable."

She rubbed where his words seemed to arrow straight into her heart.

"You go ahead and fight that as long as you need to. I tried, yet I'm still wearing this." He showed her the band on his finger. "But don't think any of this was what I wanted or that it came without a cost to me."

"So what am I supposed to do? Just be fine with all of this?" She waved around a wild hand, tears of betrayal and despair filling her eyes.

"Healing takes time. Not everything goes back to the way it was. I am intimately acquainted with that reality. But we can recover from this, Freja. And we can still have a very good life."

She shook her head. "I don't want to try."

He sucked in a breath as though she'd shot him, which gave her zero satisfaction as she walked out.

Part of him knew he was dreaming, but the flash of her yellow shirt disappearing into the trees was too real. Too terrifying.

In his head, he was thinking he should hit the intercom and tell Kurt to bring her back, but his wheelchair was rolling recklessly down the path at speeds he'd only attempted in races on well-swept trails. Yet not fast enough. She was already gone into the darkened woods.

"Freja!" Out of sheer frustration, he threw himself from his chair—

The ground rushed up to knock his breath from his body. His head glanced off the wheel of his chair where he'd left it by the nightstand. It burned like hell, but not as much as the ignominy of falling out of bed.

He swore roundly as he tried to orient himself, pushing to sit with his back against the side of the mattress, still sweating, heart pounding, trying to catch his breath.

"Giovanni?" Freja burst in and pulled up short in the doorway, backlit by the hall light.

He could only see the top half of her since he was on the floor on the far side of the bed. She wore a slinky nightgown as pale as her limbs. She came in a few more steps.

"Where are you?"

How humiliating. "Here. On the floor."

"What happened? Are you hurt?" She came around the end of the bed.

"Sir?" Now Kurt was here. Fantastic.

"I'm fine," Giovanni growled. "Go back to bed."

"I'll call you if we need anything," Freja told Kurt as she shooed him from the door and closed it. "Do you want help?" she asked.

"I don't need help getting back into bed, Freja."

"I didn't ask if you needed help. I asked if you wanted it. You did call me," she pointed out in a huffy voice.

"And you came?" His scathing tone prompted a profound silence.

"So you don't want me."

"That is a loaded question and you know it." He dropped his head against the mattress. "Do I want you in my bedroom? Yes. A thousand times, yes. Do I want you witnessing my clumsiness? No."

There was a long silence and he sensed her hovering by the door as though trying to work out how to react.

He hadn't moved off the floor. The hardwood was unforgiving through his boxer briefs, the bar of the bed-frame digging into his back. Nothing about this moment was comfortable, so he made it even less so.

"I dreamed you were running away. I was trying to come after you."

He heard her swallow. She moved to perch on the chair in the corner.

"I was lying awake thinking about it," she admitted. "I'm so angry with you, I don't know what to do with it all. I've never been a person who wants revenge, but you're right. I want to hurt you in every possible way." She didn't sound angry. She sounded profoundly sad.

He closed his eyes, defeated by a circumstance that had snowballed so far beyond his ability to control, it was no wonder she'd been flattened by it.

"Do you want me to put on the light?" she offered.

"No." This was safer. He quit sulking and rolled onto his good leg, able to lever himself up enough he could grab a handful of blankets and drag himself back onto the bed. He adjusted his briefs and sat on the edge of the mattress, trying to read her pale expression in the faint glow from the nightlight in the bathroom.

"You're never clumsy," she murmured. "I'm always amazed at your strength and agility. You're like a gym-nast."

"Will you come here?" He pushed aside the bunched

blankets and patted the edge of the bed. "It's not a trick. I just want to ask you something."

She rose and drifted toward him like a wraith, unafraid despite the swamp of percolating emotions between them.

"So trusting," he murmured as she lowered to sit beside him.

"I've always felt safe with you. That's why I'm so angry. I didn't believe you would hurt me, but you did."

"*Is* that why you're angry?" He picked up her hand and threaded his fingers through her slender, twitching ones. "Or is it something else? Tell me what happened, Freja."

She gasped and tried to jerk back her hand, but he held on even when she rose and tried to pull away.

"Is that why you called me in here?" She gave her hand a firmer tug.

He kept his hold gentle, using two hands to trap hers in a careful cage, but, "I have to know, Freja."

"You didn't want to know when it happened," she choked, roughly trying to shake him off. "I don't owe you any explanations now."

"No, you don't. But I'd like to understand." His heart was throbbing, the dull ache that had been in him for months pounding like hammers of fire driving icy spikes into his heart. "Sit," he coaxed. "Take your time."

She stood with her hand limp in his, face turned to the window, her profile ashen and still. For a long time, there was only the faint sound of their unsteady breaths.

Finally, she said in a voice that echoed with loss, "I went for a scan and they said she wasn't developing properly."

"She." He had to consciously keep himself from crushing the fine bones of her hand, but his hold on her firmed, as though he could keep her from being dragged into the pit of pure agony he heard in her voice. She was pulling him into it with her, though, and he feared they would never emerge because he had to ask, "Was it anything to do with me? Because of—"

"No." Her voice was shredded with pain. "I asked if it was because I'd been under stress and they said it was no one's fault. Just bad luck."

There was no comfort in that. It was still an abysmal sorrow.

"They said I could terminate or let nature take its course. They sent me home to think about it, but that night it started to happen and I went to hospital until it was over."

"I'm so sorry, Freja."

"No, you're not." She bitterly tried to shake off his grip again. "I cry every day and you've never once—"

"I cry," he said raggedly. He pressed the back of her hand to his wet cheek, so wrecked he didn't know how to deal with it except to work out harder, lose himself in books about her as a healthy, curious child. He compiled reports and translated documents and stalked her online. Anything so he didn't have to think about what they'd lost.

With a sob, she pivoted closer. Her other hand came up, feeling his cheek, finding the damp track running into his beard. She made a choking noise of surprise.

"It was such a miracle that she even happened." He could barely speak. His lungs were filled with acid. "It's like I'm being punished for what I've done to you, but it shouldn't have cost *her*. I keep thinking if I'd been there, maybe I could have done something—"

She pressed his face into her stomach. "I think those things, too. There wasn't."

He wrapped his arms around her and she cradled his head, and they shuddered under the grief that rocked them. They keened and shook and shared their anguish. After a time, she crumpled weakly into him.

He rolled her onto the mattress and they fit together like the complementary puzzle pieces they were, the way they always had.

"I don't want to make love. I just want you to hold me," she said between sniffles.

"I know. I will." He pulled the blankets across them and ironed her to his front, her damp face tucked against his aching throat, her sawing breaths cutting him in two.

He told her he was sorry. Sorry he wasn't there and sorry they'd lost her. She said, "Me, too," and pressed harder against him. "I could have lived without you if I had that connection, you know? I felt so alone after she was gone. Like you were really gone."

"Freja," he breathed, not telling her to shush as she sobbed piteously in his arms. And he didn't tell her he would be in her life forevermore because she wouldn't believe him.

But he would be. As he stroked her hair and eased her into sleep, he silently made her that promise. *I am here. I am yours. Always.*

Freja became aware of being too warm, yet incredibly comfortable, the way she used to feel when she slept with—

Her eyes were still gritty with last night's tears as she dragged them open to see Giovanni's bearded throat.

He was awake, watching her through heavy lashes as his strong arms cradled her protectively. He was rock-hard against her stomach.

She quirked a brow at him. *Some things never change.*

His mouth dented at one corner with mild self-disgust. *Boys will be boys.*

The sweetest rush of affection suffused her. Something deeper, even, that she shied from acknowledging because she was still so gutted by hurt and betrayal. By the loss of *this*. Sometimes, when they'd had nothing between them but skin, she had believed in happily-ever-after. Then he had been gone. He had *left*. That's how it had felt, like an abandonment. She had felt so alone in these months without him, she could hardly face each day.

Last night had helped, though. It helped a lot to know she wasn't alone in her grief.

Last night's moment of need was over, though. She ought to roll away. Her defenses were still down and if she gave in to the compulsion to set her mouth against his skin and signal other needs, she would be in over her head again in no time.

"I can see you trying to make up your mind," he said in a voice that held a morning rasp. "We'll take it slower this time."

His statement instantly infuriated her. "To where? Just because I'm thinking about sex, doesn't mean I want to stay married."

"Is that all you want?" A gruff laugh cut from his

throat before his thick arms flexed to shift her against him, the subtle friction enough to bring every cell in her body to life. "Because you know I'm always up for that."

They were nose to nose and she could have given him a hard shove, but she kissed him. With aggression. Daring him to reject her. In fact, she threw her leg across him in a way that was pure muscle memory. Straddling him in the morning had been as routine as their shared breakfast and coffee.

He didn't roll onto his back to drag her atop him, though. He pressed her onto her back and loomed over her, one hand fondling her breast, teasing her nipple through lace as he kissed the hell out of her. His beard was surprisingly silky. An added sensation as he thrust his tongue between her lips so blatantly, she grew weak with yearning. A helpless noise throbbed in her throat.

He lifted his head and asked, "Is this really what you want?" His hand left her breast and gathered the short silk of her nightgown onto her stomach.

When he discovered she wasn't wearing underwear, he swore and thrust back the blankets.

"You've been naked under this all night?" he hissed in outrage.

"I always— *Ohh.*"

He traced into her damp curls, parting her swollen folds, sending a rush of throbbing need through her whole body. She groaned and tried to close her legs against the intensity.

"Oh, no," he growled into her neck, using his body and his good thigh to keep her flat on the bed, legs open. "But be quiet or Marie will hear you."

He closed his mouth over her nipple and used his tongue to rub the rough lace of her nightgown against the swollen bud. At the same time, he eased two thick fingers into her slick channel.

"Giovanni," she hissed in acute pleasure, combing her fingers through his hair.

She played her hands over his shoulders, found his earlobes, made him bring his mouth to hers so they could kiss again, but as had often been the case, she was way ahead of him. Moments later, she wound up shattering, her cries of ecstasy muffled by his passionate kiss.

His touch grew tender, his kisses gentle. When she blinked open her eyes, his gray eyes were swirling like molten metal, turbulent with unsatisfied desire.

"Thank you. I needed that." His touch made a final circle of her damp, still sensitized flesh, sending a latent contraction through her. "I always want you, Freja. *Always.* Never doubt that. But I want more than this." He removed his hand and drew her nightgown down her thighs. "I want you to trust me with more than your body."

He had disarmed her so many times this way, leaving her trembling and pliant. This time she had to shake her head and say, "I don't know how I can."

"I know. That's why I thought we should wait for this." His rueful gaze went down her body and the tick of his cheek told her of the supreme control he was exercising over his urges. He dropped a last kiss on her mouth, one that had her parting her lips the way dry earth opened its pores to take in the rain after a drought.

When he pulled away, they were both breathing in unsteady pants.

"I'm going to shower. You'd best find your own across the hall." He sat up on the side of the bed, briefs straining to contain his rigid erection.

"Giovanni." Her hand impulsively went to his spine, where there were old scars from long-ago surgeries. "Thank you for last night. I needed *that*."

He caught her hand and twisted so he could press a kiss into her palm. For one second, she glimpsed a grief so profound, she wanted to pull him back into bed with her.

But he pulled away, transferring himself into his chair before he rolled into the bathroom.

She lay there a long time, hugging his pillow so she could breathe in his scent while she wondered if she really could do as he asked and trust him again.

Giovanni heard the helicopter as he was dressing.

He was still edgy with arousal and annoyed that they had to return to civilization so quickly. The original plan had been for Everett to quietly escort Freja to the SUV without any drama whatsoever. Giovanni had intended to whisk her quietly from the city and have as much time as they needed to reconcile before they were thrust into the spotlight again.

With Freja, however, one always had to expect the unexpected. That's why Giovanni had followed his intuition and said to the driver, "Pull around to the alley."

So Giovanni braced himself for just about anything as he moved into the lounge, finding only Everett at the island, sipping coffee. Marie was cooking. Freja was on the veranda, sitting at the small table that caught an hour of sunlight when beams angled into the valley, low and bright, first thing in the morning.

"Are Mummy and Daddy still fighting? Or have you kissed and made up?"

"You and I have had a good run, Everett. Don't ruin it by making me kill you." Giovanni smiled at Marie. "We'll eat outside with Freja."

"Freja is on a call with her intended," Everett supplied. "He wanted proof of life or he was going to provide these coordinates to anyone who would listen."

Giovanni shot him one dour look, then smoothly headed outside.

"—feel obliged to give it back," Nels was saying.

"You will not," Freja said firmly. "The financial side of our agreement stands. You'll still have a job, too." She flicked a defiant stare at Giovanni. "I won't stand for anything less considering the emotional distress you're enduring with the press right now."

"My concern is for you. You're definitely safe?"

"Completely. And I'll explain better once I'm back in New York. I'm really sorry for drawing you into this." Moments later, she ended the call and handed the device back to Everett, saying coolly to Giovanni, "I didn't have the skills to keep all that you've built from falling apart. Nels took it on in good faith and I expect you to reward him accordingly."

"About that. If he behaves himself and doesn't fight my retaking ownership, then yes, I will happily keep him on. But you and I are staying married until all the *i*'s are dotted and *t*'s crossed. If you want to divorce me after that, and sue me for more than what's in your prenup, that's fine, but I didn't amass this fortune by trusting blindly."

"No, it appears you built a lot of it by preying on other people's trust." She sent a critical glance at Everett and the house as she picked up her coffee and sipped.

"Giovanni assured me that you wouldn't expose our classified activities. Yesterday's video broke the internet so we have a lot of explaining ahead of us. Can we count on you?"

"I don't know. Let me check with my handlers in Pyongyang."

"Bidduzza." Giovanni took her hand and gave it an admonishing squeeze. "How many people did you tell that you believed I was alive?"

"Just Nels. And I only asked if he thought it was worth my hiring a private investigator to look into whether you could be alive, since I'd been given ashes and a death certificate, but hadn't seen your body. He said I was having trouble accepting my loss."

"Did you tell him or anyone else that the ring had been stolen?"

"No. They would have said I misplaced it since the rest of the jewelry was still there. But it made me wonder *why* you'd gone into hiding. For instance, if you were in financial trouble, you would have stolen the jewels to square off with your creditors. If you were being chased by the law, you would have made a better effort to take money with you, not leave so much to me."

She glanced at the house again, perhaps rightly deducing that he had as much money off the books as he did on. He had plans to donate this and other properties like it to amputees and other charities. He wasn't a tax dodger, but he could clarify that another time.

"It felt a lot like you were hiding from *me*, especially after we had that awful fight, but it seemed a pretty drastic way to end things." The line of her mouth wavered and her brow crinkled. "The most logical conclusion was that you disappeared to protect your life, in which case it made sense to act as though I believed you were dead. Getting engaged seemed to reinforce that illusion and since Nels was willing to take over your business interests and I happen to trust him, he made a good choice."

Giovanni had taken one look at the engagement announcement and had nearly thrown himself off this veranda. Not once had it occurred to him that she'd done it out of concern for him.

"Also, I thought if I made this production of a marriage, you would either show up or you wouldn't." Her mouth pursed in dismay. "At least I would know where we stood."

"And I'm the fool for thinking she had the capacity to be an operative?" Everett scoffed. "Freja, darling, how would you like an extremely well-paying career that provides ample opportunity for travel? Because I know people who would love to meet you."

"Don't. You. Dare," Giovanni said from between his teeth.

"But she could be so helpful when she goes back to North Korea," Everett said. "Does he know you've been looking into that?"

Giovanni's heart stopped. "No, he does not know that. What the *hell*, Freja?"

"You're worried about whether *you* can trust *me*?" she asked Everett, splaying an outraged hand on her chest.

"I'm going to get more coffee." Everett rose. "Nels is gay, by the way." He patted Giovanni's shoulder. "Deep in the closet, but super gay."

"What a horrible person! I know it was you who stole the ring. I can tell by your cologne," she called to Everett's retreating back, looking at the chair he'd vacated and left askew. "And the fact you didn't push the chair in at the desk."

Everett was gone and she sat back with a disgruntled look.

"Are you out of your mind? You're not going back to North Korea." Giovanni's riches could accomplish many things, but he doubted he could get her out of there again. Not without costs that were higher than monetary ones. "Just because you were treated well the first time does not mean they would roll out the red carpet if you returned. For God's sake, Freja! At *best* you'd wind up in a work camp."

"I didn't have you, I didn't have our baby. Sung-mi and Byung-woo are the only family I have left. Don't judge me for wanting to see them."

"I don't. But you have me now."

She flinched and looked to the far side of the valley, profile troubled.

Time, he thought with frustration. They had never had it, they needed it now, and he didn't want to wait. He wanted everything put right between them. Now.

"Everett might be able to call in some favors and make some inquiries. He's worth having on your side."

"Are you trying to bribe me to keep my mouth shut? I won't say a thing about you and your dumb spy games. You don't have to threaten Sung-mi and Nels, either."

"That's not what this is."

"Sure," she said flatly, clearly disbelieving him, but Everett came back and they talked about what they would say at the press conference.

Freja didn't bother packing. She had clothes in all of Giovanni's residences including the penthouse in Rome, which was where they went.

All his residential staff had been instructed to close up and go down to skeletal once she'd gone back to New York. It had felt so strange to return to America. She hadn't been away that long, but she'd been a completely different person and was again as they returned to the last place they'd been together. She saw everything with fresh eyes.

The place had been kept up, of course. The plants were healthy and there wasn't a speck of dust anywhere. The housekeeper was busy restocking the kitchen, smiling cheerfully, though wide-eyed with astonishment that her employer was alive.

But the top-level security and tinted windows and soundproof doors weren't just protecting Giovanni's wealth or privacy, Freja realized now. The quick escape routes via helicopter or the manually controlled service elevator weren't just for fire safety.

Giovanni made a call to his barber, who appeared with a flush on his cheeks as though he'd run the whole way.

While they disappeared to make him presentable, she

dug into her closet for one of her couture day dresses, choosing a three-quarter-length shirtdress. Its navy color was brightened by small white polka dots and a crisp white collar and cuffs. She kept the look simple, using a straightening iron on her hair before tying it back with a navy ribbon. She finished her light makeup with a soft pink gloss.

When she returned to the lounge, Everett was there, nursing a drink.

"I thought you were talking with Giovanni," she said, trying to explain away her dismayed double take when she saw him.

"No need. He and I have always been on the same page—for the most part." He sipped, watching her over his glass. "Were you on your way out?"

"No." Had she thought about it? Absolutely. Giovanni had been right when he had said they had a habit of running too fast. Too hot. Too hard. The way she had burst into flames under his touch this morning was completely typical.

The temptation to let that familiar urgency sweep her up and carry her away was strong, but she didn't know if she dared set herself up for another heartbreak, not after the first one had nearly destroyed her. She definitely didn't know how to trust that it wouldn't happen again.

"No?" Everett needled, as if he read all her misgivings clear as a neon sign. As if her desire to stay or go was any of his business.

"Is that why you're sitting here?" she asked crossly, making an unnecessary adjustment to a throw that was already draped perfectly over the back of the sofa. "Are you guarding me in case I decide to bolt?"

"Yes."

His frankness startled her, but she only muttered, "Well, isn't that just like Giovanni to ask for my trust, but not offer any in return."

"He didn't ask me to do this. I thought of it all by myself."

"The nineties called. They said the cold war is over and the KGB is a pop band now."

"I'm starting to see the attraction." Everett drained his glass and set it aside. "Giovanni is a man of principle and duty and tremendous loyalty, so he did everything he could to honor the commitments he had made to the job we were doing, but from the moment he met you, his priorities were impacted. I didn't understand it, but I knew from your first night together that I was losing him to you."

"So you stole him back? How mean-girl of you." She clasped her elbows as she moved to the windows and looked out on the view across the rooftops to the Colosseum and the Roman Forum.

"If only it was that easy. I genuinely thought you might have had something to do with that explosion. He was beside himself, though. If he hadn't been in traction, he would have crawled out of the hospital to go to you. The stubborn bastard wouldn't even speak to me until I got that ring back onto his finger. The only reason he stayed in hiding was for *your* safety. When I had to tell him you'd lost the baby... Let's just say it was a very bad day."

"And yet he didn't come," she said with lingering anguish tightening her throat.

"Has he told you anything of what we've been doing?" Impatience edged into his tone.

"He told me it was more important than I am." She clung to her sharp elbows. "Maybe it was. It doesn't make any of these lies easier to bear."

"So you're going to punish him for it? Leave him because of it? You'll destroy him, Freja. You have that power. Do you understand that? Your engagement to Nels—"

"Everett." Giovanni spoke in a quiet voice that was so lethal, Freja's heart clunked with alarm in her chest.

His clean shave and fresh haircut left Giovanni so imperially handsome, a stab of emotion hit her eyes. Attraction soared into her blood along with joy at his mere existence here and pride that such a gorgeous man could be called hers. Her *husband*.

If she dared to give him another chance.

"You are no longer part of this marriage," he said to Everett. "Never interfere between me and Freja again. Do you understand?"

Everett threw up his hands. "I'll be gone after the press conference."

How long would *she* be here? That was the decision she had to make, Freja realized with a pang of distress.

"You look lovely," Giovanni said with an appreciative slip of his gaze down to her navy pumps and back. "Perfect."

"You look nice, too," she murmured, still experiencing the pull of physical allure he always exerted over her. "Are we holding it downstairs? Or…?"

"Yes. My collar is wet so I'll change my shirt." He spoke in a distracted tone, rolling forward as he did. He picked up one of the hands she was trying to untangle from the other. "Where is your wedding band?"

"New York. This was in the safe and seemed a better choice than the engagement ring. It's your mother's anniversary ring."

"I know." He turned the white-gold eternity band encrusted with baguette-cut diamonds.

"If you don't want me to wear it—"

"I do. It's a good choice. Thank you."

His gaze was a depthless quicksilver pool that she could have fallen into, but Everett cleared his throat.

"The sooner we do our thing, the sooner I'll be gone."

Giovanni's mouth twitched wryly. He dropped his hands to his wheels.

"Giovanni," she said, forcing him to pivot to face her. She drew a breath that burned like the arid winds off a million miles of desert, but a bubble of something big and optimistic filled her throat. "I'm glad you're alive."

CHAPTER EIGHT

FREJA STOOD AMID the blinding camera lights and flashes, one hand on Giovanni's shoulder as he and Everett balanced on the razor's edge between truth and fabrication, never mentioning their extracurricular activities. They claimed Freja's very public engagement had been a ruse to support Giovanni's supposed "accident" and passed off these horrendous few months as an elaborate plan by an eccentric billionaire to thwart a death threat while the culprits were hunted down.

Thankfully, it was over quickly. Everett took his leave and Freja didn't realize Giovanni had pushed the button for the rooftop until the doors opened at the helicopter pad.

"We're not staying here? This is just like you, springing a flight on me out of the blue!" She gave a frantic wave of her hand. "Nothing in our calendar, just, 'Get in and shut up.' You're worse than my father when it comes to moving along on the spur of the moment. At least he gave me time to *pack*."

"Everett had your things retrieved from Milan." Giovanni pointed to her distinctive, monogrammed luggage going into the cargo area. "And I just said in the press conference that we would be spending time at home for the next week or two. Where do you think my home is, Freja?"

"I don't know! You have a dozen of them."

"Sicily." He was taking a tone as if all of this was obvious. "We're going to my villa on my family estate. I can't leave the country until Everett has me sufficiently resuscitated for bureaucrats to issue a new passport."

"Oh. I knew there was a villa there. I didn't know you thought of it as 'home.' Why didn't you take me there before?"

"I was working," he said with his *don't ask* shuttered expression that always hit her with the force of a wrecking ball.

Her heart shrank and her skin grew too tight as she climbed aboard and buckled in.

Giovanni came in and anchored his chair, releasing a frustrated sigh as he did. "There are things I will never be able to talk about, Freja. You will have to accept that."

She tried to shake it off with a small shrug, keeping her profile turned to the window.

They were served a light meal as they flew. She choked it down, but the pilaf tasted like glue and the silence stuck in her ears.

They landed behind a villa that sprawled atop a hillock overlooking a sweeping slope to the sea. Everything was bathed in a fading mauve light while the setting sun painted a red line against the horizon.

"This is beautiful," she couldn't help saying as they moved along a paved path flanked by shrubs strung with fairy lights. The air was balmy and feather-soft, flavored by the mature orange grove and the earthy scents of the surrounding vineyards. "The house looks quite new, though."

"It is." He veered down a paved path to a bricked area surrounding the pool. Quite a ways down the slope, off to the left, stood a shoe-shaped house. Its gray stones were lit by floodlights buried within its surrounding gardens. "That's where I was born. Where we would come in the summer and Christmas, when my father wasn't dragging us elsewhere for work. It's regarded as a heritage site so I couldn't remodel it to accommodate my chair, not without destroying its character."

"That's—" Incredibly sad. She'd always envied people who knew where their home was, but to be able to see it and not be able to enter? "It looks occupied."

"Staff use it." He pivoted and leaned into pushing himself up an incline that skirted the pool's blue glow, leading her to an open double-door entrance.

His housekeeper greeted him with teary warmth and welcomed Freja with belated congratulations on their marriage. Since they'd just eaten, they said they would dine later, after they'd had time to settle in and relax.

Like all of Giovanni's homes, this one was scrupulously tailored to his chair, with a full contingent of people ready to look after his every need. The decor was simple and soothing and sumptuously comfortable, encouraging relaxation. The huge estate was fenced and security patrolled, he informed her when she expressed concern for the open doors.

"This isn't New York. The cat burglars are actual cats from the vineyard looking for a morsel or a scratch between the ears."

Her suitcases were already in the master bedroom when they got there, but there was a small selection of clothing in the closet, too.

"I've never seen these," she murmured as she fingered through bohemian skirts and sleeveless knit tops. "When did you order them?"

"Sent from Milan after one of your initial fittings, I imagine. I expected we would make it here eventually."

"They're so casual." Comfortable and relaxing.

"Even when I have social commitments here, they're low-key events. We dress down for dinner." He showed her the shorts and collared T-shirt he retrieved from a drawer.

The tension that had been gripping her for ages began to release. She stepped out of her spiked pumps and tugged a crinkled cotton peasant dress from a hanger.

"I thought you might have come here after…" He didn't finish, but she knew he was referring to his own funeral. "Why did you go back to New York? Why did you buy your own place there?"

Because she hadn't been able to face any reminders of him.

"So many people were asking about the business. It seemed more convenient to be there, especially once I asked Nels for help. He wanted to include me in the decisions he was making. And this… Your life, being your wife. It seemed like it hadn't really happened. I hadn't been Signora Catalano long enough to know how to pull it off. It was easier to go back to where I'd put my life on track twice before."

But had she? Oliver's townhome hadn't been her life. Nor had university. Haring off to Europe with

Giovanni hadn't offered the sort of stability and purpose she had longed for. What sort of life did she even want to pursue?

"We could make this our home from now on. I'll still have travel demands, but not nearly so many." He followed her out of the closet.

She sat down on the end of the bed, crumpling the dress onto her knees, lips parted as she tried to think of how to respond.

"Don't say you don't want that," he commanded gruffly. Maybe it was a plea. His voice was low and held strain, as though he was speaking while having a bullet removed from his chest. "We could try again for a family, Freja."

With a small sob of longing, she hugged the formless dress to her stomach.

She did want that. A baby. Children. She knew that now. She wanted a family. People who were hers.

She didn't realize she had closed her eyes until his hand touched her knee and she blinked her lids open.

"Did the doctors say anything about... Are there concerns about future pregnancies?" he asked apprehensively. "I don't want to put you through that if—"

"No." She bit her lips together. She had asked those questions herself and found cold comfort in the answers. "They didn't identify any serious health issue and said my chances of a successful pregnancy next time were exactly the same as any other woman's."

He nodded in distant understanding, hand caressing her knee. "That's something to think about, then. Isn't it? Trying again, when we're ready?"

She didn't need to think about it. She knew that much

with unshaken certainty deep in her core. Pushing the dress off her lap, she scooted backward onto the bed.

"Can we try right now?"

"Freja." He closed his eyes, expression twisting with agony. "We need *time*."

"I need *hope*," she argued raggedly. "I need to feel something that isn't emptiness and agony and self-doubt."

"*Tisoru*, you know that's all this would be. Hope." His voice was tortured, his hands in fists on his thighs. "A thin one! I can't make it happen every time. You know that. If you're sure about wanting a family, then let's do this properly. We'll renew our vows and see a specialist and find a way. It will be a journey we take with intention, together, every step of the way."

"A chance is enough for now." Was it? Not really, but, "If it's meant to be, if *we* are meant to be, like you said yesterday, then it will happen for us again."

"Don't do that, Freja." His expression turned grave. "That is far too much pressure to put on a relationship as fragile as ours is right now. Don't do that to us."

"I need something, Giovanni! A sign. A message from the universe to convince me that I should stay with you, because my head is telling me I should be in New York by now, forgetting I ever knew you."

His breath hissed and he swore at the ceiling.

"This morning used up my lifetime's allotment of good intentions." He threw away the clothes in his lap and his biceps flexed as he joined her on the bed. "If you want to make love, I will make love with you. *Always.* But understand that I view this as a resumption of our marriage. You will not get rid of me so easily next time."

"I didn't get rid of you the first time, you idiot!"

"Call me names if you have to." He dragged himself to loom over her. "Pinch and bite me. Get all that anger out because I don't want it between us anymore."

"You put it there! You did this."

"I did." He sounded gruff, his good leg was crushing her thigh, but his lips were tantalizingly sweet as he pressed airy kisses along her jawline.

"You said I was overreacting. That I was smothering you and acting like a jealous shrew."

"I did." He set those tender kisses over her eyes, closing them, and rubbed his lips against her brow. "I was worried. I wanted you away from me, off the street so no one would guess who you were. And you tried to protect me afterward anyway. I don't deserve you, Freja. I know that."

So many soft, soft kisses that stirred more than sensual excitement. They crept close to the heart she'd been guarding so very carefully since the beginning. Oh, she had been falling in love as fast as she'd fallen into bed with him. Too fast even to recognize what was happening and put words to it. Then they had been married and all the small secrets began piling up, eating at her, causing her to hold back her tenuous new feelings.

She had fought and fought and fought not to love him, but stunted as his disappearance had left her emotionally, she had continued to yearn for him. For the only man who made her heart lift and race.

She loved him. She had known that when she chased him to Dubrovnik, desperate to know where they stood.

She was still desperate, wanting to fill herself with him. She skated her hands across the ripple of his mus-

cled chest and drank in the rumbling hum of his plea-
sured noise.

His lips seductively touched one corner of her mouth
then the other, finally giving her a tiny peck that was
nowhere near enough.

"Why do you always tease?" she scolded, cupping
the side of his smooth cheek and urging him to kiss
her properly.

He did. Slow and thorough until she moaned in the
agonized ecstasy of having him here with her. But for
how long this time?

"I'm not teasing, *bidduzza*. I'm savoring." He released the first button on her dress and kissed the inch
of breastbone he exposed. "I'm reacquainting myself
the way I should have this morning. Why are you always in such a hurry? We have time."

"Do we?" she asked baldly. "Because I have never
believed that."

He frowned.

"You only married me because I was pregnant. You
were shutting me out. I thought you resented me."

"Ah, Freja. No." He rested his forehead against her
chin.

On that fateful last day, she'd asked him, *Do you
love me? Do you even want to be married?* She couldn't
bear to ask it again, fearful of how he would respond.

"I didn't see how we could last when things were so
tense and awful," she admitted painfully. "When you
were disappearing and keeping secrets. I followed you
that day to end the suspense of *when*."

He made a noise of defeat.

"I wanted *that* to be over so I could be here." He

slipped another button free. "I won't shut you out again." His lips went down as he opened more and more of her dress. "We have time. I promise you."

She wanted to believe him. She did.

His hand slid beneath the edge of her dress and cupped her bare breast. She gasped, arching as he plumped the swell, exposing it to his pleased gaze.

"My beautiful rebel," he said with affection for her braless state. He dipped his head and sucked her nipple.

How many times had she dreamed of this? Imagined him in the bed beside her, making love with her again.

"I missed you," she confessed in a whisper and ran her hands into his hair, savoring him, too. Because they might last or they might not, but she had him now and she wanted to love him with every part of her.

Everything slowed then. Each caress was drawn out, each kiss achingly tender. Each layer of clothing peeled away bit by bit until they were naked with nothing between them but desire that scorched their skin as they moved against one another.

He spoke to her in his beautiful language, kissing every inch of her until she was weak with longing. She did the same, holding back her pleasure so they would experience it together when she was sprawled upon him, taking him in. Joined with him again in the most intimate way. Finally.

In this moment she believed, as she always had, that they were anointed by ancient gods. There was nothing more sacred than the feel of him inside her, their rocking as universal as the waves rolling up the sands of a beach and the sway of trees in the wind.

But this union was only a stolen moment from time.

A gift and a curse because eventually the crisis hit and even though it was magnificent, it marked the end.

And even though she was sated and bursting with love for him, and even though he cradled her in his arms as they caught their breath, she felt them slide apart and had to press her eyes closed against hot tears.

"You have to love the modern news cycle," Freja said over breakfast the next morning. "Your return from the dead has already been overshadowed by a golf club that has finally allowed women to join, a bitcoin embezzlement, and a kitten rescued from a ledge on a skyscraper."

"How do I compete with such a hero?" Giovanni lifted his head from the market numbers he was studying on his tablet. "Surely I'm more photogenic than a window washer?"

"He was a firefighter and any man's appearance improves tenfold when he holds a kitten or a puppy. It's a proven social media fact. Ugh," she added with a dismayed flick through her feed. "Trolls are saying your faked death was a stunt to sell more of my books."

"Ignore them," Giovanni insisted. "Turn that off. I want to show you the estate."

"I have to answer a few emails first. The publicity team for my book is having a bird that I didn't warn them about any of this." Freja frowned. "*Tsk.* And even though my first book isn't out yet, I'm being asked for a follow-up. A tell-all about our marriage. No, thank you." She swiped dismissively, but her tablet continued to ping. "This is ridiculous. Are you being inundated with invitations to charity galas and holiday mixers? I don't even know most of these people."

"The advantages of a new phone. I'm sure they'll find me in due course." He had had a mind to skip re-entering the social whirl in favor of a honeymoon, but he'd forgotten about her book tour. "I'll make some calls today, begin the search for a new team of assistants. The most inconvenient consequence of pretending to be dead has to be the loss of so many well-trained staff."

"That'll teach you. Don't do it again," she said dourly.

Amusement tugged at the corners of his mouth. "When are we due in New York for the book launch?"

"November first. Will you be alive by then? You don't have to come."

"Of course I'll be there. Do we factor in a visit to Paris on the way? Surely you need a new wardrobe for it?"

"Does anyone 'need' a new wardrobe for anything?" She kept her chin tucked as she lifted her lashes to send a scathing glance at him. Her gaze dropped to the screen and her nose wrinkled. "I'm not even sure how many appearances I'll have. I managed to cancel most of my interviews when you disappeared. Now that I'm not actually a widow, I'm being asked to reinstate them and do more. I'll try to keep it to a minimum."

"My calendar is your calendar. Enjoy your moment in the sun."

"I burn easily," she dismissed.

He had missed this. So much his chest felt strained, trying to contain the bubble of lightness inside him. He had missed her facetious asides in that honeyed voice, her white-blond brows that pulled together in concentration, and the fine, angel-blond strands of hair that lifted with static, begging his hand to reach across and smooth them flat.

She looked up when he did, then rolled her eyes and dampened her palm with the condensation on her juice glass to flatten the flyaway strands herself.

He bit back a chuckle, unable to think of a time when he'd felt so content.

Lovemaking after a dry spell had that effect on a man, he supposed.

He sobered as he acknowledged it was so much more than that. Sex with Freja was as exquisite as ever and he was enormously gratified to be intimate with her again, but he was worried about the expectation she was placing on them. He wasn't even sure if bringing a baby into this relationship while they were still finding their way was the best thing.

Not that he could say so. It would break these fragile threads of connection they were weaving between them with the return to physical closeness. That's why he'd given in—aside from the sheer pleasure in the act. He knew his limitations and the chance of another natural conception was extremely low, but the intimacy of lovemaking would begin laying the foundation of trust they desperately needed.

He brought her hand to his mouth so he could kiss her palm.

"What was that for?" she asked, blue eyes dazzled, mouth tilting into a pleased smile.

"You're beautiful." It was the simple truth. Gazing on her, he felt physical pain at how incredibly lovely she was. At how much it meant to him to have her in his life again.

Her gaze softened to an intense vulnerability, the kind that threw a tremendous weight of responsibility onto him, one of such magnitude, he didn't know how to live up to it. He had wanted to rise to it, though. That's what had taken him to Dubrovnik.

He had been hurrying toward his wife and child and a shimmering possibility that went beyond the buoyant joy of orgasms and banter and *I'm glad you're alive*. It was deep and wide and so powerful, it could destroy him if he let it. If he embraced it and lost again.

His inner walls shook, but fear clenched icy fingers around him. Fear of yet another loss. He took an emotional step back even as she dampened her lips and her mouth trembled as though she was about to say something. As though she waited for him to say something.

"I say yes to Paris. You deserve to mark your accomplishment with something special," he said.

It was a mistake. He knew it immediately, even before the light had died from her expression. The thing he feared losing was gone.

"I'll think about it." She rose and offered a smile that didn't reach her eyes. "Let me make my calls, and then you can show me the estate." She walked away.

Freja's first pregnancy had been a complete fluke. Logically, she knew it wasn't fair to hinge their reconciliation on something so capricious as another miracle, but even though everything had changed between her and Giovanni, nothing had.

Oh, he had time for her now. In that way things were

as magical as their first days together. They swam and toured his estate on an all-terrain tractor fitted for him to operate with his hands. He had a topless Jeep that was also tricked out with a hydraulic ramp so he could drive it while sitting in his wheelchair. He stayed out of the busy city centers, but toured her along the coast, and they stopped to window-shop in small villages and ordered espresso and biscotti at outdoor cafés.

He even took her inland to Piazza Armerina, the town where her father had wandered an ancient Roman complex for a week while Freja learned fencing in a grassy park.

"The infamous bikini girls," Giovanni said when she suggested he turn that direction, referring to the famed mosaics in the ruins. "I was taken there on a school outing. My extremely high expectations were left unmet."

She chuckled. "I liked the circus pictures and all the strange creatures, but my attention span was exhausted within the hour. Thus, the fencing lessons."

"I read all those books of your father's yet never quite understood what drove him to pursue such a vagabond life. It was his living, obviously, but my father traveled for work and I still knew where I was from. I had a home to come back to."

A tendril of her hair had escaped from her ponytail and caught at the corner of her mouth. She dragged it away as she said, "Yeah, but if you never have a home, you'll never be homesick."

"Is that true?" The car geared down with a small growl as he slowed for traffic. He glanced at her. "Are you missing America now that you've made a home there?"

"I miss Sung-mi and Byung-woo," she said with a crooked, *What can you do?* smile. "I kept waiting for New York to feel like home, but I actually felt more in my natural habitat when I was traveling with you, waking up in a new city every other day. Granted, you travel very comfortably," she allowed dryly. Private jets and luggage handlers made all the difference. "But even though your unannounced itinerary changes were really annoying—you do need to work on your communication skills—being on the move feels very normal to me."

"I don't want that life for either of us anymore. I want you to feel like this is your home."

She had pieced that together over these days of his proudly showing her every inch of this admittedly beautiful and ever-changing island.

"Is that unrealistic?" he asked in a guarded voice.

"I don't know." Part of her was thinking, *Home is where the heart is.* That's why she'd been content moving around with her father and living in a type of lockdown with Sung-mi.

By that logic, all she should need was Giovanni, but her heart was pining.

Because he didn't love her the way those people had. And if he wasn't willing to open his heart to her, then she didn't have a home with him.

CHAPTER NINE

GIOVANNI WAS READING through CVs from his headhunter when Freja walked into his study. Rather than the beach bum attire they'd both fallen into while here, she wore jeans, a pale gray top and a light blazer with pockets—the sort of clothes she wore for travel.

"I thought we decided to stay in for dinner." They'd only finished their late lunch an hour ago. "You look pale," he noted. "What's wrong?"

"I—" She closed the door.

He clicked off the tablet, met her by the chair where she sank down and tried to wrest the fingers of her one hand off the other. She wasn't wearing his mother's ring or any other.

Everything in him stilled.

"I've decided to go back to New York. There's a flight from Palermo in a couple of hours."

"Something with the tour? Everett will be here with my passport tomorrow. We were going to stop in Paris."

"I don't—" She shook her head and said in a small voice, "I'm not pregnant."

The words rang through him like a sonic boom, leveling everything inside him. He firmly set aside whatever emotions rose up in waves around that news and said, "We both know my limitations."

The timing was wrong, too. He was no fertility expert, but he understood the basics and they'd only started having sex a week ago.

"Freja." He reached out to still her twisting hands. "There's no rush. We have time to try again, find ways to tip the odds in our favor."

"I thought if I got pregnant again, it would mean our marriage is worth continuing." She stood up and paced anxiously across the room.

While he fell back in his chair and fought to keep panic from overwhelming him, he did what he had always done in times of heightened stakes and deep emotion. He condensed all of it into a ball deep in his core, stomach tight as he forced himself to ignore it so he could think past it.

"I told you that we shouldn't put that sort of pressure on us," he said forcefully enough to make her stiffen. He softened his tone. "We can see what happens for now, try more seriously later."

"What if it doesn't happen? What if that's the only reason we stay married and it doesn't happen?" she asked with a little sob of despair. "Think about it. You dated me to investigate me. You married me because I was pregnant. You told me we had to stay married until you took control of your company. Tomorrow you get your passport and can resume your life. And you want to share it with me? Try for a baby?"

"Wanting a family is a good reason to stay married."

"But if it doesn't happen, what do we have? We were

never suited. Isn't it better to end it now? Don't you want to marry someone you love and have a real family?"

"For God's sake, Freja. You're not even giving us a chance." He had to hold on to that cold, angry tone or the agony would shatter the steel walls holding his emotions inside. "This is not fair. I can't make that happen on demand. *You know that.*"

"This isn't about your physical limitations! It's about your emotional ones. I asked you months ago if you loved me. You still haven't answered me."

Because death had bled love out of him once and losing their baby had done it again. He had been trying to keep what they had to something he could manage. Something that didn't have the potential to destroy them both.

And what if he *couldn't* give her a baby? He couldn't bear to put her through the anguish of that. Or of losing another pregnancy. He'd already put her through *so much*.

"I think this is for the best," she said, voice papery in the silence. "I'm going to go."

He had to let her. Didn't he?

"Have you lost your mind?" Everett said when Giovanni told him Freja had left for America last night. "You went through all of this and you *let her go*?"

"News flash. Women are no longer chattel. They do what they want. And I put her through the wringer. She'd had enough."

"Is that what she said?"

"No."

"What then?"

"None of your business. I told you to butt out."

"You're always so surly when you haven't slept." Everett moved to help himself to a scotch even though it wasn't even noon yet. "Are you coming back to work for me, then?"

"No."

"No?" Everett turned with a knowing smirk. "Why not?"

"Oh, shut up. I had to wait for my passport." He dropped it into the satchel hanging off his chair, the one that already held his phone, tablet, and wheelchair repair tools. His private jet was fueled and ready when he was. "I thought about having her dragged off the plane, but…"

He had hoped she would change her mind. So he could stay exactly as closed off as he was. So he would know she loved him before he had to confess to it first.

He pinched the bridge of his nose. "What happens if I tell her I love her? What changes? Nothing. I'm still me. Still in this chair. Still dragging her around the world to attend board meetings or whatever bloody thing comes up. She wants a baby and so do I, but there's no guarantee with things like that. Failure is hell. So what do I offer her that isn't…a promise of pain?"

This was what had kept him awake all night. Despair. A complete lack of hope. He couldn't give her happily-ever-after. There was no such thing.

"I've been told to butt out," Everett said laconically. "But what do you want from her? Because she's pretty and all, but she's just a woman. She's not offering you any guarantees that she can produce an heir, is she? Or never wind up ill or needing a chair? Find someone else."

"How obtuse are you?" Giovanni asked with affront. "I

don't *want* anyone else. She doesn't have to *give* me any-thing. I just want her here, in my life. Then all the pains and disappointments of existence are bearable at least."

"Again, I don't want to overstep," Everett said, scratch-ing his upper lip and serving up his remark with buckets of irony. "But is there *any* chance she feels the same?"

Giovanni wanted to say something biting, but a ray of sunshine peeked through the thick walls inside him, throwing light into the darkness even as its heat touched on raw places and stung.

It was painful, but it tugged him to take one more chance.

"Make yourself at home. I'm leaving."

Freja was missing Giovanni even before she got on the plane to New York. She sat down next to a man who snored the whole way and tried to hold back her tears.

She reminded herself he didn't love her. Leaving was the smart thing to do, before they were too entangled for her to leave this easily again.

That's what she told Nels when he picked her up at the airport and asked, "What happened?"

He took her back to the apartment she'd bought and told him to use because he was being hounded by the press. They shared a bottle of wine and she fed him the lines about the death threat, keeping Giovanni's secret, but she apologized to Nels for using him.

"I was using you, too. But… I have to say it. You can have the man you want, Freja. I can't. So why are you squandering that?"

She didn't have a good answer. Fear? She had never let that hold her back. Distrust? She understood and accepted why Giovanni had hurt her. The only way to find out if he would do it in the future was to give him another chance.

Her brain went around in circles and, in a desperate bid for distraction, she agreed to do a reading from an advance copy of her book. Her agent found a bookstore willing to throw it together at the last minute. They put up a few posters and she mentioned it on her social media accounts, but it was so low-key, she didn't even dress up for it. She wore brown plaid pants with ankle boots and a sage-green pullover with sleeves that fell to her knuckles.

She begged Nels to come with her, certain no one would show up, swearing, "I'm fine with talking to an empty room. This is a test drive for the other appearances I have lined up, but I'd like some feedback."

The shop was in one of Greenwich Village's character buildings, the kind that had been through a thousand iterations and would go through a thousand more in service to the changing demographics of the foot traffic that passed it. Presently it catered to the pseudo-intellectuals who appreciated the reclaimed floorboards and fair-trade coffee and the reading area in the loft that offered free Wi-Fi.

The overstuffed furniture in that loft had been pushed to the rail and a dozen chairs brought in. They were already full when Freja arrived and the harried staff were frantically stealing stools from the coffee bar and carrying chairs from someone's office. A queue had started on the stairs that ran all the way out the door.

"Those people aren't all here for me," Freja said to Nels, pointing out, "They're all holding my father's books."

"Still a nice show of support."

"It is." She forced a smile, thinking her publishing team would love that it was turning into a standing-room-only event. She knew this should feel like a triumph of some kind, but even though Nels stayed nearby, she felt very…lonely.

They moved her a little closer to the rail so the people on the stairs could see her, and they introduced her.

Freja smiled at the crowd and began to read her own words:

"'Some people view life as a battle or an adventure, one where you fight to overcome adversity in hopes of a thrilling victory. Some see it as a garden, where you weed out what doesn't work and nurture what does. They tell you to stop to smell the roses.'"

There was a small ripple of laughter, thank goodness.

"'My father saw life as a journey. Traveling was his life and thus it was mine, but I always saw myself as a passenger. I didn't get to decide where we were going, but I didn't mind. When you're with someone you love, it doesn't matter where you're going or how long it takes to get there.'"

She faltered slightly, having forgotten she had written that. She cleared her throat and continued.

"'Pappa was my constant, even though the rest of the relationships in my life were transitory. When he died so unexpectedly, I was devastated, but there was a piece of me that accepted the loss as normal. No one is permanent. Eventually, you have to say goodbye to everyone.'"

Did she, though? It was striking her that she had done this. She had pushed Giovanni away. That's why she had gone to Dubrovnik that day, to say goodbye. She hadn't believed there was such a thing as building a life together. Yes, there had been things between them that had to be overcome, but it wasn't all on him to convince her they had a future. She could make that choice and pursue it herself.

"'So I knew...'" Her voice was wavering in and out as emotion overwhelmed her. "'I knew in my heart of hearts...'"

She began to shake. She couldn't do this. Why had she let him go? She wanted to go to him right now. *When you're with someone you love...*

"Freja." Nels touched her arm and nodded to the floor below.

Giovanni blocked the aisle between stacks of books. He hadn't shaved and his hair was ruffled. He was never a man to wear his heart on his sleeve, but as everyone craned their necks to see where her attention had gone, he had eyes only for her. He touched his fingertips to his mouth and blew her a kiss.

The whole crowd sighed.

She released a teary laugh.

"I'll go down," Nels whispered, squeezing her arm. "You can do this."

"I didn't expect my husband to be here." She sniffed back her tears and took a deep breath and pulled it together. "But I'm so glad he is."

She set her fingertip under her own words and picked up where she had left off.

"'I knew in my heart of hearts that I would not be in North Korea forever. That my journey would continue eventually...'"

* * *

Freja was tied up for hours. While she read, the place was so silent, the couple of times the barista caused the espresso machine to hiss, the poor woman earned a dozen dirty looks.

After a lengthy round of applause, people wanted selfies and her autograph in her father's books.

"I'm so sorry," she said when the crowd finally thinned out and she was able to come down to Giovanni.

"Why? You were working. Your fiancé kept me company."

Nels went red and started to stammer. "Freja and I have talked and we're not—"

"That was a joke," Giovanni assured him and offered his card. "Call me tomorrow. We'll talk properly about the handoff, which will still be very much hands-on."

Giovanni was already thinking he wanted as much time as possible with Freja and, judging by tonight, she had commitments of her own.

"You were spectacular," he told her as Nels left them alone.

She brushed off the compliment with a flushed smile. It faded slightly as she asked, "Why are you here?"

"To see you. Can I buy you dinner?"

"I'm not hungry. I could use a stiff drink, though," she joked.

"There's champagne at the apartment."

"You want me to come home with you?" She dipped her chin, pleased and not at all as surprised as she was pretending.

"I do. Right now."

* * *

Freja took a few calls in the car and apologized again as they entered the penthouse.

"*Bidduzza*, you have been very tolerant of my work. I'm happy to support yours. In fact, I'm so proud, my shirt shouldn't have any buttons left."

"Even though I left Sicily the way I did? I've had time to think, you know." Time to regret leaving so abruptly.

"Come here. I want to tell you something." He rolled closer to the sofa and moved onto it.

She followed and sank down next to him. He angled toward her and took her hand.

"Stefano and I were only thirteen months apart. Because of that, we did almost everything together, but when he turned fifteen, he was allowed to get a real job. It was a summer student position and he swore it was no better than glorified babysitting, but he was not at home weeding the vineyard to earn his allowance the way I was. The envy I felt that summer nearly ate me alive. I was excited for the next year when I presumed we would teach fencing together."

She saw the shadows closing in on his gray eyes and swallowed. His thumb moved restlessly across the backs of her knuckles.

"He took after our mother. She was exuberant like him. Quite playful and funny. He got her black, curly hair and pointy chin. I have our father's eyes and jaw. Papà was a more circumspect man. He had to be, given his position, but it was his nature to be very measured in the things he said and not to give away too much. I used to wish I was more like Stefano. He didn't mind sharing his thoughts and never let the weight of the world settle on him. He knew how to laugh. And girls? Oh, they loved him."

"You do fine with the ladies," she pointed out.

"Ah, but the only lady that matters had a crush on him first." There was only rueful affection in his tone.

"You loved him very much."

"I loved all of them so much I didn't know how I would survive when I woke after the crash." His eyes grew wet. He didn't hide any of the agony he felt to this day. "I'd never felt so alone. So left behind."

"I'm sorry," she whispered, cupping the side of his face.

He held her hand there and said, "When I realized the crash had been deliberate... I had to do something, but righting one wrong wasn't enough. It became an obsession. A way to avoid addressing how empty my life was. Then, one day, there you were, a glimmer of gold in all the silt. But it was so complicated."

"I know," she murmured.

"When the possibility of a baby came up..." His eyes misted afresh. "I hadn't let myself love in a long time, but I felt the roots of it starting in me. I've never wanted anything more in my life than to have a family with you. You, Freja. I could see it so clearly, I could taste it. And then it was gone."

She swiped at a tickle on her cheek and her fingers came away wet. She leaned closer and he set his warm arm across her shoulders, nose to her temple.

"It locked me up again. It's really hard to say it. To admit that I love you and want your love. I'm terrified of how vulnerable I am to the pain of loss, but losing you, even to a damned airplane and a day of travel... I want you in my life, Freja. I need you."

"I want that, too," she admitted shakily. "I love you, too. So much. I'm sorry I left. I hated myself as soon as I did."

"Well, that will teach you." He gathered her into his lap. "Don't do it again."

Six months later...

"Everything looks perfectly normal except..."

They both lost their smiles. Giovanni's hand squeezed hers tighter. Freja swallowed.

"What's wrong?"

"Nothing. See for yourself." The technician pointed to the screen, then pointed to another spot on the screen, counting, "One, two. Twins."

"But..." Freja trailed off, speechless.

"This is very common with in vitro fertilizations..." The technician sent a glance to Giovanni's chair.

"But this was artificial insemination. I'm not using fertility drugs. They didn't implant embryos, just..."

"Ah." The technician looked closer. "There's only one placenta. Looks like you just got lucky."

They stayed lucky. Their identical twin girls were born three weeks early at a clinic in Sicily, healthy and strong. They went home with their ecstatic parents a few days later.

EPILOGUE

HIS PASSPORT READ Benjamin Everhart. It was fake, but a good one. The border guard waved the small vanload of tourists along with only a cursory glance at it.

A few days of touring the sacred Paektu Mountain and Heaven Lake later, the van entered a small village. They were checked into a hotel approved for foreigners.

Everett double-checked he had the novel in his jacket pocket, then walked downstairs with a handful of airplane peanuts in his hand. The things he did for a friend.

He shoved the peanuts in his mouth and was gasping and losing consciousness before he'd reached his assigned table in the restaurant.

He woke in the clinic, an IV attached to his arm, throat still scratchy. An official stood by while a circumspect nurse checked his pulse. The woman disappeared and Everett motioned to the official that he wanted the book out of his jacket.

It was a British spy thriller. The official flipped through the pages, stopping to inspect the photo Everett was using for a bookmark. It was an image of Giovanni holding both his daughters. Louisa was trying to eat a button off his shirt. Teresa had one little fist tangled in

Freja's hair as she crouched beside her husband's wheel-chair. They were laughing at their girls' antics.

This was the tricky moment. Everett held his breath, wondering if the official would recognize her, but he only glanced at the blank backside, then stuffed the photo between the pages. He handed the book to Everett.

Everett set the photo on the side table and pretended to read.

Twenty minutes later, the doctor came in, gave him the North Korean brand of an antihistamine pen, and discharged him. Everett neglected to pick up the photo on his way out.

The next morning, as they were about to climb aboard the van, the same official pulled him aside.

Damn. That was never a good sign, but Everett kept an unbothered expression on his face.

A Korean woman offered him a small package and a silk scarf with cherry blossoms embroidered on it. The scarf was delicate and seemed valuable, but the woman motioned that this was to protect his still raw throat.

He got the message and put it on, bowing his thanks.

The official inspected the tea, sniffed it, and allowed him to board the bus.

When he gave Freja the scarf she cried into it, but for once Giovanni didn't scold him for interfering.

* * * * *

COMING SOON!

We really hope you enjoyed reading this book.
If you're looking for more romance, be sure to
head to the shops when new books are
available on

Thursday 3rd
September

To see which titles are coming soon, please visit
millsandboon.co.uk/nextmonth

MILLS & BOON

Coming next month

CHRISTMAS IN THE KING'S BED
Caitlin Crews

"Your Majesty. Really." Calista moistened her lip and he found himself drawn to that, too. What was the matter with him? "You can't possibly think that we would suit for anything more than a temporary arrangement to appease my father's worst impulses."

"I need to marry, Lady Calista. I need to produce heirs, and quickly, to prove to my people the kingdom is at last in safe hands. There will be no divorce." Orion smiled more than he should have, perhaps, when she looked stricken. "We are stuck. In each other's pockets, it seems."

She blanched at that, but he had no pity for her. Or nothing so simple as pity, anyway.

He moved toward her, taking stock of the way she lifted her head too quickly—very much as if she was beating back the urge to leap backward. To scramble away from him, as if he was some kind of predator.

The truth was, something in him roared its approval at that notion. He, who had always prided himself on how civilized he was, did not dislike the idea that here, with her, he was as much a man as any other.

Surely that had to be a good sign for their marriage.

Whether it was or wasn't, he stopped when he reached her. Then he stood before her and took her hand in his.

And the contact, skin on skin, floored him.

It was so...*tactile*.

It made him remember the images that had been dancing in his head ever since he'd brought up sex in her presence. It made him imagine it all in intricate detail.

It made him hard and needy, but better yet, it made her tremble.

Very solemnly, he took the ring—the glorious ring that in many ways was Idylla's standard to wave proudly before the world—and slid it onto one of her slender fingers.

And because he was a gentleman and a king, did not point out that she was shaking while he did it.

"And now," he said, in a low voice that should have been smooth, or less harshly possessive, but wasn't, "you are truly my betrothed. The woman who will be my bride. My queen. Your name will be bound to mine for eternity."

Continue reading
CHRISTMAS IN THE KING'S BED
Caitlin Crews

Available next month
www.millsandboon.co.uk

MILLS & BOON

THE HEART OF ROMANCE

A ROMANCE FOR EVERY KIND OF READER

MODERN

Prepare to be swept off your feet by sophisticated, sexy and seductive heroes, in some of the world's most glamourous and romantic locations, where power and passion collide.
8 stories per month.

HISTORICAL

Escape with historical heroes from time gone by. Whether your passion is for wicked Regency Rakes, muscled Vikings or rugged Highlanders, awaken the romance of the past.
6 stories per month.

MEDICAL

Set your pulse racing with dedicated, delectable doctors in the high-pressure world of medicine, where emotions run high and passion, comfort and love are the best medicine.
6 stories per month.

Celebrate true love with tender stories of heartfelt romance, from the rush of falling in love to the joy a new baby can bring, and a focus on the emotional heart of a relationship.
8 stories per month.

Indulge in secrets and scandal, intense drama and plenty of sizzling hot action with powerful and passionate heroes who have it all: wealth, status, good looks…everything but the right woman.
6 stories per month.

Experience all the excitement of a gripping thriller, with an intense romance at its heart. Resourceful, true-to-life women and strong, fearless men face danger and desire - a killer combination!
8 stories per month.

DARE

Sensual love stories featuring smart, sassy heroines you'd want as a best friend, and compelling intense heroes who are worthy of them.
4 stories per month.

To see which titles are coming soon, please visit

millsandboon.co.uk/nextmonth

JOIN US ON SOCIAL MEDIA!

Stay up to date with our latest releases, author news and gossip, special offers and discounts, and all the behind-the-scenes action from Mills & Boon...

 millsandboon

 millsandboonuk

 millsandboon

It might just be true love...

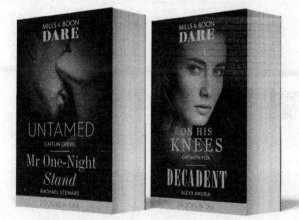